Tragedies of Modernity

Cultural beliefs, mediocrity and trouble of civilization
Tragedies in success path

Tragedies of Modernity

Transitioning for better life

FREDERICK W. SONPON

TRAGEDIES OF MODERNITY
TRANSITIONING FOR BETTER LIFE

This is a work of fiction. All of the characters, names, incidents, organizations, and dialogue in this novel are either the products of the author's imagination or are used fictitiously.

iUniverse books may be ordered through booksellers or by contacting:

iUniverse
1663 Liberty Drive
Bloomington, IN 47403
www.iuniverse.com
1-800-Authors (1-800-288-4677)

Because of the dynamic nature of the Internet, any web addresses or links contained in this book may have changed since publication and may no longer be valid. The views expressed in this work are solely those of the author and do not necessarily reflect the views of the publisher, and the publisher hereby disclaims any responsibility for them.

Any people depicted in stock imagery provided by Thinkstock are models, and such images are being used for illustrative purposes only. Certain stock imagery © Thinkstock.

ISBN: 978-1-4917-5601-0 (sc)
ISBN: 978-1-4917-5602-7 (e)

Library of Congress Control Number: 2014922222

Print information available on the last page.

iUniverse rev. date: 01/29/2015

They had real fun! Now it's time to return home. By Nine P.M. they are set. The president went his way. And Gmasnoh and Tesio are going their way, too, riding first pass the Ouachita Mountains area to take some photographs.

While on the way there, passing the Kiamichi Mountain ranges, right over the little river bridge in Honobia, a great spot for photograph, Tesio is bending a special terrible curve without reducing his speed by then because he is enjoying the music playing inside the car.

Surprising, while bending the terrible curve, because it's a long curve, not knowing a tow truck had since broken down at the place. And it has been since forty minutes ago. The police have just arrived to the sport trying to remove same.

By the time Tesio left the curve--and while concentrating again changing his music by plugging a memory stick instead, because the first music skipped, and when he lifted his head by then he surprisingly spotted the damaged tow truck. Very promptly he tried applying the brakes but that couldn't really hold. Gmasnoh yelled. "This is the end of us!" Truly it was too late. Only the echoing of her voice you could hear from a distance away during that moment.

The police came strictly at the spot. They were taken to the same Oral Robert Hospital where they had since been working. Nobody could believe it. At last, unbelievably, the two went into coma for nearly a year now. And the both parents of theirs left home to see them at the hospital.

However, on the twenty-fourth day of the following year around July, they have been surprisingly pronounced dead. Mournfully, however, Doctor Scott and Williams in collaboration with the family and the US Government peacefully buried them.

Dedication

Samson S. Tiklo and Amos Karr, Jr.

ACKNOWLEDGEMENT

Anna Forkpa, Zuanna Vincent and
Fidel N. Sonpon and Josiah Joekai, Jr.

1

The summer came. Niffu town is burning in huge sunrays. It's a lay town barricaded by breadfruit, mango, and orange trees. Even in the town itself, the trees are like a flower because they are everywhere flagging in various leaves.

In this lay town---the population is about seven hundred people. The population of goats, cows and sheep, chickens and ducks became very plentiful than humans. Most animals feed on the breadfruits and plum fruits for which they are always gathered in town than being into the bushes.

Condors and other small birds into the bushes nearby are whistling sweetly as well. And the worst of it, the withered leaves underneath the various trees at night the animals are hugely trampling on them and making huge sound.

Two brothers: Putunah and Snoteh woke early the morning at 4 A.M. prompt in order taking their impregnated wives who are about giving birth at the time each to a popular traditional midwife. Before then at 2:00AM various animals gathered in their various yards. Since the two O'clock time that morning because of the noise of the animals they are without sleep either. They are just listening to the various sounds and fun made by the animals outside their yards while inside their rooms. Others came at the window hitting each other, especially the cows, mooing furiously high.

They are like beasts. Some are sleeping. Others are even fearfully jumping around playing. On the other hand, some are mating in a squeaky style.

What is so a fearful thing here is that, for years now, lots of strange evils have been taking place in the town which nobody could easily get over that either. Imagine at seven thirty P.M.

oftentimes women and children found themselves indoors because of fear. If a person was doing anything that moment he or she has to abandon it right away and go indoors. Only brave men or women could at least come outside their various rooms probably to sit in their living rooms, while chatting.

When the often night comes, like earlier started, it's just fear to rule the minds of the people within the town. For anybody to come outside the house either he or she must have been a very brave man or woman to do so. Some nights, the only sound you could hear is that, surprising ballets sounds on the legs of strange humans, who nobody could see either during the night, that you could hear everywhere. After the night the next morning you could hear that, surprisingly, somebody has died. Fear by then got its own caskets to have buried almost everyone into it. Why the people should keep living like that? Rather, this is the huge question that rules lots of minds at last.

A wonderful night came. And it's almost close to the morning of 4:00AM. Two brothers want to wake up and walk through the fearful darkness of the morning because of a serious problem they had on hand. Should fear rule us still or see our women die? This is the serious question to give birth soon by the two brothers to answer then.

Putunah, when his woman Nancy keeps complaining on her labour pains, he decided to go for his knife to make an attempt coming outside the house because he wants to carry his wife to a special midwife they all knew in town. And his mind has been into a mournful thinking that an evil person, if he may have come out the house could that be an attack on his life by someone strange. He thought to then remove the fear. He is behaving like a brave man in his house upon coming to the living room of his house. He seemed so serious with his foreface the veins plaiting themselves on him.

He left the woman inside the room. He is about to come outside his house firstly before he could go for the woman later.

He is like someone about to be chased as he was getting prepared to get outside his house that morning of four o'clock. He took the knife, while holding it tightly at rear, attempting now opening his front door in bravery then. He is about to jump out by the time forcibly. All he thought is that, if it's for him to die as long his wife is in labour pains the moment he is prepared to die.

Jeeringly, he had the knife pointing before him as he is holding it tightly, bouncing on his toes. All that he thinks is that by the time he gets out and anybody wants to attack him he is prepared to kick back at the person. He's highly poised to attack his presumed enemy.

After few minutes he got out the house. Luckily when he got out, only the goats and cows he saw running from him. His heart pounded in velocity on him. He coughed. He did that and a cow mooed high. And that moment he was between fear and bravery. After few minutes then, his perspiration became normal, feeling as good as before. He feels as victory is won by him that nobody or anything had thought of attacking him either.

Now he got to take his wife to the midwife's residence, then. He went inside. And but the illusion of huge fear once epitomized him changed when he had put up a smile. He went for his wife inside the house finally, because the woman couldn't easily walk by herself again. She is in labour pain. He placed one of her hands on his shoulder while holding her tightly then, taking her to the midwife.

Snoteh, on the other hand, is attempting coming outside his house too. By the time he attempted opening his front door, a cow mooed high. He yelled by calling on his dead mother's name. And Putunah--the brother, interestingly, has answered him saying, "Here I'm. We are about going to the midwife because Nancy is in labour pain."

"Oh! I and my wife are about doing the same. Nandee is into labour pain as well."

"Then get her ready so we can all leave together." Putunah urged.

Putunah finally stepped out his house with his wife Nancy. But something very funny happened for which he lost his concentration a bit again. He kicked something on the ground that is very disgusting. He was trying to ignore that yet, while then continuing the journey but he couldn't still. Heavy cow manure was that surprisingly he kicked on the ground and he was yet to know. But what had got him to notice same is that, a lay breeze came and the scent of the stuff blasted his nose in disgust by force. He was then obligated motionlessly to decide doing something about.

"Wow! I hit something very stupid. I guess it's a damn cow toilet I kicked."

"Where is it, Putunah?" Nancy asked.

"But Nancy, can't you even smell the toilet too? I can smell the mess now on my toes and why then you can't?" He said and smiled as well in the darkness.

"But the scent hasn't reached my nose yet, Putunah."

"I'll ask the Almighty now to help you to know. But for me, it has already bombed me nastily. The mess stinks. My whole toes went into it."

"I'm so sorry, dear. Probably it's because of my condition for which I'm losing my sense of smelling yet." Nancy said. Putunah complained and hissed, while he's contemplating of cleaning the stuff from his toes.

First of all, he allowed the woman to rest a bit at the doorpost upon taking a bench to her that he took quickly from inside the house.

"But Putunah, you're to do this for me quickly. Please let us go. My pain is a bit increasing." Nancy said. In response Putunah said, "What's the matter . . . hush you woman? I'm already trying my best." He frowned in the darkness.

"It's true. But you need to apply a quick step by cleaning that thing so we can leave promptly. I know you're doing your best. But this is my worry that the midwife has waken to do other things for herself. In fact, the midwife usually leave town as early as five O'clock in the morning to go into the bushes in order to get herbs because she doesn't like for anyone to see her each time she is going into the bush to collect herbs. And the clear day is coming."

"I'm aware of your condition. And you can already see me helping in the process, isn't it?"

"It's true."

"Why then you keep squeezing me and getting me even boggle instead? I'm doing my best."

"I'm sorry." She said in apology. By then she felt sheepish and idiomatically fell on him for which her body seems a bit heavy. But it's something he got to do by all means.

On the other hand, Nancy is complaining on Snoteh. "I won't blame you of slowing your steps either. Why for God's sake our town is of no development yet? No vehicle road for anyone with a problem like mine to be able to sit into a car at least getting to the location of a hospital?" In response Snoteh said, "I'm really in sympathy with you about this, isn't it? Why complained?"

"I know that. Just that I want us to be a lay fast in reaching at the residence of the midwife. This is all my worry, please."

"Okay. Let it not be your worry either. I'm doing my best already."

They all landed at the place finally. Silent joy filled Putunah's heart yet. Surprising, the midwife, as usual took the two women under a group of palm trees stuck up together, underneath them to deliver the two women at once. First of all, she got on her kneels while displaying in a funny way chanting.

Something so funny about her is that, each time she is about doing such work, she has always prayed to the Almighty—in her Kru vernacular she called him "*Nye-suah*" firstly. Second, she begins to call on the spirits of her forefathers which are called the gods.

And after chanting and praying she is now seriously putting lots of mixtures together. She wants to get her herb material well-prepared in that for her work soon to begin. She had a sharp country knife by her too.

Before she could start up the mixing of her herbs, she lit the campfire very close to her quickly. She did that for her to see clearly what she is doing by the way then. After like fourteen minutes, she keeps poking the fire. Now she is feeling so pleased over her work because she could see clearly.

But whistling near the place into the bushes, are the crickets. They made dotted lights all over the place. They are in a theatre of joy because illumination from them seemed so wonderful to praise as well as the way they are jumping here and there perhaps.

Niffu Town became very dark despite it is now at clear daylight. It has been since then the women got into labour pains the darkness engulfed the whole place. And it's badly few minutes to twelve mid-day.

The midwife has been sweating profusely. To wonder, however, the cases of the two women seemed a bit complicated than anything in her career since then.

Heaven became alerted consciously. What is a blessing by then is that, the first cry of the babies interestingly brought day light after by 12:30 Noon.

Nancy had born a boy that is named Tesio, while on the other hand a girl is borne by Nandee named as Gmasnoh.

It was an incredible moment anybody couldn't easily have described. When the children were born lots of men went to the yard of the midwife. There some said the two children should be taken to the evil forest and abandon there. And some also said it's the gods that came by then to resolve peacefully the many problems of evils.

However, the belief of those whom said the two children be taken to the forest is that meant, they are not real human rather to be living among humans.

Jeering, this ugly belief has made it when any woman happens to born a twin one person could be taken to the evil forest and abandon. It has even happened before a woman had threesomes of children at once in the past and only one person was considered to survive. But upon consultation with the gods by the shrine men it was approved that the children should live.

At the time, seven years had since passed. The children met up with a kind of evil in the town since then. But everything is about to end, as they are now seven years old.

It is this seventh year the gods of the land thought to bring lasting peace to the people of Niffu. The elders at the time thought on consulting the gods of the land to solve the many problems of various evils. And the shrine men said the gods told them that the children will also help in time to come in their development in town.

It's so incredible to describe. However, the entire town for the past twenty and more years now, it has been a ground for ritualistic evils. A woman or man who happens to walk alone either to a farm could go missing surprisingly. It got the gods and elders angry for said thing to be put to a stop.

Finally, lots of men left town one evening to consult the gods. It's in the same seventh year of the children. They took their sacrifice materials of different sorts of things at the shrine. And Tesio and Gmasnoh were just seven years old. But they got to feel what has been happening since then. Sometimes when they are outside playing with their friends the parents would yell at them to leave the play and go take bath to enter their houses.

"We have come to sacrifice to you our gods. There are so many evils in our land. Our women and children don't any longer travel alone on roads by themselves again. When a person either male or female walks alone that person is being hunted since then by ritualistic men. Hear our cry! We are crying over you people because we can't continue to live like this throughout our lives. We believe if this continues like this, which lots of children or men and women may keep running away from the town for safety never to think of coming back here again. It's evil that, we have to try and get rid of such now. Our gods, we know you can hear. And now you have to come to help us! If our earth which we live will have no peace for us, then why should we be humans again? Gone are the days we have to continue living like animals, cutting one another life short. How long will you continue to be asleep? Should we all be as spirits of yours before we can find safety or what?" Elder Bartee took some water from his mouth and through it on the ground. He is by the head of the shrine Momsio, while looking at him chanting. There he stood up and said same without meanness either. He seems so contumacious. He is like one of the gods even. His colleagues around him are looking at him in fear.

Momsio collected the sacrifice materials some from the hands of Bartee and wasted much of it over lots of graves near the area.

Group of elders, which grouped themselves together already, believed to be the strongest amongst men in the town, were all seated at the shrine, looking at Momsio in fear. You could see the goats and chickens' blood and other food stuff wasted all over the place.

Momsio chanted. Looking at him you could say that he's a representative of the devil. His chalk lines on his body are prodigiously fearful indeed.

They made a return to town later. The night came. Now the gods in respond to the sacrifice conducted for an answer of peace thought it wise, sending a spirit as messengers of theirs to town that night after they left the shrine.

"Your problems are now over. We know how you have all being suffering the stress of the too many evils in town here." A threatening voice of powers from the gods is gallivanting in town the night fearfully delivering message of interest to everyone. "Prosperity and peace you've wished for is now available to the land of your forefathers where you're. This I have come to give you. Every head that is now listening to me, I want you take note of this that there would be no more trouble in the land of your birth that be here again. But, there are customs every one of you, if you don't know now you have to know, that you are to always obey as of today on. Don't you, as people of this land, know that most of the civilized laws of our nation we have since depended on none can any longer solve the many problems of our human's carnages here? If, as of today on, you have been told not to eat a particular animal or food or neither you fishing either into a particular creek, nor follow another man's woman or a woman to follow another woman's husband either, you're to obey. Moreover, no foreign person shall be allowed to get married to anybody in town here either. It's about now maintaining order and peace in the life of every family of the land. Our father' spirits sent me to give you the instructions. Please let everyone go by the traditional rules daily from the gods, as of today on." The strange spirit worded. Surprising, even as a leaf probably falls to the ground, could the sound of it be that so high presumably for anyone to feel as if the gods are physical that night to be watchful about. The whole place remained much stilled.

After that fearfully threatening voice of admonishment, when day came clearly, a particular lady came to visit the parents of the two children.

At the time the juju or medicine men and women have early the morning again slaughtered two cows as sacrifice to the gods for the acceptance of their call for peace. The whole population in town danced, believing that their forefather's spirit came purposely to have had the many problems of the land resolved. That year there was even good harvest. The fish and forest animals were even good friends to humans. By the time a person either goes fishing or hunt, he or she becomes happy.

Tesio and Gmasnoh had grown up since then very smartly. Tesio that last night when the spirit of the forefather came, he was highly attacked at heart with huge fear and trembling. And for Gmasnoh, she had made, as a shelter her father Snoteh's body for her safety. For Tesio, what he did was that he got stuck to his mother's body, while hiding from the voice presumably.

Eight years had gone by. And Tesio decided finding the chief elder that morning at his house. His aim is to understand certain issues about the customs. Before he could ask the elder, he said to him that they should walk back to his house where they can sit to discuss the issue. The elder did that as a respect to him because he seemed so powerful and developing well about upholding every bit of the tradition in the land. He became a very strong boy traditionally.

"Let me ask you this, dear. Is it that, are we to be as examples with the customs-making exercise that has to do with a person should be at twenty-five years old before he or she gets married in town here?"

Elder Bartee became speechless a bit. Tesio is sitting on his own bamboo plaited bed. No sponge on it either. As he was sitting it keeps making noise underneath him.

Bartee has thought to have then patted Tesio firstly on his forehead. After that he said, "The customs are good for the society. Nobody should think ugly about them. And they are for everyone's upkeep. That aspect you talked about is not for you and your cousin only to obey same. Stop taking it for a joke either. Especially the way you and Gmasnoh are born consciously suggests you shall be great people in life which nobody is going take for a joke either here. The gods told us that you and this girl have to go to school. And our eyes must be on the two of you. Maybe you can't understand what I meant to say now but the time shall come for you to understand it well. However, the purpose is for you both to be for us helpers. We want a change of our statuses here. Especially, we want development here. Because of that there is no need for early marriage business to come near the both of you either. So everyone person has to go by the customs."

Tesio had his wrapper on his shoulders sitting on the bed listening keenly. Only mosquitoes that morning are fusing with his ears, biting. He tries driving them off. But some proved impossible to go away at once.

"You need to help me to twig this thing better." Tesio said and paused.

"You got all the best to ask for understanding in every customs, Tesio." With tightened or stiffed eyes, while looking into Tesio's eyes, Elder Bartee said lamely.

"Tesio, I'm an elder that's very strong--a traditionalist you know of. Take note of this that the tradition will protect the both of you, if you can keep every aspect of the customs. It's not as foolish a thing to see me here, son. You and Gmasnoh have to understand the true nature of custom-making in a given society where we are."

When he said that but Gmasnoh quickly came into the house to them. She decided at least to leave the window area in her parents' house where she has been listening to them.

"What did you just mention, Elder? I need a lay understanding too about that really." she broke out.

"I'm saying the customs are not intended in any way to reprimand anybody, especially the both of you either. But the deviltry of most of those here must stop. It's something of prime concern for which there will be daily new customs to guard the footsteps of everyone to behave well. We can't continue to make evil as a sport here. Do you think it's on this part of the earth did Satan fall. Definitely it's a no!"

"Is that you really mean to say for the customs exercise . . . is all about?"

"Yes—"

"Alright. If I may be permitted to ask you again, do the gods mean that for us only? If yes, but I see that as no matter not upholding them either."

"Son," Bartee is still speaking, "even the group or intermarriage here is another example of what we want for peaceful organization in our land. You know it. We always want to be building up the spirit of togetherness all the time."

The elder patted Tesio and he winked his eyes also in happiness.

"Alright--" He smiled. Elder Bartee wiped a mist from over his eyelashes. "That's a good way that our people by the gods could promote peace?"

"Yes."

"But my elder, how can these work for us perpetually, where we can remain committed to the tradition? At least, I and my sister need to take some oaths right away, as a sign of true commitment to the tradition." Tesio innocently said. He became so serious on the face while looking into Bartee's eyes.

"It's good just what you have asked. You have really impressed me. It shows how serious you are about upholding you people's culture. But the time shall come at least at fourteen years for you both to take some oaths about your protection and others." Bartee said, and Tesio jumped up at his seat, demanding the oath-taking right away. When he said it, Gmasnoh went out the house. She is feeling so funny that they are discussing as men and nobody could had given her the attention really yet.

Tesio pounded the table before the elder like a man, proving how serious he's to take a traditional oath of not marrying outside the elder's arrangement upon the instructions of the gods.

"Look, let me die, if I happen to grow up and refuse to uphold every bit of the customs or tradition, especially to say that, I'm going to marry a foreign woman apart from a woman from the town here. That's a taboo. Let the gods chuck me to death."

"Stop it! My son, there is no joke inside a snake mouth either---especially about this. Everything you'll say here can't be taken for a joke either. The gods are everywhere around, even here by us listening. They have very big eyes spiritually.

And they are very powerful, if I may say either. But fear nothing. They are powers for peaceful organization of everyone."

"Surely?"

"Yes. But you won't see them. They are our forefathers' spirits in the land that have been guarding us."

"So, Elder Bartee, as we are sitting do I have one of the spirits living inside me or at the house here?"

"Yes. They live in the house here with you each time for something bad not to happen to you and your cousin either." He said in serious without a smile either. He dabbed Tesio as well.

"Really?"

"Yes."

"Okay. Let me ask you again this: what's the true meaning of the customs exercise by the way in a society of ours?"

"First, I want you understand this. The spirits are powers that have even made the witches that used to kill anybody at will to have ceased in their behaviour." Tesio giggled. "That's true, because I can remember the oral history my parents gave me is that, the citizens here any family member into witch either living within the family he or she could decide on quelling a member at will. It gets me to wonder about the culture of our people here. Do you think Satan used to have a base here also or that's here he fell from heaven?"

"That's a fact, Tesio. But all that had stopped since then by the elders. Now we would remain forever united," he said jokingly. By his assertion Tesio got seriously pondering on what he really meant to say.

2

Elder Koffa being a friend to Putunah, he woke one early morning purposely to speak with him on something on his mind. Usually he did that every morning. He walked about three minutes and reached at Putunah's abode. He was firstly that, rather welcomed inside. He sat into one of his bamboo chairs and got his hands relaxed to his knees. And his skin is still bared without any trace of hair either. But he is an old man. He has a kind of country soap that he rubs to make instantly the hair to be removed from his skin. He did that as usual.

However, few minutes after Putunah decided to offer him some sliced kola nuts and some pepper very well-cubed.

It's so sweet, dried pepper. One thing so interesting about the pepper is that---the smell alone could cause anybody surprisingly had smelled it by then to develop so much anxiety for it. In preparation upon drying it at first, next you have to pound same into a mortar. It smells like heated groundnuts.

"For the past days now at night my mind has been telling me something ugly. It's a part of the customs." Elder Koffa broke the ice with Putunah.

"What's it about the part of the customs you want talk about? Imagine I have been feeling as the tradition is a sight for sore eyes perhaps. Take note of that." Putunah said.

By the time he spoke Tesio came inside to where they are. He knew the father and his friend are in conversation seriously talking a matter relative to the tradition. He bombed into them and sat by his father. It made the father Putunah a bit galled but to ask him to leave, giving them a chance. Tesio obeyed.

"Now the way it looks to me concerning the part of the customs where a person has to be at twenty-five years before he or she can think of woman or man's business that needs a lay revision by the gods." Koffa said and paused a little. "Koffa, what's this other matter you're talking about? Can't you even remember before how little children at a very early age were impregnated? That part of the customs frankly is about doing away with early marriage situation because we want the young people in particular now, and in time to come, prioritizing western education. If, we don't maintain that our future would continue to be in jeopardy. There could be unending poverty in our land which there would always be the lack of development on an overall too. So, this thing is better as it is." Putunah said.

"It's true! But let's look at that a little. That's all together not as bad to be either, but something needs to be revised about it."

"Is this a reason you have come to see me or what? Don't you know that the traditions of any society help to hold the people together? Please, I beg of you to leave that alone."

"Look, Putunah, you are an elder and I, too, is an elder as you are. I know that there is no society without a tradition can prosperous to be as great as it may, but ours about the premarital vow is awkwardly an impediment. And never to see it remain as it is now. You shall know the truth I'm talking about if you can't understand me; now when the time shall come don't you blame me either."

"Please, let's lay low on this yet. I'm begging you. You know how long the customs have been guarding our steps in keeping a relation with the gods?" Putunah sturdily said.

"But don't forget that not every slow step of a great tortoise is good for him either. If, we don't act now, when time shall come if not revising the customs, I can see a big trouble to come."

You could see Koffa twisting here and there in the hallway of Putunah's house. And Putunah remained tacit yet. After like three minutes he broke out saying, "Nothing much can I further say again about this at all! Just that it's bothering my mind for which I couldn't sit at home without telling you either. But I'm done."

"Koffa, don't be angry with me either. You've raised a very serious issue for us to discuss later with other colleagues of ours than being it only the two of us to talk about it, please." Putunah said unenthusiastically. Koffa bobbed.

After the long chat, Koffa decided going home because he has to go on the farm few minutes later upon reaching home and when he shall have eaten his breakfast. He was so happy to have seen his friend and they yakked the morning very nicely.

Before his departure Putunah requested his wife to give him some dried bonny fish from the drier upon behest to do so then. The woman folded the fish into a wide leaf she went outside she brought.

Koffa is happy that, when he gets home by the afternoon hour his wife would cook it with some cassava later. Koffa is elated by the gesture of his friend and smiled so much over it.

He reached home finally. His passion for early morning breakfast has built up in him high. It's the breakfast perhaps he knew about for which he has been at Putunah's house and they chatted so long. It's like his stomach had taken in enough of air for which hunger became very huge with him.

He is yet few steps to reach at the house. And he decided calling his wife from inside the house. Before he could call her, he coughed, as a way of telling the woman that he's now close at the house. And the woman heard him coughed and she became alerted.

"Ma Tanneh," he is almost to bump into the front door of his house, "you try now and open the door. I want to get away as soon as I'm through with my breakfast to go on the farm."

She's a bit delaying. When she heard him she woke from her bed to get the rope of her wrapper firstly fasten same on her body. By the way then his angle is building up in him. He has been for a lay while now at the door knocking. But no avail yet. His feature is changing. Jealousy, a disease of any lover, developed inside him that the woman probably is delaying because she's with a man inside the room, whereas she is looking for her wrapper's rope.

"Do you want to see me dead by hunger before you can come and open this door?" he pounded the door again and again.

"Ah, what's this? I'm looking for my wrapper's rope to tie on my waist and to come to you." Parlee Munnah said while frowning.

"But do you have a man inside the room or what? You keep delaying, why?"

"Why should you say that to me? In fact, you'll have to burst the door open."

"Oh, that's what you saying? But who is this woman I married since then that keeps causing trouble for me?" He hissed as usual at the doorpost.

Finally she opened the door. By the time she opened it, she went at the back of the yard quickly. He was then being swallowed inside the house. After few minutes, he came back outside again just to inspect his yard yet.

"Haven't you in fact swept around this house yet?" He took his own hand, rubbing it on the bamboo bench outside. They are plaited in a bundle. And they paralleled in structure as well.

In response the woman said, "But I did that."

"You must be joking! Furs are still over here. How can you clean-up and there are still dirt, in fact? Please, don't play on my annoyance. I beg of you." He pushed up his mouth and hissed.

"I did clean up, Koffa! It's just that the animals are too many these days. You, all the men in town had made them so plentiful. Why should you guys make them as property and forget to trade them off constantly? And so, they got furs everywhere because during the night time they are just playing and kicking everything here in our yard."

"Look, you've been living like this with the animals since then. It can't be as strange for which you didn't clean up either."

"What should I still say? I told you that I have already cleaned up. Like you said, Koffa, if I'm to wake very early every time purposely be cleaning up furs, will you pay me? You haven't one day given me a stipend either---for doing that." She said and cut her eyes at him. He was nowhere close to her either to notice her while frowning and doing otherwise.

Koffa isn't satisfied with her response either. "What kind of lazy woman is this? Oh, my God! She has really become a problem of my life these days. See it here!" He's pointing his finger at the dirt inside the house. "Why there are even goats' toilet and the furs everywhere in the yard? Are you blind?" he said quietly to himself.

He decided at last to talk louder for her to hear him better. He went to the kitchen and looked at the food table and saw nothing like his food on it. He trembles. It's like a dream yet, as he is thinking whether she did give out his food to anybody.

"In fact, what have you been doing all this while, when day broke since then? Perhaps did you get through with preparing my sliced cassava?"

He didn't get a response still. In so doing, he decided to walk up to her and stood at the doorpost. It has become a different story again.

The sliced cassava which is often prepared in the morning is a cultural food. Most men consume that before later could any think of going either on the farm or fishing. Embarrassing the moment, she has surprisingly given out the man's food to her son without his knowledge.

"Your son," her tone is low, "Wisseh ate the food. I thought you said I should warm the soup and cassava at the time to have given it him, Koffa?" The woman said grudgingly. Koffa became shivering in body for what she did. His nerves are shaking on him. He is so incensed. "No. That can't be true. You're joking—"he said by force. He pounded the table with his hand. He got the woman petrified about that. He remains yet, asking for his food.

Elder Koffa got soured inside him, like I said. What should he do? However, with no feeling of decency at the time in him, he's angrily moving about inside the room to collect his belt to come and pummel her. The woman is outside feeling battered at heart about his high calling perhaps.

"Hey, you leave the back of the house and come here to me!"

"What's the meaning of all that, Koffa?"

"Do you know what you've done to me?" he's sighing, meaning how seriously is the hunger.

"I'm so sorry, Koffa. I didn't mean that either. But, it's your son who ate your food. I gave it to him. And that shouldn't really be a problem now again---I really hope so."

"Look, who are you to tell me such? I believe you're joking with me. Stop the stupidity and bring my food here to me now!" He said with a frowning face still. "It's even about time I consume it to go on the farm. As you're saying such, if true, do you expect me to go on our farm?" He padded. He is a bit doddering, as if he has reached his old age already.

He is still inside the room struggling to get his belt. He is that so anguished. He is trying to find the belt but the belt couldn't yet be found. He remained a bit stilled to figure out where he has left it.

By the time the woman decided going at the back of the yard where is the cassava garden to dig up some cassava to cook for him quickly. She's so sorry for what she did. But the husband feels so disappointed.

"I'll surely beat the hell out of you. And you have long been doing this but that isn't going to work with me again."

"Ah, Koffa, what's it? Are you to beat me up just for food matter, when you know the boy is your blood as mine, too?"

"Shut up! You woman, I want you now shut up! You supposed to tell me that?"

"What's it, Koffa? Okay, I'm making an appeal to you so that I can be allowed dig up and cook some cassava very fast for you."

"Shut up! Get out of my face now! You should have been here before me to say that mess. In fact, I'm coming out there to you soon."

Despite his lousy behaviour, he's still inside looking for his belt among the clothes confusedly. Koffa is fusing with her while inside and said again, "If, you don't learn to always follow my instruction you might be replaced with another woman soon. I promise you this now."

"That's your habit. Should I fear you for that?" She made a rebuttal to him about his ugly statement.

When she said that surprisingly, which nobody could think, but the clothes hanging on the rope inside the room have almost entangled the head of Koffa. Luckily he found the wonderful belt at last. He rolled it up around his palm quickly and started coming outside. His aim now is to whip her with it. Arrogance by the way then has rumpled itself inside him. He couldn't even have a second mind either to desist from being in anger with her either.

The woman is still digging up cassava. She is so seriously making sure to get that quickly done.

"Where are you?"

"I'm here behind the house." She has reluctantly said.

"What are you doing there? Bring my food here now!" Koffa still brayed on her. She is so annoyed for his lack of understanding.

"What are you saying, Koffa? Do you want me turn to the food so as to see you chew me up--or what?"

"Oh! That's the unruly thing you are saying to me? Look, am I to joke with you again about this?"

"But there is no food here which I continue to tell you about! What do you want me to say? I'm about to cook. I expect you to go walking around again."

"You mean that—"

"Yes!"

"You should just allow me reach to you now. I'll hurt you." Koffa said quietly and she didn't at all hear him either. He's pounding the ground with his toes, walking straight at her in the back where she is.

"You must tell me now what have you done with my food." He said that loudly.

"Is it by force? Do you still want to know? I told you that I'm about digging up some cassava for you in the back? Relax your impulse, dear." She said, while looking around herself by then because she knew he may have come forcibly on her like the way he's sounding.

"I'm already close to you." Koffa said quietly.

At times what he does, especially when he's so hungry at night is that, he wakes her up to go and cook for him. She is like a maid into her own house, quite frankly. It's so annoying but she got to do that because that's the culture. She would just hiss to herself quietly but forced to honour the request whatever.

Now so jeeringly the moment to describe, the two are racing, as he is going after her to forcibly get his food out of her. Koffa is making sure to hit at her.

3

["He'll kill me . . . oh!"]

["He'll kill me . . . oh!"] The wife shouted twice, while pleading with her neighbour to come to her aid as she's chased away by him to whip her.

Interestingly, Munnah, for what is noted, she's probably being blessed that moment as the man tries chasing her and he couldn't just reach her by then. His bones were sounding on him as he is running like an old man. And he's of a problem of rheumatism that often got him walking like a really old dolly up man.

So good for the woman, however, some goats in a number of ten came in a railroaded way between the two. They are lover goats that were in the act of matting when they surprisingly came between the two and halted Koffa a little. He has also broken his leg on one of them. He kicked about two but he couldn't still make it to pass through. Despite that he maintains his tenacity to seeing being hit at still.

The woman used that time when the goats came between, finding her way quickly into Putunah's house. He had nearly hit on the back of her brutally. It's like heaven was alerted that moment to spare her grace perhaps.

"What's it? Now tell me! My friend, what's it?" Putunah intermittently asked his colleague upon forcefully coming close to him, while he, Putunah, is standing at the doorpost. First, however, he allowed the woman to pass him by.

While there shamelessly, Koffa who was about falling said, "It's that woman inside your house there. I must deal with her now."

Putunah decided to intervene. "Both of you're too big for this! You can't be chasing your wife like your equal. Koffa, what has happened to you these days?" Koffa's breathe trembles the clothes of Putunah, when he came very close almost to fall on him after he stormed his toes at the doorpost. One of his teeth almost broke. Luckily his friend Putunah was there to have held his hand. His eyes went wide at Putunah. Luckily, he gained balance before him but carefully speechless like a hunting tiger a bit.

Munnah, while sitting inside the house of Putunah, and she spotted him at the portal almost to have fallen off--and she quickly said, "You are a damned shameless man. I don't know how will your son behave if you can behave like this?" She said hissed in anger. Koffa almost push Putunah aside just to see him go inside to pummel her. But Putunah held him like steel. He couldn't pass through him either. Now he became a presiding general to himself in shame. Nothing else he could do again, rather to behave calm.

Obvious, the situation is so shameful for anyone of the two either to have openly quickly had explained to Putunah yet, what had gone wrong by then at home which got them there either. He is blushed.

However, for almost three minutes, neither him, nor the woman could think of explaining either. Who should have been the first person to explain the issue to Putunah when he asked, became very hard to do any either. The woman tries to cover up the story because he is her husband. But the guy doesn't have a shame either.

After the two rested a bit Putunah decided to ask some question about the thing that went wrong for which they chased one another, for. "Madam," Putunah came close to her, "is something wrong?" In response Parlee Munnah said, "Please try asking your friend before you first."

"Oh! That's what you are saying to me? I beg of you, please tell me what the matter is." Putunah said, while pretended smiling as well. He's feeling so embarrassed the moment.

Before the interrogation the entire yard of Putunah is at a gridlock with individuals who wanted to inquire about the issue. Some were clapping hands to have seen them have a face to face fight. It's as a melodrama the moment, seeing lots of people standing inquisitively.

"Koffa, I know that there is something seriously wrong, isn't it?" Putunah said pretentiously. He asked and smiled as well.

Koffa is delaying speaking on the issue still. However, Putunah is a smart old man who understands the tradition. As such, while looking at the way the both are, especially Koffa being an elder, he decided to balance himself in soothing the man first.

For the tradition, any problem that may have been between a man and a woman, the man is always right. Because of that he decided not to be focused with calming her either. He wants his colleague comforted than the woman. Reason being, she is the complaint. Usually the complaint, if is a woman, suffers a bit injustice of the king. It's a tradition full of sorts of ironies.

"This woman before you should have done something for me this morning. She should have warmed my food. She did and gave out my food. And it has been my hope that upon eating to go on the farm later. I should have burst her head up since then before her arrival here. She refused to do what she was told to. Putunah, I want you be my witness in the time to come because I would surely divorce this woman soon—" In a quick rebuttal Parlee Munnah said, "Let him go ahead now! If food matter is the reason of paying my dowry at the time to my parents, let him go ahead!" The woman responded with tears into her eyes. Putunah penitently smiled in shame.

"Hey, wait you woman!" Putunah tries friendly to resolve the matter. "I'd surely try later to deal with your husband about this. In fact, the elders will have to know about this. Therefore, please be at peace and try going home now."

"You've to always advise that your friend Koffa." Munnah said.

"But Koffa is it right the way you did?" Putunah asked.

There is still an angle being expressed on Koffa's face. His nerves, because he's bright in complexion, were greened in disgust showing his muscularity.

"Putunah, I intended removing the wax inside her ears. Each time I tell her anything of this kind from today on at least she'd be able to listen well. She seems berserk." Koffa unruly or disrespectfully said without any bit of thinking of her as his wife either.

"Cool off a little, Koffa." Putunah pleaded. The woman remains still respectfully mute.

Putunah turns to the woman to sooth her. "I'm so sorry, dear. Let me tell you this that, this be the husband of yours is a troublesome man. I want you go home now and do as he earlier told you to, ensuring that he has some food upon that to be able to go on the farm for the family's sake to cut some palms, please."

"Okay. I'm leaving but you've to tell him to be that considerate at times. A man doesn't behave as the way he did, as if he's an animal. If, he wants to be as though he is a goat these days, you'll have to advise him to desist." Munnah said.

"That's okay. Please go home now." Putunah concluded.

Munnah frowned at Putunah a bit. She did that because she expected him to have said something very concrete or of value, for her against the husband than that he had said.

She has quietly then wiped her face off tears. She is butting out the door. The partial way in which Putunah chose to handle the issue had got her so much dejected. However, she left for home finally.

After that Putunah and Koffa thought to start a new conversation. First of all, he has decided to advise him yet. "I want you stop doing that. You're no more a boy now. It's disgusting to see you continue like this each time against your woman, Koffa." Putunah said and Koffa bobbed.

While in the process of chatting Barrie Musa, who hailed from Lofa County and runs a business since twenty years now in Monrovia came in the house. He wants to buy some cows and goats in Niffu by the help of Putunah, which he has always done for him. He is urged to sit.

Before he could come inside the house he got a hint of what both Putunah and Koffa have been saying on the issue of the woman. He decided to add his word too. He didn't even investigate yet but he had the mind to jump to conclusion that the woman misbehaved by not doing what the husband had told her.

Musa owned the majority shares into a slaughter business, which is being managed by his brother on Bushrod Island. One thing about his family members in business is that, they are trusted people. Business is all that they can do in life.

However, the Island is found between the Providence Island and Centre Monrovia. The area has a very huge urban population. Because of the population on the island, he makes a lot of profit in his business for which he's always in Niffu to buy cattle.

He's a very tall bright man that has convincing talks on his lips because he's a businessman that is often in talk with his customers, while convincing each just to buy his meat.

His ancestries are from the Republic of Mali in West Africa. He's a very generous Muslim man. His wife, who is his strength for his business activities, Demawa Musa, has deference for him. But at times she can just in outburst developed anger inside her because he couldn't give her a free time either. She is always at the business place counting money the whole day. It became her daily life situation. She feels her whole life is shrouded by the act of making money which could be considered as her god. And anybody presumably, as she fears at time, one day openly would approach her like that either.

Something so terrible about Musa is that the way he treats his wife. When he's about going home during the evening hour, after the whole day selling, he got her into his car as if his child without her having a free time to herself either, where she could visit at least a friend close by her dwelling. She is a very beautiful Fullah tribal woman from the same region with a look of an Indian.

Damawa fears him only a bit because he's to the woman as if a father. At an early age when she got married to him. She didn't even enjoy any fatherly love apart from her old dolly husband that got to give her that. And she couldn't even afford to see him be hurt one day either.

There is something very ironic by then to speak of about the relationship of the two. The age range between the two is thirty years.

"In Lofa," he breaks the ice upon seeing his friends brainstorming on Koffa's issue, "we are controlling the population from doing evil; we are instilling discipline, especially in our children and women too. We established the Sandi and Poro secret societies for the entire population to be disciplined. It's a bush-school to teach behaviour standards to our people. And the worst thing here with you guys which I can't really yet understand is that, why would you tell your wife something she refused to do it? Woman is subject to work for a man; if, for example, you don't know that now, please get to know it." Musa comically said.

"Please don't make us to laugh. You're sounding very interesting to us really. And I think that is really a fact about what you have said." Putunah said.

"Wow—" Koffa added.

"You should have punished your wife by then." Musa added again.

"Really?"

"Yes."

"Okay. I thought those of us here in Niffu are probably jokers even by spawning customs daily for the population's protection against evil." Putunah friendlily said. By the time he said it they all chuckled over his statement.

Tesio and his cousin Gmasnoh upon hearing the news and upon leaving the waterside area they are now positioned at the back of the yard to discuss it. They felt sorry and serious about it. Why will two persons behaved as the way they did? It got Gmasnoh feeling so stupid about it.

"I saw Koffa and wife fusing. I'm confused of the reason should the two behaved like that. Why should old folks as they are, but won't desist from such act by the way?"

"Yeah! It's hard to talk. Let's leave that to discuss our school matters." Gmasnoh said.

"That would really be that fine to do so, please." Tesio added.

"Well, I've something very interesting to tell you, Tesio."

"What's it?"

"My heart has been speaking to me that I must try studying to be a doctor someday in the near run." Gmasnoh ambitiously said. Tesio chuckled.

"Do you mean that, Gmasnoh?"

"Yes. That's my purpose of schooling for which I have to exert every effort now in that to achieve the goal."

"Really—"

They giggled over it again.

"But let me ask you again. Do you mean that . . . imagine as small as the both of us are for you to be thinking that way? If you don't know probably, but it's a hard study you are to go through, ain't you even aware?"

"It's no matter by that either. Life is all about making a try. I can make it." Gmasnoh said. Tesio is sitting by her. Gmasnoh is also smiling.

"Wow! You sound so interesting to me. Okay, but let me rephrase my question again. What's your aim of being a doctor--by the way then?" She looked at Tesio into his eyes a bit speechlessly. She had her two hands clapped at her mouth so surprised. In response she said, "Wow! I don't expect it to be you perhaps asking me such a question like this Tesio, when you know how the terrible condition here about the lack of hospital is either."

"Yes. I do know of that. You don't have to be hurt about my question either. We are all discussing for which I wished to know. You are sounding too very good to me."

"Okay. I'm sorry. But didn't you see the other day a woman was into labour pain for which only traditional midwife tried to deliver her, but it was futile? Even by record your mother told you similarly a story about us that nearly such thing missed us. There are too much of medical problems in our town. And these are the threatening factors that have really moved me to be a doctor." Gmasnoh strongly purported with a serious smile.

"That's so good to say. But for what I see it to be now is that, I think you're still too small yet to think that way." Tesio sagely said. Gmasnoh made a rebuttal by saying, "I don't want you to continue to say so, Tesio. The human's tongue is the power of his or her life. What you confess now and perhaps earnestly work towards that would surely come to pass. Life isn't by magic either." Tesio looked at her very interestingly and bobbed.

"Really?"

"What not? It's true."

"You are also sounding really so good too!"

"Yes. I need to try my best too."

"If that's the case then you may be so that right as you've said, seeing you exert every effort about it. I'd expect that you be very serious with the plan." He padded. "Yes. I will keep doing my best in school to achieve it." Gmasnoh added. Tesio said again, "I've already decided to be an engineer, but because of the plan of yours which I find interesting. Therefore I may yet study along with you on the issue of medical and later I'd branch up, rather pursuing engineering studies. It's my desire to really be the first and best engineer in time to come here in Niffu Town. And when I'm done with my studies I shall put a road network here in our town." Tesio said constructively.

He'd got Gmasnoh to chuckle too. She's like a fool in state yet laughing ridiculously. Like two minutes after she whipped her eyes unconsciously with her palm and later became very serious again. It seems so interesting about her really.

4

Under the plum tree by the house of Putunah there is a hammer hanging between a planted stick and the plum tree itself.

This wonderful day that came Tesio is sitting a bit over the cousin while into a hammer. And she is sitting underneath it. His legs hanging down from it, as if he's at a playground swinging them at the same time conversing with her. While in the process, Elder Bartee saw the two talking. Even the day is a day of school. Because of that he decided urging them peacefully to go inside quickly. He wants them get ready to leave for school. They have been discussing issues on school matter which has so much interested the elder. He hid himself behind the plum tree first without them knowing and listened to everything they had to say by then.

Bartee came into Putunah's house about that. He opens a lecture. First of all, he heard what the conversation has been between Tesio and Gmasnoh which he wants to comment about. He's so happy that they could converse nicely like that, as if old folks talking seriously a matter. It made him riveted in body over such nice talk.

"Putunah, I must tell you this that since the civil war has ended young people by far these days in Liberia are seriously speaking a lot good about education than it used to be as our days of old."

"Really?"

"Yes. That is the case with Gmasnoh and Tesio. Their conversation is all about school matters. Imagine I got my foolish son Nagbe who can't even talk about school matter at the house. The guy is just at home eating all of my food each day and there is no school business in his head either. Imagine the day he happens to forcibly go to school like that only failing grades he brings to my house. But both you, your brother's children are good."

"Surely?"

"Yes."

"That's really fine."

"As you are my very good friend, Putunah, I really want you and brother Snoteh to take care of them always. For what I can see about them is that they would be as great individuals to even help us in town here." He said. He had his hand clapped to his chain smiling.

They are happy because not too many young people like the two have the virtuosity in that smartly to speak of school. So, he took it very importantly to make his friend not and ever, feeling reluctant about helping the children develop well. And Putunah is full of fun perhaps. All that the friend had said he still wants to ask or say something funny to him.

"Bartee, I didn't get you clearly. Did you say that the little kids were talking about school matters very interestingly?"

"Yes!"

"Really?"

"That's so true!"

"Wow! I don't even know what to say again. My heart is so elated by the saying. And you are making me feel so proud about the two of them." He said, self-importantly. And his friend chuckled over it.

The main hour of school came. Tesio and Gmasnoh have to walk about thirty minutes before reaching on the campus from the house. Now they are strolling little by little while going to school finally.

Needless to say, that the mothers at home had a lot of work to do. Besides, the two children have kept their conversation at home. So, a short-lived pity of them not being around started developing into the two because none the guys is there.

"The way Tesio isn't here either---I'm thinking of how will I make it fast with the daily work home? There is no water even in the entire house which I've to go to the creek?" Nancy said to herself. She feels as jilt as lover does at times. Not that the children deceived her the moment, but she has always wished that they be around her. It's the same with Nandee, the mother of Gmasnoh.

"Nancy decided calling out from her window to know if Nandee is facing similar situation as hers in her house too.

"Are you so busy right now, Nandee? This is Tesio's mother, please."

"Yes. What's it?"

"No, just that I've too much work right now on me. I thought to ask you if you facing similar situation and if not, you could come to help me. I've to clean up the house as well as be able to go draw some water at the creek. I'm about to even split wood and cook later for my husband and the children. That's so much work here!"

"You mean that, Nancy? I thought mine was too much than yours. Now I'm also faced with similar situation."

"Wow! Okay, let me just finish mine on time I'd be there later to assist you instead."

"Alright! I hope so, please."

After the across-house talk, the two women got busy strongly cleaning up as earlier said into their various homes. They were forced to modulate from complaining rather to cope with the activities since the children are gone to school.

Teacher Wilson Wea-bla, a famous man every kid in the school knew about, especially for his act of mentoring children, he has interestingly come to class. He has just walked about forty minutes from his village near Niffu Town to have come to school that morning. It's something he often had done from Monday to Friday in every week.

"I've a new lesson for you all today. First of all, you've to learn a new word called 'Restoration," he sounded. He's looking so outlandish with a kind of funny trousers on him. The leg is so wide from down and rubbing on the floor. No one could easily see the shoes he had on either because of the trousers. He had his hair uncut. He had on a size one shirt light green and with a blue trouser on. His bespectacled covered almost every part of his eyes until only the face itself you could see instead of the eyes. He had red, blue, and green pens with him. They are all stuck up into his front pocket on the shirt.

And the word he got on the board is so an interesting word for all of the students later to like. Just that it's strange yet. "What is it that word are you talking about, Sir?" Gmasnoh asked inquisitively while at her seat.

"Gmasnoh, may I advise that you all have to give me a lay chance yet to display to you what may be as the meaning of the word on the chalkboard. This shouldn't be your worry either. I'll better explain the meaning to you." He said. The kids' eyes went wide opened, gazing at him in bewilderment. They were like impatient to hear him speak on it. He means to provide a concept that would give the meaning of what the word entails in a biblical context in that to blend it with the social-economic situation of man's surviving-fight on earth.

He was done with putting his dotted analysis about the single word on the board. He turned to the students for response.

Tesio's hand is raised. He was given the permission to ask his question. "If I may ask you sir, what has been a problem in human's life that calls for a need for that word of 'restoration' you got on the chalkboard really has to do with man's life?" Tesio soberly asked.

"Tesio, can't you see the kind of life we all pass through daily," he's turning his head about, "which is full of stresses and pains? Poverty is the evil that is going around or fighting against every human's life, isn't it?"

"Thank you, sir! So, Wea-bla, I'm confused as a kid to know still, because you should be aware that we are yet immature to fully understand you about this concept you trying to provide. What does that big word got to do with us?" The teacher looked at him seriously, focusing on his eyes smiling, and understandingly thought that his mind is still maturing, though. However, few minutes later, Mr. Wea-bla makes a respond by saying, "Alright. When I'm finished with explaining, the connotation will be as cleared as anything for which you won't even be able to ask too much of question either. Just relax a little."

Tesio said no problem. He went to explain. "We, as humans biblically are fully restored from sins by the mercy of God being available to all men because we now live under the grace period that's by him. But the physical, so you want me still stress this, which is a hard struggle that we all got to always go through daily? For example, when day breaks either it is all about the twisting and turning for a survival by every human at every home. That means you need restoration for the day, termed a survival in concept."

"Thanks! But let me know again, if you would like me to ask." Gmasnoh said. "Go ahead!" Wea-bla became very poised. "Why should all this suffering be on man?" Gmasnoh purportedly asked.

"The root of human's suffering is derived from the old---the spiritual side of life. Imagine man was once created perfect, which everyone does know about during biblical studies. But what is now a burden is the physical state of living a better life. It's left with man again to provide for himself than it used to be."

"Wea-bla, are you today teaching a Bible lesson or what? Because we should be having a Bible instructor in class to teach that to us perhaps---and that isn't you either---that which you know of."

"No. I'm trying to teach concept to every one of you. The word shouldn't be a problem perhaps to anybody here. I'm introducing that because I know the importance of life. For every human being the life of him or her begins at the childhood level to adulthood. We have to know this. If you know the need for which everyone has to struggle in that to be somebody, it won't be a problem either. It's because of that I thought it wise to mentor you all who are the foundation of our human's society yet."

"It is a mentoring from the gods you've to give us or what?"

"Please, I don't want to talk on traditional issue here. I don't really know what tradition is because all my days I have been in school in the Netherlands. I know only the creator of the universe than the gods you're talking about."

Gmasnoh is a bit mute. She is looking at his eyes. She feels like shivering in goodness to what he's saying. There's something which had enthralled her then. And that has to do with the issue of the teacher not knowing what the tradition in the land is.

You could see Wea-bla boastfully bouncing around at the same time pointing his fingers at the word on the board which he had made dotted analysis of it. He feels really proud that he's talking sense to the kids. And they couldn't fully yet understand what he's been saying.

"Are you saying to us that perhaps when a person seriously works hard to be a thief either, he or she gets the same credit in life about that too? I'm confused of what you really mean to say." Tesio said.

"No, get me clearly. Neither do I want you misinterpret me either. What I'm saying here is that for every one of you guys to make a difference towards life as a whole. You have to have the concept that you have to struggle to achieve the goal of living a better life. And it begins by schooling. Please get me rightly. I do not want you speak of being a thief either."

"I wish to apologize, sir." Tesio said.

Wea-bla laughed. "But I still have to make you understand what life is all about really."

"I think that would be a great deed an importance to us." Gmasnoh said. Wea-bla became obligated consciously to speak his mind still about the issue. "God said," he's now standing in an aisle close to Tesio, "let us make man in our image, and in His image man was made good. Or, are you all here saying to me that the God's image is like suffering to man to sit idly while dying in poverty? Truly that might happen to anybody because she or he doesn't want to take a better step towards success either." He said and paused.

"But taking a step, as you have said," Tesio stood up before the class upon getting permission to speak, "if I don't have the foundation as my father and mother didn't have at the time to have brought me up good because there is no money, how can I make it still to hit the mark of living a good life?"

"You can still make it to be somebody."

"Like how, sir? Reason being there is a parable about the tortoise that says that tortoise wants to jump but it doesn't have the right leg as other animals to make a jump either. And this is the situation with my family financially. How can I then make it when poverty first got hold of my parents and now me?"

"If that's the reason you asked I want you to know that there is no more the case for anyone to find everything as easy it used to be on earth before during early creation of the world again. The garden of Eden which we learned about during biblical days is no more an existence."

"Wow!"

"That's the fact. I expect that your biblical teacher should have told you that since then, isn't it?"

"We know that. It's true!"

"So, will you guys get your hands folded on, where not to find a better way out of this life anymore because of poverty? Let me tell everybody that there has been no easy means or would ever be any easy way out for any man or woman to find life easy again."

Everyone giggled. There is huge exuberant from the faces of the kids. They all became very eager to understand fully what he is now saying to them.

"Visually, sir, you're sounding spiritual about the word than it should have been as an ordinary subject to us either. And you are also sounding too importantly as a value to listen to for our lives. In fact, are you a clergyman, if I may ask?" Tesio soberly asked."

"Let me again say this that everything that man does on earth now and in time to come, is about economy. If you want to be a doctor either, the underlying factor or concept of pursuing that goal is about economy. And nobody has a monopoly over knowledge. When you learn you can be the best. Go after it." Wilson Wea-bla said. And Gmasnoh bobbed.

"What do you think, my students, will I've to go to school those days to have a PhD by the way then? See, I'm working for a pay because I'm able to impact knowledge to you. The idea here is that, from day one I chose school because I don't want to stay in poverty. I wanted to economically restore my life to a value. And poverty makes you feel as valueless, a being. I got the power now with me which am imperatively consciously a forceful weapon of friendliness that I hold for any man to love me, for. I want you be that seriously working daily developing your lives, too, rather to learn to be your own power." He said and giggled over it.

He's so grateful that he has provided a great deal of important concept that would live with each of them. It was as if a melodrama the moment to see.

Few minutes later, he got out the class quickly. He has been running against another instructor's turn. And that instructor came in and taught for an hour.

It is about 1:00PM now. This is the usual hour that the school knocks out for the student populace to go home.

Many students became very hungry the hour and rushing home to find food. Everyone took his or her bag while going out to the building portal. First of all, Gmasnoh ran to her cousin who has quickly gone to the other side of the building to say hi to a friend called Dorsla. She found him. After few minutes, very interestingly by then Tesio cuddled hands with her while then swinging same smiling, walking till they reached home finally.

Their entry into the house became so much happiness for both the mothers who had then thought earlier missing them.

Quite interestingly, the first person met at the doorpost of the house was Tesio's father. Putunah saw them from a distance coming back home then and stood at the door awaiting them.

Being at the house Putunah decided to ask of what they have done at school on that day perhaps. And Tesio couldn't just wait on his father to fully rest by asking him a question on whatever he wants to know either. But he's breezed emotionally to have disclosed of the lesson. He stuttered by saying, "Pap, the both of us learned a new word." Gmasnoh by then asked him to wait a little. She wanted to be the first to say that. "We learned a word called 'restoration' in school today. The meaning is nothing but a suggestion that every man or woman on earth is somehow being confronted by poverty unavoidably. And if he or she doesn't struggle to get rid of such evil he or she becomes valueless perhaps." Gmasnoh said. She held Putunah's right hand.

It got Putunah to laugh first. He had a husky voice put up while laughing ridiculously. He didn't believe it.

In response he said, "You guys have now become one of those clergies that I knew before when I was in the City of Monrovia. I hope you're not going to bombard me with something quite differently that would scare me, oh?" He said and paused for a little while. He knows how ambitious the two are. They are always asking question about every little thing each had a doubt about to know it.

"Daddy, that was an issue the teacher introduced in class and he had lots of responses from us about that. But he's a very smart and interesting teacher." Tesio said. "Well, the both of you now have the ball in your court. I'm so happy that your teacher was able to tell you the truth." Putunah said.

Putunah keeps laughing till tears ran down his eyebrows while his back his turned to them, falling down the way to his maws. And the very lively of the two is Gmasnoh. "Pap, in fact, you and ours statuses right now suggest nothing other than once the talked about the issue of poverty in class. We are penniless people for now. As you, our fathers of our families are dead broke, Dad. It's so bad which today we catching the hell of hard times." Gmasnoh unruly said. She even frowned.

"Oh, you are joking! Why can you be so lousy about this like that? Anyway, what you have said is the truth. And I want you both graduate soon from such ugly state of life." He said while still smiling. He's reminded of his shame of poverty. But what could he and brother do again in life really now that they are almost at the doddering stage, which is old age? He's a bit blushed due to the aide memoire but he pretended not to be either. So he had both an anguished and happy looks corresponding on him. He's smiling too.

He wiped his face off tears. He became very nonchalant than ever. "Get to know this, you little children that it's such a reason to believe in yourself as you go to school in time to come where you to correct the problem of poverty. Restore your lives first and later your generation can feel as good that you did." He tries shamelessly to sooth the two. They smiled.

"Dad, you're right. Our teacher had told us that already. Therefore, we'd keep doing our best to be successful. Be assured of that. This is a non-turning back moment of our lives we can't just miss in any way seeing it change either."

"Thank you ever so much! That's what I want you all should persistently pursuit the truth about life through obtaining education now. And I'm so happy that you're proving it rightly."

Putunah said and patted the backs of the two, urging them inside the room to go and take-off their uniforms. As they were going away from him, you could see him wobbling with his head in remembrance of what the two had shamelessly told him about.

Because he's so embarrassed, having the children rebuked him perhaps, later he said, "Dimmitt! Should I think that these little children are putting up a good fight with poverty? Or, are they to behave stupid and saying all sorts of shit to us? Anyway, I noticed that they have the right minds to do the best by helping us realize our dreams too? I can't get over their shameless talk against my brother Snoteh and me. Do they think we ain't since then that serious in life to have been in school or probably working or what? Just that the opportunity they have now wasn't as the way it should have been for us. Things were so bad at the time of our youth for which we couldn't that make it to school either." Putunah complained to himself. He turned to look at them still nesting inside the room gradually.

Putunah walked to his living room and got relaxed while holding his head with his two hands. By the time he sat his brother Snoteh came inside. He asked him to sit. Putunah was looking at the brother thinking that he could ask him a question as to what may have gone wrong with him either. Perhaps Snoteh wasn't even concerned about his look either. But his wish has been for the brother to ask him what went wrong with him so he could have explained it to him.

5

The next day became very wonderfully bright yet in the morning. And for the afternoon it is glowing as well joyously. Most of those in town decided to pour to the beach to swim. This is something often done during the Hamilton when the weather became sultry. The magnanimity of the atmosphere is highly indescribably sweet as really a sight for sore eyes.

During such time often tinny bonny fish pulled on shore forcibly by the ocean tides became very plentiful. So early in the morning before the late afternoon or even during the day itself, lots of women and children in part begin picking them from the shore. And they are often dried up and eaten with cassava upon boiling it.

At the beach there is lots of fun. A friend to both Tesio and Gmasnoh is making her way to their house. Rosa Tweh is her name. Before her departure from home to her friends' house she saw how hot the sunray was. She has therefore thought it wise to let go her seeing her friends very quickly. All that she wants them do is by finding a way out upon her reaching to the house to go on the beach instead. For her, however, the father refused to go on the beach. As that, she thought the fathers of Tesio and Gmasnoh may not refuse as her father did.

She has reached finally at the house. They were not outside but she heard them conversing inside the house. And she stood at the portal banking it quietly. All she thinks is that for her to, by all means the moment, since obtained the approval of the father at home now, for her friends to join her then. Glaring, there is so much excitement in her body about that really.

"Could we," she is referring to Tesio, Gmasnoh and herself, "make our way to the beach?"

Tesio recognized the voice but pretended not to. "May I know who are you speaking please?" Tesio anxiously asked. He's inside the room. He's almost to recognize the voice. In response Rosa said, "I'm Rosa. I'm seeing the ocean showing huge fate of friendliness for which I came to call you guys up."

"Wow! That has also been my wish, Rosa!" Tesio said while inside the house. He went out very quickly and stood at the portal first to see her. She smiled. "Where is your Cousin Gmasnoh then, Tesio?"

"She is inside with her dad who came to see my father on a very serious issue."

"That's alright."

She called Gmasnoh inside the house. She came and stood with her. "But Gmasnoh, you can see the weather being so nice. Are we to go on the beach if you can at least talk with both of you dads about this?" Rosa sagely requested same.

"What do you just say, Rosa?" Gmasnoh so alluringly asked as her two hands are into the palm of Rosa. Tesio is standing looking at them.

"I'm saying can we make a try now so as to go on the beach to swim?" Rosa re-echoed. She got her right hand this time round on the left shoulder of her friend.

"That should be a very good idea. In fact, let me go inside now to talk with our fathers. I'm hopeful one of them will go with us. Only my father that I know is busy and may not go with us."

"Yes. You guys could friendly convince your dads to take us to the beach, isn't it good?"

"That's pretty, Rosa." Tesio said and danced over it as well.

The three of them confederated a bit. All are deeply overwhelmed and expressed the desires to go.

Tesio has himself stooped. He and Gmasnoh are going inside quickly to have their fathers informed. Interestingly, Snoteh passed to the other side of his brother's room which had a door and went to his house and sat at the back porch of it close by where he had passed, between the two houses, while weaving his fishing net.

"Dad! Can't you hear me?" Gmasnoh emotionally said. She's struggling to locate her daddy inside the house still. She doesn't know that he has passed to the other side and weaving his fishing net either. Before she could get her father's attention and approval, luckily Tesio and Pap Putunah were together conversing on the same issue inside the same house.

"Tesio, can you locate for me where is my dad?" In response Tesio said, "He's just right in between the two houses weaving his net." She then felt so nonchalant to avoid being in such a roaring mood anymore. She took a gasp.

"Nan-dea-ju!" Putunah said that twice frivolously. That in his Kru vernacular meant my 'mother's child', which is usually said when he needs a help from his brother. It's so heart-touching in nature. And many persons say that when they are seriously hit by trouble. At will anyone could just say to sooth instead. That he did. By that he thinks his brother may by all means be arrested by pitiful feeling to let go with him and the children as well.

Snoteh is that so suffused like I said with a work he needs to complete as soon as possible before the following day comes or the night crows on him. Consequently, he had appealed to the conscience of Putunah in order to continue with his work yet. Failure to have then completed such task, which has since three days now been posing a huge challenge to him, that means he won't at all go fishing the following day.

"Alright. I'd go with them. Just do your job." Putunah said.

"Thanks! Then, see you all later." Snoteh added.

There is something so wonderful about the beach. During the dry or sunny season in every year it becomes the popular thing beginning at October the population enjoys. It's so a cultural festivity that sorts of sporting activities became so popular.

Stimulatingly to say, the boys in town learn to play football, and wrestle, as well as carry out running race so much admired by everyone. By that exciting jamboree little children learn a lot more about some of the cultural activities. At the beach, there is jumping rope exercise too. Besides, most children learn to perform the act of building blocks houses as fun into the sand. Because it's close to Christmas Season happiness often spawns itself seeds of admiration by then.

Needless to say that, the wrestling has two forms. Either two persons who one way of other, being it sometime past either, offending each other or put up a heated argument and maybe abused each other either and happen to go on the beach by then, one of the elders who may have seen them before when they did such, has to prescribe the punish right there at the beach. And that punishment has to be by a fight prompt between the two opposing parties.

Some individuals with a very good talent about the number of ten persons are asked by then to fight too. It's like wrestling by itself. And most of the elders even passed through this other form of discipline before as they are now part of the elder council, having each anytime got the guts to punish any undisciplined child or group children in that way to a fight.

Otherwise noted again, but a kid who even got so ranting with a friend because of a particular situation and decided to insult the other friend either upon an argument is heated--- they are to fight. It is such a way most of the elders think that could discipline be installed between the two persons, which one part of the two could say at last, either he or she is sorry to the other upon the fight went on or one person wins and got stopped.

While Pantoe and Putunah are being seated under a coconut palm, awaiting a boy who has been requested to assist them that he picks some coconut, and looking otherwise not at the boy—but at a distance, he spotted two individuals who went into an argument before and abused each other.

First of all, he decided to let Tarplah pick some coconuts for them. Known about Pantoe, he always had behaved so forceful in asking little children to do something for him. So peremptorily he said to the boy, "Hey, Tarplah, you come and pick us some coconut fruits." Kotatee Pantoe had ordered. Tarplah became distraught in body. He didn't even dream of that either. But few minutes later, he came to himself and close in at them very quietly where he has decided to ask by saying, "Sir, did you say should I pick you both some coconuts?"

"Yes. Please go up the tree now to help us refresh on some coconuts."

"Alright." Tarplah said anxiously in fear.

The boy didn't even waste time he promptly took-off his shirt, embracing the coconut tree while barefooted, and got climbing it. He's like a roaring tiger climbing to a prey up a tree because it has been his popular thing to do daily perhaps. And naturally, the trees lined like plantation trees which doesn't even belong to a particular individual except the entire town's people. So anybody could leave town at any time and pick any of the fruit.

Pantoe, an elderly man with a long white beard, proudly seated with a whip into his hand he decided using as a means to punish those two guys before he knew have abused one another. He hates such unruly act of indiscipline by children.

What's so for anyone to adore about him is that, he has a way of punishing any bad child who may have done something wrongly---for that matter---and living in the town. Nobody dares deprecate him about that either, to say, he doesn't have the right to punish any child who happens to do wrong perhaps. Anybody or his colleagues of elders doing so, stopping from doing what he wants to do, as long his act is about disciplining a child who's believed culturally, a property of the community, the case would have been settled later between him and you by the elder councils in town that means, such person wants to obstruct his justice system. It's a trouble to confront you by him. Consequently, he became his own traditional law enforcer by will.

The two guys he has behest refused to go by his instruction because he is at a distance for which none could recognize him yet. Railroaded by then he walked up on them.

Tesio and Gmasnoh followed him too. They are group of guys playing football together. He interrupted the play and said, "Hey, gentlemen, stop what you are doing now!" He'd a whip into his hands. That he's intending using to have ordered the guys. And by the time he said it, some guys around on the beach apart from the ones playing the ball, all came jingling to protect the fight just in case any of the two being ordered, probably none could think of escaping to town either because of fear not to start the fight.

"What did you just say—" Plah asked Pantoe sacrilegiously. He's frowning for what the old man said to let him take off his shirt and fight his opponent. And Plah, to wonder, is a bit angry and scary. The old man is always lumbering to him by his act of justice. If he had the will to beat the old man up, he could do it. His heart is pounding on him.

And when Pantoe is about doing what he ought to do nobody is to think of stopping him either. They are playing and the old man decided halting them just to see a fight then, prompted.

Clumsy, the crowd standing by upon corralling them is hooting.

"Yeah! Did the both of you call yourself men? Then, start to fight on. Plah, try and beat Mantee up. He's always doing that to his friends." The crowd unconsciously and yet unanimously bellowed.

Mantee is emaciated. He has a slanderous body but in spite of that he's so strong. He gained most of his power as a result of his daily act of farm work he goes about. He had beaten lots of his friends standing by on several occasions each twice or more. Therefore, as long it came to this particular fight, they were nemesis to him. Everyone had gotten on the side of Plah to see him beat him up mercilessly.

It's really astonishing to Plah yet. He stood up mind-bogglingly to himself. He thought the old man is that joking---the manner in which he got the two together.

A question of what have the two of them done before which the old man has had to order a fight between them is proving impermissible to come to mind, though. But the old man is trying first to remain them of their sins.

What is a fun to really see here is that, Plah's heart is pounding on him as he took-off his shirt. Why should that surprising fear come into him that became a question in vacuum he couldn't have answered like that either.

No matter what, and Plah is to get himself ready now to fight. His escape from it seems inevitable to come to mind. First of all, he took a look around him to see if there was any family member standing by. And surprising to his eyes then, jeeringly, he has spotted his girlfriend. They have been school friends since then. He used to write secret love letters to girl telling her that she is his secret admirer. Now the girl is before him to see him prove his ability to a fight—something that is morale culturally. His heart right away pounded in him a mountainous fear by the time he spotted her and others, which is not as compared to previous moment of fear that was developing earlier inside him. And so then, sweat keeps pouring out of him as if he has carried on with the fight already. It seemed greatly strange by his fearful sweat which has quickly moistened his clothes on him. The girl laughed. He stupidly looked back again.

As a man who believes in his own strength but yet he's feeling shame. He's thinking that he was to be beaten by then. That silliness quickly shrouded his head. However, looking around him, he gained a lay bravery rather to fight.

In an acrobatic way, he bounced up three times to prove his readiness. His girlfriend said he should fight. She has shown him a sign to go on. So quickly then, he's epitomized a bit by happiness in that he can now make it, no matter what, to fight.

"Both of you got to take-off your shirts now!" Pantoe yelled again. And Tesio and Gmasnoh so inquisitively got going around the crowd to see in the circle as they are about to fight. Tesio is smiling. His fighter has been Plah. And for Gmasnoh just anybody who could win the fight becomes her great interest by then.

The fight started. In a second they held each other bodily as the heads were laid sideway against each other furiously. In few seconds, as they are in a melee already, interestingly unknowingly to Plah, Mentee the opponent pushed him off his body. It got him misplaced his steps almost to have fallen to the ground. But so swiftly, he gained his balance. He bounced on his toes once again.

But Plah is so strong and swift. He's prepared to do everything in his power. He has to prove the different really, because everyone knows how strong Mentee is. While he was bouncing, Mentee swiftly came on him and cleverly knocked him down to the ground. His back is laid flat on the bare sand like a castrated dog. He roared. The hand bones of the two of them knuckles are hitting together, making a huge cracking sound the moment teasingly. Punches got huge. Luckily, Plah won the fight thirty minutes after as expected of him.

Earlier noted, when anyone goes into such fight like that, as long there is a winner, the two people might be forced to friendly say sorry to each other and promise never to think of repeating such act of insulting each other again. That moment, friendliness became its own school in paradigm for unity amongst the few young people on the beach. In other words, repentance became a noble statesman by idea, embraced by the two individuals, as they are all smiling embracing each other never to think of fighting again. Few minutes after, Plah and Mentee started to wipe the sand off their bodies. As usual, they continued their playing of football once again.

Pantoe took Tesio and Gmasnoh back to where Putunah has been seated after the fight has been over.

"Who did win the fight?" So bluntly, "Plah beat his friend," Gmasnoh said.

"It was wonderful, dad." Tesio padded.

"But please take my advice from today on. Don't you ever run to individuals each time that may be fighting either! I hate that. When you learn to always do that someday you may be hurt." Putunah said. Gmasnoh and Tesio bobbed.

"You're right, Dad. Really, I'd like to be as the guys someday, especially Plah." Tesio said self-importantly.

As he was talking he woke from his seat, now displaying in amusement the way he'd probably someday fight when the time comes. He promised to fight like a Chinese-man, being that day probably declared by the elder as the strongest man in town, as Tesio thought.

Juvenile tendency has yet, inexplicably, a worthwhile or a noble man in his life. No trace of maturity could you even see. Reason being, at Tesio's age he is behaving as though a five years old boy even though he is almost at the stage of being more a teen soon. Putunah and Pantoe laughed, as he is behaving the way he wishes to one day do in his fighting style. They are feeling fine to note that he's a smart guy with a great sense of greatness by displaying of what he would do when the time shall come. That's the endless presumption from him by then that he would be declared as the strongest man in the whole town they live.

"There is no problem by that, my son. If you wish to be the strongest among men upon flogging all of the young men in town someday, as you said, you are most welcome. It's part of our culture. You'll have to even go through that someday as you are growing up." Pantoe put it sagely, too and smiled as well.

While still smiling they thought to divert from what they were talking earlier at least to something quite differently.

"Please, dad, give me enough of coconut water. This one is extremely nice." Tesio requested. At the time Putunah had some coconut fruits opened before him. Each of them was already drinking the sweet water out of what each had. Tesio and Gmasnoh are drinking at the same time humming to the sweetness of the fruit. He melodiously gobbled up the first one the water with no time to waste either and his eyes opened wide in eagerness for another again.

"Dad, I'm done with it. Could you just give me some more?" Gmasnoh requested. She's licking her lips off the sweet. Putunah just winked at them and shrugged. He promised to give what they requested then.

The desires by the two of getting another coconut fruit, looking at the father, is steeping up more confidence that the father is going to by all means provide what he promised inevitably. And few minutes later he did for sure.

6

Thirty minutes later, a very beautiful lady came on the beach to swim. The first thing she decided to do is to speak with the two elders. The passage to the beach is close by where they are seated.

"Pap Putunah, how are you doing?"

"I'm good and you?" Pantoe and Putunah look-see and said. In response she said, "I'm okay, dads."

Putunah said as he had one of the coconuts to his mouth while yet filling his belly with the sweets. In spite of only the greetings he decided to ask the lady first to know her mission of coming on the beach--what that purposely is.

"May I inquire from you, Taryonnoh; is there any matter, please? Did my wife send you to come and call me, Taryonnoh?"

"No sir! I'm here to a swim, Pap Putunah." Taryonnoh said amusingly. She got Putunah to giggle.

"That's good. Now could you at least give me a help by taking my kids with you to swim as well?"

"Okay. Pad, that can't be a problem between us either. You don't have to really beg me to do that, please. They are my brother and sisters I need to help without your instruction even."

Taryonnoh is looking into his face smiling when she said. Putunah dabbed her.

What so interesting here is that, she'd on a funny swimming trunk. And she couldn't just by conscience hide her juvenile status either. She is so nicely into the stuff. She should have feel as old as the old folks she is meeting always feel about women presumably. They always wanted for women to be clothed in an outlandish or uncool way, forgetting about the modern times they found themselves into. But Taryonnoh doesn't care about what they choose to do or think about her either. Reason being she has been living in the city of Monrovia and regarded a lot about fashion wears than the way they are thinking should be eccentric in her style either.

As the girl was leaving while taking the three children with her at a distance Putunah said, "Just that I don't want you carry them very close to the falling tides. Be very careful to watch them swim, please." Putunah pleaded with the lady.

"It's no matter, pap. Be assured that I'd do my best to take good care of them." She replied.

Tesio gesticulated in happiness by smiling. Gmasnoh followed and the fathers all smiled. Pantoe decided to discuss something concocted about the girl. And he always did that. In a gossip he said, "Isn't that girl who five months again gave birth to a son?" Pantoe purposefully voiced.

"What are you talking about, Pantoe?"

"That girl is just a fine girl but she isn't serious. She has a child for which I want to tell you about her behaviour on that. And I saw you looking at the girl in amusement?"

"Stop it! She is a baby girl and why will I be looking at her as if I want to make her one of my concubines like you always doing in town here?"

"Oh, that's what you are saying? Please don't tease."

"I got to."

"Okay. Let me tell you something very important that I know about that girl."

"What is it? What do you mean, Pantoe?"

Putunah's ears remained wide opened, as if a propeller, while listening to Pantoe who is seriously fictitiously about to tarnish the girl's.

The ugly story which Pantoe never wanted to disclose of to his friend Putunah is that, when the girl entered the town upon leaving Monrovia City, he wanted to go and pay her dowry furtively to her aunt. It's quite horrible. And the girl came to Niffu since three months ago for the Christmas Break that is due in a month's time. The girl and the aunt all refused and shamed him about the talk. That has made him angry to tell lie to just any friend he feels wanted to jump the boat by the girl purposefully wishing either, approaching her maybe.

In his further comment he said, "One good day came when Teacher Wea-bla complained her to her aunty about her disliking school. She refused after the teacher tried over and over, seeing her being that serious with her lesson instead of having a kid."

"Really?"

"Yes."

"But the girl isn't from here either. She has just come from Monrovia. What's it that you speaking about?"

"She has since been one year here in Niffu. When she came she went to the village and it's just few days ago she decided to be in Niffu Town itself. She came from Monrovia where she is now staying with her aunty. She is here for long. I don't think she will even go back to Monrovia again."

"Are you sure of what you are saying? Sometimes you are always bringing up stories just to tease anybody's mind. Please tell me the truth this time round."

"Why will I tell a lie about her either?"

"I think I need to authenticate the fact about the matter for myself really."

"Look, Putunah, she isn't that serious at all. It's highly regrettable about her that I know really." Pantoe said. Putunah dejectedly wobbled with his head in repudiation yet about her act.

"You can see her so beautiful but there is no sense of rightness about developing her life for a better future either."

"Dammit! I can see a reason she looks so early matured like that. No. . . . That's disgusting! Really, some humans are very crazy at times oppositely about self-development."

"Yes, Putunah! That's common these days in the society, especially for our children of the 21st Century. We, imagine doing our days of old we never had that opportunity they have today as young people for school either. They have all the means to learn well and be as successful as Doctor Ben Carson or Bill Gate, but most of them are behaving stupid?" Putunah added. Pantoe smiled.

"Why smiled Pantoe? I never knew that. I wasn't even going to have letting her touched my kids either. These are very serious guys. I don't really need her lack of seriousness around them anymore. Pantoe, don't get me wake from my seat now either to go stopping her from touching them either again."

"No. Just leave that. She'd start to behave well soon as long she is here. We the elders will discipline her by the time she goes against our will."

"I hope so!"

In the process of talking surprisingly, but Taryonnoh looked back at them. She felt funny in spirit about the way the two are conversing. Putunah noticed her and decided to point his finger at Tesio differently pretending as if he's not talking to her.

"Pantoe, that boy," Putunah is thus referring to Tesio, "is very smartly a serious guy. My next plan soon, as they are soon to complete secondary education, is for my brother and me to send them away to Monrovia for college sojourn there. I've my extended junior brother there; they'll rather be with him for school." He got his friend Pantoe to smile.

"Why smiled? They'll even be of great help to us in time to come." Putunah in a sugar-coated tone proudly padded.

Pantoe decided to ask him a question as he had spoken on the issue of city life. "But, if I may ask, Putunah, are the children cognizant of the tradition of our land, which says that no one goes out of town now, finding ends meet or better life either, and fails to come back to fulfil his or her traditional marriage ceremony at home?"

"Stop that, Pantoe. What's the meaning of all that really? We have been talking about softening the tradition. I want us to forget about talking about this now because there won't be a problem either. Let sleeping dog lie yet." He's saying the issue should be laid to a rest yet, since he and Koffa before spoke about it and Tesio can't any longer go to the shrine because of that. And he's strongly hopeful that the matter is going quietly by resolving itself with the gods. The mind of adjuring same, by carrying out the necessary sacrifice to that, he's not even thinking about it yet. Usually, as a child comes from the shrine and is part of the bush-school, there is no way easily can the person adjure a specific traditional issue either. But there is something that can be done to reduce most of the punishment if a person happens to violate a bit of the customs or tradition.

"Look, Pantoe," Putunah is pointing his fingers at his friend, meaning to relax his question yet, because it seems embarrassing to him, "I don't want you to amplify this issue on my brain. The tradition or minus tradition but I want a better life for my children by way of obtaining Western Education."

"That isn't bad. The idea is splendid which everyone here had since embraced same. If, you don't want me to talk about it again, I want you now begin preparation to call for the reduction to that traditional belief, Putunah."

"You're thinking of traditionally reducing the punishment of any of the customs, is it by mouth-say or what? You have to meet the elders who shall go to the shrine to meet the gods on that."

"What are you saying when I told you already to lay low on this thing? In fact, Tesio, as of this day won't think of going to the shrine again. Get my words to this!" He got up while talking. You could see him pointing his finger at his colleagues as if he's angry either. But he's not. That's the way of him talking seriously a matter that he does often.

"Don't be angry. But this act of yours of behaving ignorantly is not my matter either. It is an issue that requires men meeting to decide the pros and cons of it. The worst part of the new tradition that I don't really support is that, which says before any of our children leave for any city, he or she is to take an oath of commitment." Pantoe said. "It's ridiculous to say so. No! They can't be in school this time round to continue such exercise of even going to the shrine. In fact, Pantoe, the children need always to study hard. Their exams are close. And the school talked about scholarship issue sometimes ago for which my brother and I won't continue to see them, going to the shrine. And in fact, this twelve grade year has become not an easy year for them. They are likely to receive scholarship to leave Niffu to attend college in Monrovia. That isn't something to embrace by every one of us in town and relax the various traditional acts yet?" Putunah frankly said. Pantoe bobbed.

They have decided upon talking a long while speaking on something differently than earlier what's talked about. They are smiling while walking back to town.

7

All heads are up as early on the first Tuesday in November. Gbarlee Swen, a wonderful friend to Nandee, Tesio's mother that morning came to visit her.

Surprising to everyone by then Tesio is on his bed shivering to his body. He should have gotten ready to go to school instead. But it got impossible for him to. He is rather very ill.

Really that illness is a surprise to everyone. Reason being Tesio and some of his colleagues the day before they all had played together in the yard at night.

Nancy and Gbarlee came at Tesio while he is on his bed shrouded. Earlier she got the news that he's that sick. "You can see him right now of how Tesio is very warm in body." Nancy said.

"Just wait a minute Nancy. Let me do my own examination on his body. You know I'm the best herbalist in town right now." Gbarlee said and Nancy smiled.

"Alright. You can go ahead with that."

Gbarlee dabbed Tesio on the body. Now she got to know that he's badly attacked with high fever.

"Nancy, I want you kindly get me some pepper right now. As you are doing I am also going behind the house to get some herbs for him, too. He's highly sick." Gbarlee pleaded with Nancy. She peremptorily went for the pepper as she was told to. Not that the pepper is faraway but she needs to dry it up over fire on top of a pot top. That she often had done it by drying her pepper even for her daily soup.

To note, if it is properly dried up by then she would next be able to pound it into a mortar as usual. Few minutes later, as she is being told, she got it placed on a pot top in order to dry it up—for sure.

Just in that time Gmasnoh came to tell Tesio so they could go to school. When she arrived at the house Nancy was at the doorpost. Gmasnoh saw her turning around here and there with the pepper she has warmed already and was about putting it into a mortar to pound it.

"Is Tesio ready for school now?"

"He's not well to go to school today, Gmasnoh." She said quietly. She was very low in saying it---because the hazardous scent of the pepper upon warming it had decimated his nose in smell badly. She was even coughing when Gmasnoh thought to ask her the question unknowing. Gmasnoh didn't get her clearly yet. She even started coughing too over the scent of the stuff as well.

"We got to go now! Is he inside?" She repeated calling again because she didn't get what Nancy had said. "In fact, you couldn't beat the pepper outside the house instead of you doing it inside the house this morning?" Gmasnoh padded again. For that question Nancy didn't even care to answer her either.

But luckily she had passed her from the door. She is seriously poised in seriousness while walking inside the room. In a soft tone, interestingly, Gmasnoh is still asking for Tesio, whereas she's already into the room. Tesio entire body became blanketed with a bedspread. Gmasnoh is so then very surprised, seeing that Tesio is shrouded in bed still. It got her shocked.

"Oh, my God, but this can't be an illness!" She called Tesio's name repeatedly while he remains still covered.

Nancy came to her. "Your brother is very sick." Nancy said in response.

"You mean . . . that the merciless thing of illness has attacked Tesio? But we did play together yesterday night. Imagine we were jumping here and there in the moonlight. This is highly a surprise to me! Wow, I can't get over this!" She said and had her hands cupped to her mouth in bewilderment.

She sat on the bed with him idiomatically to tease. By the time she sat the bamboo bed made a huge sound underneath them. She quickly woke. But Tesio urged her to sit. And she did that again.

However, she thought earlier that she was about spoiling it either. Dumped to sorrow, she was still dabbing him on his legs. After like ten minutes she thought to leave him. "You'll soon be fine, Tesio. Don't you just worry about anything of school today because I'd be there to inform the various teachers, especially the class sponsor that you won't be there today! I'm so sorry for all this. But you shall be fine again." she'd friendly said to sooth him. Tesio bobbed. Lay tears dropped from his eyes unfortunately. He has always wished to be in school with her. Unfortunately he couldn't perhaps.

"When I get to school," as Gmasnoh was about leaving the room, "I'll tell Mr. Wea-bla in particular that you ain't well at all. Definitely, he'll see a reason consciously to pardon you for the day. And I'm also of the conviction that he may come to visit you later." Gmasnoh said. Tesio nodded.

Tesio decided to ask her a favour yet. "Could you, in my behalf, at least talk with our mother's friend Aunty Gbarlee to offer me some treatment now? I need that herb treatment in order to gain my health very quickly, please."

"You're right! In fact, is she around?"

"Yes. Just check at the back of the house you will see here there. She is gone to prepare some herbs for me but I want her to do it very promptly."

"I'll quickly now get to her." Gmasnoh promptly went at the back. She and the woman spoke on his issue and she promised to treat him very quickly.

She walked back again. "Don't worry yourself. She is about completing the mixing exercise of the herbs."

Noted, Gbarlee is a very good herbalist. Her treatment of a person attacked by illness as malaria becomes instant by the time she's done with treating the person.

Gbarlee is done with compiling the herb as thought, except the pepper she needs to add into it. But Nancy is still pounding it into the mortar to bring it later to her.

As a wonderful woman, she thought to install in Tesio hope yet. "I'm hopeful shortly that you would be fine again. Just watch that after everything is being done by Aunty Gbarlee, that is upon you taking your treatment, surely, you shall be fine again either to go to school." She said while between sorrow and fear for his life. And she smiled lamely.

"Alright! Whatever you wish for me, like you said, that which Aunty will do for me, I'd believe it now." Tesio said and pulled under his shroud while still shivering.

Now Gmasnoh woke, walking to the doorpost in sorrow. It's unbelievable. She's deeply sorry.

What really surprised everyone here is that the illness came as astonishment. She is highly paranoid, having her brother not been able to go to school with her either.

Now Gbarlee decided to call her friend Nancy finally, bringing the pepper to herself. You could see her putting the pepper into the herb at last. It looks so boiled-green. The pepper changed the entire stuff into such a colour.

"Nancy, the pepper is well-pounded. Did you do it into the mortar or where?"

"I did that just right in the mortar."

"Thanks. It's done well, Nancy."

"That's' true. But nowhere else did I do it besides the mortar." Nancy said and smiled. The hazardously sweet scent got the two of them coughing.

Tesio's eyes became very red. Gbarlee asked him to wake up and go with her at the back of the yard right by the bathroom. What got his eyes red is that of the herb which he knows contained a lot of pepper. But in spite of that he's an intrepid guy. He's just pretending about the pain that is involved with it but he couldn't just avoid it either.

They were finally at the back. Gbarlee held the stuff into her left hand and she was about blasting it into him. First of all, she requested that he takes off his trousers. And he got it at his kneels. He bent over and Gbarlee put it at his anus into him.

For almost fifteen minutes tears blurred Tesio's eyes. He's howling over the pains. And the pepper is so strong into the herbs. When Gbarlee was done with it she washed her hands. She walked back to where her friend Nancy is. That got Nancy to have anxiously then asked. "Did you finish with him?" In response Gbarlee said, "It's done." Nancy smiled and said, "Thanks."

Gmasnoh got on campus finally. She's so downhearted about her brother's fever for which he is absent. Smartly, instead of her explaining verbally what had gone wrong with her brother to Wea-bla, she sat quietly somewhere and penned her thoughts.

She saw the teacher writing something on the chalkboard. She walked quietly to him. And she was about sliding into his pocket quietly the note. Wea-bla jerked. "What's it Gmasnoh you are putting into my pocket?"

"It's something about my brother who couldn't be here because he's sick." Wea-bla didn't get her clearly yet. "Please, Gmasnoh, it's not time for fun. You almost scare me up. Go and have your seat, please. Anyway what did you put into my pocket perhaps?"

"It's a note. I want you kindly read that and you will get to know why Tesio isn't here either." Gmasnoh purported. And she smiled over it.

"Oh, what do you mean dear? Is he sick?" Wilson Wea-bla reluctantly asked. "That is the matter wrong with him right now? He is so much sick and trembling on his bed. Really I couldn't get over it because we did play the night yesterday." Gmasnoh said. Wea-bla got so downhearted, having received the news. He, in particular, so much admires Tesio. And so, he's a bit hurt about him not being around.

"We will all have to see him after school later." He promised. "Okay." Gmasnoh responded and walked to her seat.

8

Very interestingly they are now big. They are fourteen years of age. What is so a happy moment to describe is that, they are in grade twelve. And they are soon to graduate that year.

Report cards are to be given out to the students. A week before this day the school had its picnic. This is such a wonderfully final recreational exercise. After that in a week's time the school has to close. It is highly amusing as food and drinks would be very plentifully shared by everyone as a way of saying goodbye to each other, as schoolmates yet for the year then.

To wonder, because the school is a community one, the administration tasked every student at the time to have made contribution for the picnic. Every student was entitled to bring at least two cups of rice each, a piece of fish or meat, a bundle of wood and so on. And they did.

One week passed since that time. School is about to close this special day that came. Being so full of excitement, the Registrar keeps looking around herself hoping that Tesio and Gmasnoh be quickly there in the hall. She is a bit complaining to herself why they don't even regard time yet. And this is often the case with those from the town. Time is never an essence to their lives.

The registrar went to the portal and stood there. Five minutes later, to her dismay, she saw the two luckily marshalling towards her. At least she got a lay relief at heart.

"What is that the both of you are coming so late? You should have been here on time because you all have very important tasks to perform in behalf of the school during this closing exercise." She sagely said. Tesio smiled.

"Sister Kpanyen Swen, we are so sorry for this. Just that we wanted to get ourselves preen because of the task you told us before we are to perform." Tesio said. They became walking into the hall.

And the Registrar thought to exotically introduce to the student populace somehow, as they are there already. "The best amongst our student populace," Kpanyen cuddled her hands with Tesio and Gmasnoh, as she is speaking, "may you please come inside and sit at the front end." She said. Gmasnoh is also seated.

Once a rumour of Tesio being as the dux materialized. And Gmasnoh also came second to him. Because of such splendid performance they are given scholarships. They are to travel to Monrovia after a month soon for college sojourn.

Usually in Niffu such splendid performance by a student could be as a basis for a whole day and night play by the entire town peoples. In so doing, the entire town decided to play for them. They were taken home by a dancing crowd.

Interestingly, Sayon who has travelled from Kenya to Liberia upon completion of studies in Civil Engineering came home since a month now. He should be marrying to a woman he brought with him. Sayon hailed from Niffu. He met his girl Mwontu during studies in Kenya at one of the best Universities.

What is so jeering is that, Sayon wasn't around when the new customs since then came to being. Reason being there is no one that is allowed to marry a foreign woman either. That is, the person must have come from Niffu other than any other place. But he has unknowingly almost violated the rules. It became a very big issue when the elders couldn't easily have handled the matter for almost a month now till the gods acted this same day Tesio and Gmasnoh graduated.

The story about Sayon is that, the gods came up with a decision to say Mwontu NSangi should leave the land and go back to Kenya. In obedience of his people and tradition, as mindful he is then about his own life to that, Sayon sent Mwontu away for true and married another girl, as being requested by the town people within Niffu. As that, a heavy sacrifice was conducted before, when luckily his soul is believed had been freed from the presumed dangerously nightmare that must have almost befallen him.

And the verdict, as the elders came from the shrine provided, which has been from the gods said that, the day and night should exclusively be for Sayon since he had obeyed them and getting marry to a new woman that had been approved by the gods through the elder council then.

Wle-dee, as the new woman, is the lucky woman by then to marry him. That day the entire town people got lots of chalks painted on her body while the women and children were all dancing around with her. They did that for almost the whole day, when later at night quietly unknown to Sayon himself, she was taken to their new home. There they had the best of time to have celebrated in love. That day, surprising to Sayon, the woman never knew about man's business either. It's that day he chewed her apple, as if Adam and Eve in the Garden of Eden before did to themselves. And it was wonderful to the two both that night like guys from a different planet other than earth.

However, it coincided with Gmasnoh and Tesio's graduation. So, the play for them has been postponed to the next day.

The next day came joyously finally. The weather is sultry. During this time of the year most trees in Niffu the trees are spawning new leaves despite the hot temperature of sun. And the ground underneath where the leaves are oftentimes, despite could everyone sweep in his or her yard, but shrouded the whole ground blurring visibility from a distance, except a person who wanted to see under the trees and came close, while standing under them, could notice a ground either. The mango trees in particular were just bearing new fruits, as the old leaves went away with newer ones shooting out.

Lots of women and children are gathered. They are all seated. They are in the centre of town under a big historical plumb tree named after one of the forefathers before who took his town warriors to a war and they became victorious at last. His name is 'jlopleh."

"Yesterday," Elder Bartee stood up at the podium, "what Tesio and Gmasnoh had done for our town can't be explained by a human's word so easily. It was quite wonderful. This is what we all expect of every young people educationally perhaps."

"Yeah!" The happy audience bellowed.

"So, let's rally around every child or Gmasnoh and Tesio as usual while still they are pursuing higher education. They are about going to the city of Monrovia for college life." Everyone giggled.

"Let me tell you this moment that beginning today now and night ---by the approval of the gods, we are playing till day. If you would like or not, this is an unending festivity that everyone needs to be aware of. On the third day of the play here---the last part of it shall be the fight between Tesio and our enemy----that is the Balo Town people who had sent their son, provoking us to a war. We don't need war. But that decision of repudiation it has to be proven by way of Tesio winning the fight or beating his opponent." Bartee said confidently. It was a huge laughter again.

Surprisingly, however, all those seated, everyone's eye was raised at him in bewilderment. He cleared his throat of mucus that has been making him put up a husky voice by then. He gained balance later again.

Lots of people by then keep crowding still at the meeting place.

The program has started and deepening into huge formalities of talking by different speakers.

Near the tree where they are gathered is a big house most of the caterers are working at the back of it. Hugely cows and goats are toasted. Some of the women are being removing furs while others doing different sorts of things befitting the cook for the refreshment after the main program is over to be had.

Something quite interesting yet is that, Wea-bla has been invited to speak at the program. Everyone in town admires him so much. Tittering, he has always been going around holding just three stupid words to his credit. And he is very good at literally rhyming words with a purpose to teach a moral lesson. And everything he thinks about life is all about courage-saying. Because of the evilly ruined those days the town fell into, especially there is no development; he wants a change of that. And now he's making sure that the condition be as no more where permanently eradicated. As that, he thought by then, that obtaining western education is the best way out to go for change of the perilous situation mediocrity of the town and its people's lives to be that improved later. He's humour and pensive. He knows the important of manpower development as the basis for development for any given society.

Before Wea-bla is to speak, one Nimely, a culturally dramatist and his wife needed to perform--- which they are so set upon wearing funny clothes on them. At a surprised start of the said drama, Nimely and his wife are chasing each other while then passing through the audience, making their way to the podium.

Nimely is very tactful and humour. He often performed in that just to teach a moral lesson during any of his drama. As they were running or he is chasing his wife, he behaved like he is falling while trying to pummel her. And probably that has been his intent really which is what the drama meant to display then. Noted, he's trying to give a picture of how critical, despite a problem may exist at the time either between two individuals, but there should still be a way out for the sake of maintaining unity or peace, rather to instantly do away with the issue. He was falling and the woman decided to give him a hand still. The wife had then forgotten what has been the problem she had with him instantly just to assist him.

"Dad, dad," at the time Nimely was chasing his wife, "you just look out there." Tesio said while pointing at them while performing.

"We never wanted to play fun only to see you people to laugh. But it's a lesson that when teeth and tongue fused at times there can still be a room to live together. They can't forever deny each other of an existence. It's the same with our human's world. We will always need each other in some kind of way. It may be directly or indirectly. And it could also be either as rich and poor to live together. But our world is an umbrella everyone soul finds herself or himself to note of."

"Yeah!" the audience said joyously.

"That's a very good drama, Tesio. It has a lot of sense into it. Did you enjoy it?"

"What not, Gmasnoh. It's truly so educative. I'm so embroiled by the excitement of it." They smiled. And Gmasnoh and Tesio had their heads grouped as they were analysing the theme of the drama.

9

The Kru tribal Warrior dance crew is about playing her part soon. Lots of individuals that are part of the said dance crew had chalk marks painted on their faces. They had one blue wrapper in a number and with ballets on the legs too. As a person shakes his or her leg, only the sound of the ballets you could hear. Some guys with the various drums columned side each other, while about to beat their drums, keep moving here and there in preparation for such exercise.

However, the indoor program by then is almost at the end. And the time is few minutes to four P.M.

Everyone became so eager about this other part of the program to resume. Interestingly, by a surprised start, the crowd first corralled the dancers. Most of those running from home are little children upon hearing the drums sound.

Right in that time Tesio decided to walk at the back of the house where the people are cooking. He wanted to have purposely used the bathroom to pass water out. Without even looking at his step being taking yet on the ground, whereas he knew how plentiful animals are living among the population of the town, he bombed stupidly into one of the cows' manure just as his father did before when his mother was about giving birth to him.

"Oh!"

"What's going on . . . Tesio?" Gmasnoh asked.

"I got one of my legs kicked a nasty toilet of a cow, Gmasnoh."

"What? That's so disgusting! Why you didn't take your footsteps carefully?"

"That's what I should have done but I didn't."

"But you will have to go inside now. First of all take off that stuff and leave it at the back of the house. And upon that wear different shoes." Gmasnoh advised. He bobbed. Truly he did. After few minutes of wearing what he needed to, he was back and sat again for the program.

Instructor Wea-bla had the opportunity given him earlier to have kept delivering his speech. Few minutes before then, Tesio's arrival, he is almost to complete his speech-making exercise by then. The last statement he made got Gmasnoh too seriously stiff-eyed. She is looking at him speechlessly. She finds so much interest in what he has been saying.

After him lots of eminent individuals made speeches too---and most of whom speeches were admonishments as usual, as Wea-bla did same.

By the way a lady left alone by her friends while removing furs of the dead animals intended for the cook, she's been attacked seriously. Her crying husky voice got majority of those at the program racing to find her to know what is wrong with her.

The story here about her is that, while she has been removing the furs of the dead cows, but three other living cows stood by her and one of them butted her body. She had her head bowed while removing the furs when the cow quietly came on her and unruly butted her. The entire horns almost went inside her. To that, and before she could notice the particular animal coming, especially the one that hit her, it was late for her to have escaped from it. That's how her body was thrown on the ground and her legs flapped in the air together. It pierced her stomach a little.

And such thing which happened is like a curse. Animals rarely do that. As such, the animal that particularly hit at her, the people right away went after it in that to get it tied, as the woman was then being held on the ground, howling over her pains.

She has been complaining to herself persistently. Her body is so soured for anyone not to even think of touching her yet. In complaining on her pains she said, "Never will I take care of party food in my life again. This thing is disgusting to me. What did I do to the animal for which I must be singled out and butted?" She said and hissed.

Being so incensed for such, the first two persons that earlier reached her, she voiced against them yet to leave her alone, meaning for any not to touch her yet. She wanted her pains to subside a little before could any think of doing that to her.

But still, as her condition is so mournful, however, one of them acted hard-headed and touched her. And she just unruly elbowed the person. However, when her pain cool down a little she became nonchalant, having to see now somebody, this time round to pet her, saying sorry by then. She accepted. And she got so earlier, miserably, into pains.

"This is seriously a backwardness of our town which must be corrected. How can humans and animals keep living together as if, they are one breed perhaps, Gmasnoh?" Tesio said.

"I, in particular desist this! It got to be corrected, Tesio. We can't continue to see this in our town throughout either. And so, when we get higher education our resources shall be used to develop the town." Gmasnoh, who is downhearted yet, but she is smiling pretentiously when she said same. She felt funny to smile because the incident seemed funny to her. To wonder, Tesio is yet smiling over it too. But he didn't make the woman to notice him either.

A son of the soil who almost thirty years ago had been living in the United States, God blessed, he came to deliver a speech, too. His coming to that poor town of Niffu seems wonderful for everyone. He abandoned all of the comfort in the USA looking at his level of education but he wanted a change of his people's way of life.

For him, he has spent most of his life in the United States where he got schooled and obtained a PhD upon attending Harvard University. He is one of those who left the town at the time when evils became huge. At least for the level of unity since then he has so decided to return home. At the old age he was, according to him, the American setting wasn't as good for him again. He's given the chance to say something to the public.

"There is a power in the obtainment of knowledge. There is a power that when a person obtains western education that isn't as corrupt by virtue of obtaining it. It's a power one gets and nobody can take it away either. It is really a fine dictatorship in nature. Education doesn't behave as sweet the democracy that called for rotation every time. Let our children be dictators to educate themselves. Obtain it because it would become your power for life. Nobody definitely would take it away from you when you all obtain same."

He said the entire place became so squeaky laughing over what he has said.

"I don't want you laugh at me either. What I'm trying to say is that, there are intelligently the people who are educated and holding something of a form of dictatorship characteristics with them. Knowledge in that way can't be shared easily, to say, will you pass your brain to another person when the life shall have left the soul either. This is what I'm trying to tell you about. I'm even one of those dictators. But let me not take your whole time either. But unity is all that we all as humans need to have by living together as one family on earth. When there

is unity with us, development will come about. Let our children go to school. Avoid evil! And if everyone by education can be a dictator at brain wide level let him or her work towards that now. Don't fight each other. Evil will not profit you anything."

Dr. Saywonteh Wleh said. Tears filled lots of people at the place eyes. When he was done with saying all that, he quickly got pats on Gmasnoh and Tesio's backs while also hugging them seemly.

The day formalities ended. Now the night came. This particular night, Tesio, as a big boy he has to prove his ability that he could do his best as a fighter. Everything that has to do with his greatness that is all that the people keep promoting in his life.

Therefore, Dr. Wleh decided to quiz him a bit. And the elders are seated around him when he asked to know the exact time of the fight.

"I know fighting relatively is our tradition. But will the fight between Tesio and the guy from the neighbouring town be as scheduled, rather for this evening holds, as it may? Tesio, I know for sure you're a very good fighter now who shall prove your best as usual." Dr. Wleh said. Tesio smiled.

The kind of fight seems as a ritual. Every man or youthful person that seems so representative, possessing characteristics that are similarly the gods---something of spiritual power that is proven by the way the Tesio and Gmasnoh are being born, he has to go to a fight like that. It's about a person having physical power too, a way of training you mentally in time to come to be able to bear pain. Quite frankly, they meant that Tesio maintains a physical balance when he's either confronted by a threatening situation. It's a bloody kind of fight he has to face. Now he has reached the age of facing same. To wonder, his father Putunah and Snoteh passed through that before and –the Putunah broke his tooth from it before. So, the question is will he be having a mark as the father? It's a question soon to be answered.

By eight P.M. torches are lit. The elders divided between Tesio and his opponent. Gmasnoh in particular became so seriously hoping that her brother wins the fight in behalf of the town people. Putunah and his brother Snoteh, who are the fathers of the two, were with them. Only the mothers left at home. They are going on the beach that evening hour.

"Papa," Tesio is calling his father's attention as they are walking, "what's the importance of all this aspect of our culture? Every time we keep promoting a fight. That's how we shall continue to live throughout our lives then? We are becoming too confrontational even at home by this kind of culture too."

"My son, you're to just watch! Be a man. Failure on your part winning that fight means the war presumed with the Bola People, when the time shall come we may be the losers. I fear that either. I know you shall win. Never allowed your conscience destroys you so soon by installing fear into you. That's what the people of Bola want to do. They want to try our weakness. We hit bloodshed but let's prove to them that we can fight them anytime and anywhere to make a win."

"But my spirit is bothering me. I want to know if you have done the sacrifice as whether I will win this fight. This thing is not an ordinary fight which you know about."

"Please, don't confront yourself with defeat so soon. We want you to be confident that you shall surely win. Your grandfather had been a warrior before for which he never defeated himself like the way so early you are speaking like this."

"I'm not scary or worrying about winning or not. It's about knowing what the importance of such a culture is."

"Tesio, I want you go and fight so that you can obtain your juju powers after. When you obtain that power anybody who wants to harm you any time surprisingly, he or she won't succeed at all. It could be a juju for food also. It's a traditional-eye that I want you now possess by the time the fight is over. You are about even going to the city. You need that with you all the time. The whole part of it someone could one day surprisingly think of attacking you with a gun, and when the time comes you may even vanish without him or her harming you either. That's the sole purpose of the chant that I want you to have upon that fight shall be over then. Let it hang on you, especially the cow tail or Gbatu."

"Suppose I'm beaten, what will the elders and the gods do? Are we to be neglected by our people or what?"

"No. The only thing here is that the morale of you in particular and at last the family of ours would be reduced to nothingness. You will be as a person with a big coconut head on your shoulders, passing here and there without a god's protection either. And it shall be a shame for the entire town and its people. So, you just think on that now."

They are at the beach finally. In prompting the fight four individuals bodily in muscles seemed yet grotesque in nature got on the ground to introduce the fight.

The guys bitterly fought. The permission to see Tesio and Waytlo going into such fight became a reality at last. The four men you could see protuberances on their faces, pointing in disgust. They hit at each other in that to have proven a sway by one over the other.

Before Tesio could make up his mind, Waytlo came swiftly on him. He knocked him down to the ground. His bones made cracking sound on him. But he's struggling to balance himself while underneath his friend.

Waytlo, sitting over Tesio, he took a hand-fold of sand from the ground and rubbed it on his body and into his hair a lot full. Tesio became so miserable. The only thing you could hear from the people is a shout. They are feeling so downhearted that Tesio is thrown on the ground and he may be beaten perhaps. "Oh! This is a big trouble for us Tesio. You need to beat up Waytlo. Put a lay strength into you and beat him up."

Gmasnoh is so happy singing to cheer him up. All she had in mind is that her brother will somehow win the fight.

However, Gmasnoh thought to make him to build more strength into himself as she is singing. She had on her plaited leafy clothes with her body seemed a bit expose yet.

Later, in a roaring style Tesio did push Waytlo to the ground off his body and sat on him, too. They held each other fist on the ground as if tigers are fighting over flesh furiously. At last, the fight became a success for Tesio. The people of Niffu gained strong hope. This is how it was expected by then.

The other formality resumed. Tesio and Gmasnoh are to be given protection from the gods. The elders had something of juju with them.

Just what Tesio had said before when he and his father went on the beach after Plah and Mentee fought, that he wanted to be a swift and strong fighter, truly, that he did. And he has acquired the age to have done that really. Interestingly, when he has acquired his juju protection he is given a chance to speak.

"I promise to uphold every aspect of my tradition. Even, as we are about starting a new life in the city, I'd continue to do everything within my power to remain committed." To tease, he said that to the elder council when the time comes should they be the ones to even give him a wife. Perhaps he needs not to talk or be boastful about that either, because it's something the tradition required should be then. It's unavoidable for him.

"Wow! He speaks like a man." Koffa said to his colleague Snoteh while very close to him quietly. Tesio didn't even hear what he had said.

"Let me promise you that till the return home upon the time of the gods I won't cheat out there by getting married to a different woman who may not be a person from here. Besides I won't do any marriage on my own without the approval of the gods." Tesio said strongly. He sounded yet as a novice to a city life. But all he thinks about the moment is the protection of the tradition.

He had a cow tail giving him by the elder council. It is referred to as 'Gbatu' which contained a lot of powers. Besides, if his opponent first hit him while fighting, and he happens to butt you with his head, instantly you become unconscious. In order for that person to come to himself he has to **piss** on you first.

Gmasnoh too is saying, but surprisingly that, "The man I would marry in time to come shall come from Niffu Town. No foreign man is going to be a husband either to me. It's a taboo to see that happen." Gmasnoh boastfully said, too.

After such ritual, the flute and samba players gesticulated in singing. The drum specialists began playing. It became a whole choir to praise that night. Glaring, they are so then betrothed more to unity. They are like guys who just came from a special society festivity. They are so cheering the occasion as traditional cultural gurus.

10

Tesio and Gmasnoh are set at least for the last time taking their mothers to the farm. And for almost a year now because of school activities they didn't make an attempt either to have one day carried their mothers to the farm. But now they are about to do same. Their parents want for them to be successful. And so, school matter became paramount to them. But this particular day they want to prove their love towards them.

The sun is glowing. And at the same time the birds in the forest along the roadside are sweetly whistling. Some are mostly sucking flowers.

"Moms," Tesio is referring to his mother and that of Gmasnoh's mother, "is our farm area as usual the same location or not, this year? Because I can remember we used to walk about three hours to go and come back to town as usual." Tesio with a serious face he asked.

"What—"Nancy murmured. She is a bit hesitant to respond. He decided to repeat himself. "I guess both of you got me clearly, isn't it? I asked the question because the two of us are soon to leave you people in town. At least when we shall have left town in five days none of you should go on the farm yet, which we thought of by then for which we are here with you to go."

"You are very thoughtful, Tesio. But why have you decided to ask such a question? Are you so scary of going due to the distance or what?" Nancy said. Tesio smiled.

"The distance is yet as it used to be perhaps. I guess you want to know because it has been one year now since the both of you stopped coming with us on the farm." Nancy added again.

"Yes. Mom, I'm so much concerned about the both of you the kind of trouble of travelling a long distance all the time. We pray that things would be good soon by the time we complete college." Tesio said and his mother Nandee, in particular, laughed. He sounded too maturely to her which she couldn't even wait to seeing him go to the city, as purported by him, completing his study.

"But let me explain a little yet. I know you really want to know this. The area of farmland since then is the same. Please, we don't change farmland like that." Nancy said and giggled.

"Don't be hurt, mommy. I asked because we want the two of you to be a lay relax for five days when we shall have left the town. Since we are about going to the city it's our wish that you rest your body a little. You need to feel as missing us in few days." Tesio enthusiastically purported.

"You're right, son." Nancy smiled.

Despite the question they are still seriously going. They are about entering the deep forest area. Some saw grasses columned along the way are bruising quietly their bodies in disgust.

Deep in the forest they are standing by a creek. It's so filled with lots of rainwaters surprisingly. The rain fell at the source up river area. And there was no trace of rain from where they came. And so, it became a surprise to everyone. In the middle of the creek while they are about to cross several vultures flew nearby. Some sat at the bank of the creek collecting some dead materials.

The condors came perhaps to hunt for fish. A particular fish is near Gmasnoh. It is that particular fish one of the birds came forcibly by her to collect same. She shivered. She didn't believe it. And the sound of the bird prompted her disorder in body right away.

She slipped into the creek. Tesio on the bridge he tries giving her a stick into his hand to let her hold on to it. She couldn't. He and the mothers all started crying. He wants to exercise his body to go and collect the girl from the water. But he was overshadowed by rumpled fear not to try that either. The place is highly horrible. There is a lay distance away right behind the rock area where crocodiles are. When he reflected his mind on the issue of the place, he became namby-pamby. He felt he couldn't make it to swim by collecting her from the water either. Due to such incident, they were then forced to return to town immediately.

However, the trip of going to the city is delayed because of said horrific incident. As a surprise, nobody thought could the news have reached as far as Monrovia. Because of that the government's head doctor came to meet with Gmasnoh. But he had something he wanted to do other than that alone.

Interestingly, he came in a lay plane into Niffu. The place of contact has been Snoteh's house. He decided to introduce himself upon entry into the house.

"I'm Snoteh Tesioti, and you?"

"Well, I'm Doctor Barclay Stewart, the General Doctor of Liberia."

"Yes! I have been wishing to see that you are here."

"Thanks."

"I guess the government may have sent you here, isn't it?"

"That's true."

The two have decided to embrace each other by then, which they did. They are also chuckling. Snoteh is so surprised of him being around upon hearing the news of Gmasnoh. He sat and shrugged.

Before a real chat could begin fully, Snoteh first brought some kola nuts at the table. Doctor Stewart took a lot of pieces and begins chewing. Snoteh couldn't have waited either rather to begin a lecture.

"May I ask you a question, Sir?"

"Yes. What's the issue really?"

"It's not any serious problem per se. Just that I want to know if there is something very important which brought you here apart from what you just said about Gmasnoh?"

"Thanks. I heard something terrible did happen to Gmasnoh. It's for such purposely that I came to see her and the family. Besides, I came to use the occasion to speak with her and Tesio on the government's plan of scholarship which has been already awarded. I hope they would be prepared as soon as possible in few days to leave for the city of Monrovia."

Snoteh leaped, rather from his seat dancing. He is dancing little by little. His steps are cajoling really, rather to teach a moral lesson. Stewart is just laughing. Inquisitive individuals, who heard Stewart laughing like a rich man, came around to see what has been the issue of his laughter then.

However, few minutes later, he sat surprisingly again.

"Really, are you saying that my children have been given scholarship?"

"Yes."

"I do really appreciate the gesture. I need to call my brother Putunah right away." Snoteh said and rose from his seat and embrace Doctor Stewart. He sent for his brother already.

"Doctor Stewart how did you really get the news of Gmasnoh perhaps?"

"Well, you know our world is a small village. It was on radio and TV."

Right in that time Rosa came in the house to play with Tesio and Gmasnoh. She walked to her two friends. She spotted

Doctor Stewart, who she since got to read about at least. Now he has come for her to see him in person or physically. She's so happy that Doctor Stewart came to Niffu purposely to see her friends. As smart teens, they saw reason to have left the presence of the old folks and went their way at the back of the house to brainstorm on the issue of the Doctor's arrival.

"Why did the doctor come to see the both of you about?

"He's the head of all doctors in Liberia. He came with some gifts. Moreover, he's telling us about a scholarship the government of Liberia gave us that he wants to disclose of the details perhaps which he did."

"Really?"

"Yes."

"Wow, that's so great."

"Why?"

"Oh, it's a good idea for me seeing the whole government of our country sent him here?"

"Yes." Tesio padded.

Upon saying that Rosa placed her two hands upon the shoulders of Gmasnoh and Tesio. She is smiling. She was too that happy about the news given her then.

But something came to Tesio's mind yet. And what he had said at the time hurts Gmasnoh a lot.

"We need to relax a little or ponder over yet what Doctor Stewart's message is. I think it may be something ugly."

"Why?"

"Reason being government support system in our country can't be that perfect. It is full of problems. Perhaps if we could get private scholarships other than that would be so better then."

"No. You can't say that, Tesio. Things are changing than before." Gmasnoh said.

"You're right!" Rosa added. Right in that time Dorsla interrupted and came inside the house where they are. He requested to be part of the conversation too, and which he was permitted to.

"I heard you guys when I was at the window. I think Tesio the both of you have to give it a try yet. I believe that there would be a change perhaps over this. Government's support system in Liberia isn't as it used to be before." Dorsla atheistically said.

As they are talking Tesio's mother unexpectedly ran out the house. She saw a dog and goat humping. It made her so ignored.

Just in that time too, Rosa's mother came to call her. It is almost Seven P.M. Rosa quietly said excused to her colleagues and went home finally.

What is so jeering is that the night is deepening into a stage of dead in itself. By then you can see that everyone in town must all soon be at sleep.

There is an ugly story about taking bath outside when it's pass Seven Thirty Post Meridians. And Doctor Stewart needed to go and take his bath before it becomes that hour of night. Doctor Stewart is told by Snoteh to pass the night at the house finally. He had then consented.

At last, both Putunah and Snoteh's wives prepared some evening food for him. He chose to consume palm butter Soup that night. Before he could eat he went at the back of the yard into the outside bathroom first to take his bath before it's the seven.

There is a strange story about taking bath late at that hour of night. The story here is that before a boy became affected by that. Demons entered him when he mistaken took bath in rain by then.

His story here is that---the evening hour--the rain poured down heavily. And without his parents being at home because they went on the farm, he secretly went at the back of the yard and took bath in the rain. And it was just few minutes passed seven thirty post meridians. He shouldn't have taken bath outside during that time of the night. For almost four years since then he was sleeping at the graveyard. During the nine year in his menace, when luckily his people paid for his chant materials and his soul got unfettered from the demon and he became once again a human to live among humans too.

The threatening story has been in everybody's mind since then in Niffu. Nobody had the mind neither to make a mistake like that either. Tesio and Gmasnoh heard the story.

So, Rosa learned of that. Because of that the mother came to call her before it's too late, the same.

Doctor Stewart is finally done with taking his bath outside the yard. He decided to come to the dining table. During the time he said something very interesting to Tesio and his sister. And at last he thought it wise presented his number.

11

Yet, all the quagmires probably of getting up early in the morning, or either playing in the dust or travelling with the elders to the traditional shrine are about silently getting excuse into them. Gmasnoh and Tesio are traveling to the city of Monrovia for college sojourn finally.

The weather seems promising. It's sultry as usual. By then the feeling of being homesick yet is developing into the two. But as the passion for education was that very high, they are forced to go then.

Rosa and Dorsla came to meet with Tesio and Gmasnoh that early morning at Four Thirty. They brought some chickens and dried coconut fruits. They are meant as the good-bye gifts for the friends.

"We've come but with tears into our eyes—this early morning just to say good-bye. We are going to greatly miss you both." Dorsla said.

It seems exciting. Dorsla placed his right hand on Tesio's shoulder. He looked at him in the face penitently. And Tesio decided to make a lay rebuttal to what he has said. "Please, Dorsla, it's an opportunity not just for me alone. Gmasnoh and I would do our best to be successful to think about the people of our entire town. We really want to help in developing the lives of our people here, including you too."

"I hope so. But I have a lay negative feeling about what the city life can do to a person when you leave from the rurally extremely poor as this area is."

"I know of that. But what is the observation do you want to speak on?"

"Let me just say this that, I won't see you for long. I'm thinking about the friendship that you would soon forget about me. My worry is about the kind of closeness we have been having in our every day's life in Niffu."

"No, Dorsla! Why can't you wait a minute? Do you think that my going to the city is going to dump our friendship? You must be joking, dear!"

"But that's my worry, Tesio. I love you and I will greatly miss you while you may be away. I don't know how long are you guys going to be away either but I got to miss you each and every day."

"Dorsla, do you want to revise this friendship to a different thing or what?"

"It can be so either. My worry is about what you may either encounter about what a city's life does to a person at times. When you get there for you to be as focused on friendship, as it has been here, definitely I really see that as being impossible shortly."

"No! What is this pessimism is about? We've been good friends all this while! Dorsla, don't say that to me either. We should both be praying for each other. I'll definitely someday come back. And our friendship would be more than ever." He got Dorsla to laugh interestingly.

He knew Tesio didn't really understand what he meant to say either. He thought to still clarify his statement.

"I'm sorry, Tesio! But you need to understand what I'm trying to say." Dorsla said and Tesio bobbed.

"Dorsla, I do know of what is about a friendship is. And I should be worrying about the departure than you framing it differently."

"Sure?"

"Yes."

Dorsla said and pretentiously howled a little when Tesio spoke. Only his tears proved how serious he's about the friendship gaining suspension yet. And Tesio perhaps he couldn't afford to look at his face. Pity epitomized Dorsla's whole life.

"Okay. You're right for all that you have said, Dorsla. But I'm a different person. I can't be fooled either to abandon my people in town here, especially you as a very close friend of mine."

"But what's about your secret admirer, Rosa?"

"Look, she's my friend and you're the one who really know about the friendship to that extent that I want for you to even put your eyes on her. Keep the secret please." Tesio said and chuckled. He got his friend's mind knocked down to pitiful feelings the moment. He was wiping his eyelashes off the tears full because he got him to smile. But Rosa at last would expose of the secret of the friendship perhaps.

After the chat Tesio decided to embrace him. And Gmasnoh on the other hand is hugging Rosa frivolously too. For almost five minutes they are hugging each other. After that Tesio went to the canoe that they are about to ride and sat. He raised his hand saying good-bye finally.

Rosa decided to say her final words to Tesio. "Never forget about the friendship. As you may be away I promise to remain here waiting for you for us to marry someday. I believe the gods are now watching us to protect us in that to achieve that someday."

"Let everyone of us be in touch with each other. I swear in maintaining persistently the friendship, too." Tesio said. His cow tail given him by the elders almost drop into the ocean. But he was very smart and swift to have grabbed it from falling into the water.

A moment later, you could see the canoe slashing through the ocean, as they are leaving the shore moving deep-sea. Rosa got the fathers: Snoteh and Putunah to laugh by her funny assertion. But they knew that couldn't be a thing to say anything ugly to her either.

The distance in canoe from Niffu to Monrovia is about five days ride. It's something everyone in Niffu knew about. As a result the elder council asked that every place they may have stopped they should send a communication that they are doing fine and still on their way travelling. And it seems so funny by then. Reason being there is no communication network at the area. But they wanted for anybody that would be met on the way going back to where they come from, he or she is to get the message through to them.

The ice has been broken while going. The fathers of the two decided to admonish them in that to be very careful as they are going to a city like Monrovia to behave well. They know there is intertwining of people who may be on different acts of life. There is robbery, there is cheating, and there is gossip and sorts of city's life choiring stuffs that they may soon encounter to know of, as the fathers would think later.

Tesio is the one to start the conversation. He is very inquisitive. "Dad, how is life in the city? I'm asking you because both of you'd been there before."

"Tesio, I can't sit in this canoe to really explain it all. My back has got numbed since then. I'm just praying that we reach the city quickly. I can't really any longer bear it anymore because of the pains into my back is getting huge."

"I'm so sorry dad!"

"Anyway, I can still explain a little partly about the life in the city. My son," Putunah is dipping water out of the canoe throwing it into the sea, "life in the city which my brother and

I ran from sometimes ago when President Tubman died is as hell right now."

"Wow! Can a person go to hell and make a comeback to the human's world?" Gmasnoh asked.

"It's metaphoric for which I want you open your ears to understand me. I'm talking about how extremely difficult was life then."

"Okay."

Interesting, Snoteh said and the two fathers both giggled together. Gmasnoh gasped, while smiling too.

"But dad what is. . .so much the difficulties at the time for which the two of you had left the city for? Were you afraid of attending school or what? Or, did somebody put you into a temptation or what?"

"Son, who do you think is to blame when life is full of lots of imbalances? I hope you guys will make a difference as you're going there too. I believe we never had a purpose for school as you are doing for which economically things became difficult with us." Putunah added.

"Daddy Putunah, I'm still asking you. Why do you want us to go to the city then for school when you knew life is difficult there?"

"No! You have to go. The life at the rural area here isn't good as the one in the city for the both of you to note. We want you and Gmasnoh to be serious to learn."

"But dad we are doing our best already. You need not worry about that either." Gmasnoh said.

When he saw that the children are in acquiescence to whatever he'd said he went on to talk about something of condemnation which any human either surprisingly or not, could the person probably had experienced in the city.

"I don't want to keep saying this but it's such an ugly thing for which I want the both of you to avoid it in life." Snoteh said.

"What's it, Dad?"

"Avoid trouble." Snoteh padded.

Gmasnoh interrupted and said, "Tesio, why are our fathers thinking so negatively over our lives? Is it the time for that when all this while we have been trying?"

"That's okay, Gmasnoh. Our dads don't me any harm either. It's just that they want us to do the best still. That's all!"

"Okay. I think you're the one who really understand the two." Gmasnoh said. And Putunah and Snoteh remained a lay mute yet.

"Let me make a promise to our dads."

"Tesio, what's it the promise you want to make?" Gmasnoh asked. "I personally will build each of them a house."

"Tesio," Gmasnoh is adding her words, "speak as you mean truly for the two of us to do for them than only you, please. The both of us have the same set of goals, isn't it?"

"That's really correct, Gmasnoh. Don't be jealous. I don't me to exempt you, or not mentioning you either. I'm sorry that the two of us are working together on the same purpose of life. So, do you promise as I did to build our parents some houses, too?"

"What not, Tesio!" Gmasnoh smiled. And Putunah and Snoteh also smiled along.

12

They are finally uptown. Tesio couldn't believe it. He's so much overjoyed, having arrived in the city finally. His body atoms, which is his body structure is yet dancing to the goodness of the city.

"Wow! That's how the city looks, Gmasnoh? The place is like a heaven." Tesio said. "I think we will see various things that are very amusing than just electricity that got you wondering yet. You just wait a minute." Gmasnoh said.

"I can't get over it. This is worth so much revel for me, Gmasnoh. I can't believe this that we are finally now into the city."

"Tesio, I beg of you. You don't have to be so excited like a country boy perhaps. Relax a little yet." She said and smiled too.

Tesio is always behaving that so exuberant over any issue for that matter. And it's their first time really even though of coming to the city. But he needs to be a lay relax, as thought by Gmasnoh. She is behaving so sheepish standing by her brother behaving the way is he doing.

Uncle Forkey has been dreaming since then for them to have come to his compound to stay for school. And God so blessed, they are there into his house for true. He is so much excited than anything, having seen them come live this time round.

They are urged peacefully to be seated at the living room yet. Uncle Forkey's compound has lots of flowers. And the main building where they are is greatly decorated. The chairs are bamboo-plaited and nicely cushioned over that too. As yet they are novice to the city life they feeling as though he has partly come from heaven to have owned such a house perhaps.

Uncle Forkey decided asking his daughter to come and meet with them.

"Teta," he's speaking, "please come and meet with your brother and sister for now. And you're to prepare something for each of them this evening. From today on you have to make them feel as comfortable living with us."

"Okay. I will do just what you have said, dad."

Teta took the stand and did firstly a formality involving the introduction of herself then. Tesio couldn't even have given her a chance either. He is so then smiling while introducing himself and Gmasnoh as well to Teta by the way.

Teta has been told by the father to prepare some food for them. Because of that she came very close to Tesio, asking him what he needed for the night. It is the first change they are about to experience upon Teta sought their permission to have been able to prepare some French fried with roasted fish and juice, as she wished. Tesio nodded peremptorily, as if he has been finger-throated to do so for the offer then. And Gmasnoh who never knew what that is really, she too requested same.

By the time Teta is done with the request she went to fetch some water in the bathrooms. She wanted her stranger-families to take their bath first, which later could they have come at the dinner table. She is so excited, having seen a new family adding to her family number.

Snoteh and Putunah, the fathers of the two are so happy. That got them filled with happiness for which they decided to go to bed right away without even a mind to think of food either. Glaring, the long desire to have seen the children come to the city had proven success the moment, for which they are even dumped to sleep.

In making the two old men feeling as good, having come to the city, Uncle Forkey told Teta at the time to have taken them to a room which contained a mattress so lumpy. Oftentimes there special strangers stayed at night. There, however, perhaps their souls have gotten drunk to sleep.

There is a great deal of reputation about Uncle Forkey which Tesio and Gmasnoh since cherished. He got a degree in chemistry from the University of Liberia since twenty years ago. Upon his graduation and when he got employment with the Firestone Company lots of opportunities came his way then.

After two years when he got his employment the company had sent him to Nigeria. There he acquired a Master in Organic Chemistry from the University of Ibadan.

Uncle Forkey is six feet tall. He's a man of curly black hair. He has bushy eyebrows too. His height has also been a great promoter in his basketball talents. It's the game that really paved the way when he got out of high school and reached college. It helped when he had different other opportunities that he travelled a lot out of Liberia, too.

The last moment that brought him unthinkable pride is a special game one time play in the Republic of Equatorial Guinea when he went with his basketball team from Monrovia. His bonus after the game was a very fat bonus to praise by him from his team.

"I'm really happy that the both of you brought proud to our families as I did before. But I see the performance of the both of you, showing wonderfully greater yet that you are-- and would be, in time to come still. And the both of you are a bit ahead of me academically." He sounded boastfully correct yet. Tesio smiled almost persistently.

"Thanks, Uncle Forkey. I lack the words to even express now on how I'm so much happy. Staying with you, we shall really meet our goal of obtaining higher education." Tesio said and smiled. He dabbed Gmasnoh. Similarly she smiled with him.

"I'm so happy especially with the performance of Gmasnoh. She has done extremely well for which I'm even not able to tell the degree of what my love is towards her either for that. But that's it. She is a big girl that appreciate for everything she chooses to do for now."

"No. Uncle Forkey, don't make me laugh please."

"But do you know how many women from southeast Liberia who ain't serious at all? Anyway, let me not bore you. You can have your meal now and later rest your bodies after. I hope that tomorrow we may talk more than this." Uncle Forkey said.

Gmasnoh and Tesio woke from their seats and had their hands folded before them. It is as showing deference for all that the Uncle had said and to say goodbye to him as he's going to his room to rest his body.

"Thank you ever so much, Uncle Forkey." Tesio added.

13

One week upon being into Monrovia, two well-known basketball teams are about playing a national basketball final. It's a game between The Uhuru Kings and Pathorns. It's a very cultivating match everyone in Monrovia who heard about the game wanted to watch. Teta has so much interest in the basketball game. And for the final between Uhuru Kings and Pathorns she couldn't just miss it.

The game started almost thirty minutes since then. Tesio and Gmasnoh decided to watch the game with her.

Teta is so sad. Her team is being led by five points against. And it's Uhuru Kings that is leading Pathorns.

The game started almost an hour ago. Remaining time is just five minutes into the game. Teta is so downhearted.

This is a game Teta so much admired. She's so anguished by the news that the coach of her team Pathorns, is yet delaying in bringing on the court a player from Nigeria by the name of William Ogogwe. Perhaps the coach knows what he's doing. He knows a lot about his player Ogogwe. And he is a good player but he lacks stimulus to play for a long while. But Teta couldn't just afford to keep waiting that long for Ogogwe to come into the game. She is passionately driven by impatience to see him play.

Coach Johns O. Johns by then knew exactly the minute could Ogogwe come in the game. And this guy has since been playing but he was asked to rest his body yet. He will come in during the last half which has already started since then.

"What sort of game is this?" Tesio asked. He and Gmasnoh are seated by Teta in the living room while watching the game too. Teta has been so squeaky showing so much excitement about the game. And it interests the guys too.

"Tesio, that's basketball game. This is a game I really like." Teta said and quickly took her face from looking at him. She is glued to the TV.

"But this isn't really a fine game as football, isn't it?" Tesio said.

"Hey, Tesio, please wait a minute. How can you compare a basketball with a football game when you know most players playing basketball make more money and are getting rich daily? They have lots of fortunes than football players."

"You're joking!"

"This can't be a joke either. That's the fact I'm telling you. Try reading most of the time a sport newspaper or when you get to know about computer start to browse on the net to know it. Don't make me talk that much yet. Rather, I want to keep my concentration on the game yet. Please, I want my team win. And I'm so downhearted right now about the Uhuru Kings leading my team."

Tesio dressed a bit close to Gmasnoh to speak with her on the game issue.

"How sound is that game she's so much interested in?" Tesio quietly asked Gmasnoh.

"But I'm also developing interesting into it."

"Hey, stop the kidding please."

"I mean what I've said. I may soon begin learning to practice it, if you don't know. That's a very nice game. I see it as a mental-game than football as you think."

Teta wasn't even watching the two as they are discussing either. She's just looking at the game hoping that her team makes a difference as the time is running out.

To everyone's surprise then, Ogogwe did a splendid move. Exotic to view, it is this moment, which is so much a surprise;

I got to know the difference between a traditional basketball learner and a mission boy playing a basketball game that day. He knows the game and every move to make during crucial time.

Ogogwe passes and dribbling skills are accurate. You could think that it's the only career of his lifetime perhaps. But he's a scientist and a lecturer once at Ibadan University in Nigeria. And for the game he has the ability of a great player. He's a pointer, dribbler and defender inexplicably.

Frankly speaking his bouncing while holding the ball is quite exceptional. He knows what to do with the ball as he's playing to even cause a foul against his opponent.

However, he's fouled. He did as thought and he was quickly awarded some freed shots. And it had worked for him. By that is barely left three minutes where he must beat his opponent by then.

Teta has been feeling bad about the result. However, to her surprise, the hope has been almost all-restored as expected of her. Now the score is tied. She'd herself very close to the TV as if she is part of the game and on the court itself. She is almost to punch the TV each time Ogogwe made an interesting mood and he's fouled.

A moment later, Ogogwe was truly fouled again around the centre court area. He's been allowed to make some free shots again. None did him miss either.

There became the dramatic turn of the game. And all sorts of blockades are now being put up by Pathorns, when Uhuru Kings couldn't even shoot one basket again.

Teta is sweating and yelling inside her people's house. "Look, Teta, you've to know that there are others in the house here, especially your parents at rest. You should know that we need to rest our bodies for work tomorrow. See this hour of the night! Why are you yelling in here? Is it called for?"

Uncle Forkey, the father of Teta wanted her to stop the noise and watch the game peacefully. But it seems hard for Teta because she is so elated. However, apolitically she said, "It's the game on TV causing me to be that lousy, Daddy." Teta tried making her father understand the cause of her being so noisy.

One minute is now left. Ogogwe at a distance of centre court he took three shots brilliantly surprisingly, beating Uhuru Kings in an astonishing manner. Immediately he made the baskets the game was called to an end by the referee.

It's this day Tesio upon seeing that guy's splendid performance his mind changed instantly by developing interest in the game. This is a game he couldn't from the beginning understand either. But the story changed on him to like the game.

Trophies are presented to the first and second winner, as purported. After the presentation of trophies something funny is taking place at the court which nobody could easily had explained. It's mindboggling to Tesio. And he is so confused. He and Gmasnoh are glued to the TV. Tesio is moved to ask Teta to explain the meaning of all that, especially the saying of the suspension of love by the girlfriends of the defeated Uhuru Kings.

"What's that issue of suspension of relationship is all about, Teta? I can't really understand that."

"Tesio, are you referring to me or the game?"

"I'm talking about what's happening right now. How can a simple game be a matter by girls of the defeated Uhuru Kings for the males? This is complete nonsense."

"But Tesio, you don't know if that has been a date? Girlfriend and boyfriend kind of relationship doesn't mean a marriage has taken place either between. So, a fiancée could look at her boyfriend and say I don't want you. What's the matter of you having problem with that either?"

"You mean . . . because of a simple game . . . will the issue of a relationship be in jeopardy, Teta? I really feared the life in the city. I'm now praying that by the time I'm done with my studies in the city I would go back home to stay my whole time there than here. It's stupid here!"

"It's no matter! Relax a little. You don't have to speak about that either. That's what the city's life entails at times."

"No!"

"Rightly speaking, Tesio, if you wish to know better of what I'm saying here is that, there isn't anything much when it comes to being faithfulness in relationship, as long there is yet a marriage either. Look, all what you see about the players is just a simple affair, which we call a boyfriend and girlfriend relationship type. If you like you could call it fiancée perhaps. It's common here in the city. You can't just meet a girl and you tell her right away that you marrying her just a day after. For the rural area where you guys came from, there is early marriage there. And that gets lots of young girls involved in early bearing of children. But for the city where you are now you can't see that except gaming in relationship the situation you can find here at certain level yet. The days of Romeo and Juliet pattern of love are even over in the world."

"Stop it!"

Tesio said and Gmasnoh laughed over it. It sounds so funny yet.

"Did you hear what she had said? She's speaking of what civilization probably is with those in the city." Gmasnoh voiced to Tesio.

"That is what she meant to say?"

"Yes! Imagine we took oaths at home for relationship matters. Isn't that inanity?" Gmasnoh said. Tesio shrugged.

Tesio tries to think of what Teta had said. The explanation seemed strange to his senses yet.

Uncle Forkey came into the hallway after the result of the game has been announced. He's smiling despite what he said to Teta to remain quiet then. He too is embroiled by the excitement. And he is a fen of Pathorns as Teta the daughter is.

By the time he sat in the living room his eyes mistakenly saw something in the hands of Tesio. He waited a bit. Most of the formalities of trophy presentation he was waiting to see them pass over yet.

Thirty minutes later he has decided at least to ask about that.

"What's that cow tail and beads all over you about?"

"Uncle, these are powers or protections from the gods back home given me by the elders. It's a commitment to the tradition of my land." He said and Uncle Forkey laughed.

"You're joking. In fact, I'll ensure that you and Gmasnoh be ready each time to attend church services, please. That stupid thing of yours will be moved soon. Get to know this that you ain't any longer in the countryside."

"No! Uncle, I can't make it to really go to church where I may be forced to remove my powers. I've a problem with church business sometimes ago. It's such a reason I forbade going to church since then. There are lots of pastors who these days are preaching in that meant, rather obliterating cultural values. And that won't work against me either."

"You are really joking. You don't believe in the words of God which is the Bible? You need to make a change of character, please. This is the city. Why? You are scaring me up really."

"Uncle Forkey, before the Bible came to being there has been our people's culture. If, you want me to go to church that shouldn't be by force either."

He made the Uncle to right away lay low on the matter. But Forkey has decided to one day discuss the matter with him better than the way it's perhaps.

Uncle Forkey is going back to his room complaining on what he had said. "I won't even talk that much. The life in the city will force him to change." Uncle Forkey complained to himself.

14

Four weeks had gone by. Tesio and Gmasnoh since have been adapting strongly.

A particular day so joyously came. This day Uncle Forkey decided to buy them some phones since they are in the city to be able to freely communicate with relatives yet while about to start school soon.

Uncle Forkey thought to give Teta instruction to assist the two family strangers yet. "Please make sure to chatter a taxi tomorrow ensuring that the strangers have some cell phones. Take them to the offices of the Lone Star Communication network in Congo Town." Forkey instructed. Teta bobbed. It's one of the biggest communication companies with headquarters located in Monrovia.

Teta is so happy having got the instruction. Her happiness is that at the end of the day upon helping her family-strangers, getting the phones at least, there would be a lay change left for her to have done different thing with it. Now she is praying to herself that the deal hour soon that be. She is an honest girl. But each time her father sends her to buy; he hardly takes away the change. And it's becoming so used to her but she would first report it on the phone to her father before she can be allowed to have it. That she knew.

God so blessed then, the main day came. They're all preparing to go uptown. As teens yet, the passion for material things is still a problem of their lives. They couldn't waste any time either, but to go and buy whatever each could be had. Teta, who secretly told her cousins of her plans, she said that it's the occasion she wants to use to buy a gift for her fiancée whose birthday is barely a day to go. She said and Tesio frowned. He couldn't report her to the father either because he felt doing so could make the father either anguish with her. And he and the cousin are stranger-family not to be as early bringing complaint or problem couldn't come between either of them. Besides, Uncle Forkey had encouraged her to have a fiancée since then for which he feels he should be blamed for Teta's misgiving perhaps.

"Uncle Forkey, I'd continue to appreciate you for all that you keep doing for us since then. Now we are about getting to the centre city area so we can buy our phones. Isn't that a great gesture by you to praise? I'm crazily happy, Uncle."

"No, Tesio, you don't have to say all that either. Come on . . . stop the kidding! Both of you're my brothers' children and part of my family, too. Do you want to differentiate yourselves from my family either? If you don't know, you're also children to me--who I need to take care of as Teta too." Tesio and Gmasnoh giggled. Uncle Forkey came close, petting the two on the backs.

An old dolly man, with no plan of thinking whether Forkey has money with him or not, but because he is a friend of Forkey, he came from the interior with some goods purposely to ask Forkey for an assist only to have his proper medical due to what had sometimes ago dangerously happened. And it has been a week ago.

Teta ran out. At the time she heard the doorbell rang. More besides, the gateman called her name on the line to tell her that somebody came to her father. And the guy described who the stranger is and where he has come from to see the father then.

To everyone's surprise, it's Uncle Togba Slewion. He's been urged inside right away. Teta took him in the living room and gave him some soft drink first after asking him to sit. He took a gasp, feeling exuberant that he's finally in the city. His head is still dusted up from yet the gravel road dust. That is, there is no pavement from his area to the city of Monrovia. So, the dust made shroud over his head which there is no tracing of either the black strains of hair could one see on him either. Only the brown colour of the dust you could see about him. His eyelashes are like filaments shooting up over his eyes as the dust covered them up in brown colour. Teta went to inform her father then.

"Please, Uncle Slewion let me tell my father that you're here to see him or you're his guest since seated." Uncle Slewion happily bobbed.

"Dad, your friend is here."

"What's his name?"

Teta called his name. That got the father happy to have quickly made his way to him. They chatted. After a while of chatting with the friend, the friend asked Forkey that he's leaving to find some family members and to make a comeback the next day. Forkey agreed.

Uncle Forkey and wife had however left the house. He is gone to work finally. Teta and her stranger-families (Gmasnoh and Tesio) decided to each go inside where to do the final things of going uptown too, as earlier planned.

An hour later they reached uptown. They first went to the phone store and bought the ones needed as requested by Uncle Forkey. Come the next is for Teta to take them around.

As the panorama continues Tesio and Gmasnoh's cheeks remain wide. However, three hours later the formalities came to an end finally.

Teta's plan of letting them practice with Pathorns finally came to fruition. Most of the guys in their neighbourhood first started practicing with Tesio and Gmasnoh. By then they got to know the various rules and what the game fully entails then.

Before this day's practice session could resume, they were seated under the trees at the back of the yard. By then they have been reading at the same time conversing on various issues of concern to them.

Something so wonderful about the Teta is that she loves music a lot. Her popular songs are mainly by John Legend and Boyz-II Men. She loves the songs of the late Barry White, too. And when it comes to the recent artists she has Chris Brown and Akon. I mean the list is just endless.

Interesting, she got the soft notes playing upon everyone had read three hours later. Teta skips through few different artists of their popular oldies too apart from those named above.

Teta, a funny girl she is, decided to tease Tesio. She is seeing him shaking his head and making an attempt with his legs each time to get out of his hammer to dance. He's really struggling; amused by the music, he's shaking his legs by thinking of what the proper way the dance could be either. Intermittently, he would rise and sit once gain over and over. Teta is so quietly dancing in letting him doing it the same. It was real fun to see. And you can see the guy proving really as an awakening man of the city yet, who has just left the rural area. Surely Tesio has such ability of doing well by then. He wants to learn everything. Funny Teta, as she thought, that she needs him to have a fiancée at least, since he is in the city.

"Tesio, I want to find you a girl. Will you, please be willing to accept the gift?" Teta asked.

"What do you mean about that, Teta? Am I a man now for that? Please, let you not bring such a joke around me. Now my focus is about the lesson I left my home for. That you know about. How will our uncle feels when he hears that I haven't even getting in school but woman's matter have become my problem? I came to the city to study upon that I may find a job. Would you please leave me alone?"

"Hey, you need to cool up. I'm not talking about marriage. All that I'm saying here is that for you to have somebody by you. I don't want you be without a fiancée. Why will you want to be a celibate yet?"

"Not that I won't have a woman or have sex per se, but I want to remain my focus yet. My plan is about helping the people back home. Besides, the poverty that got our parents suffering, in my right mind, I want it be eradicated."

"You are the one who supposed to redeem your people or entire town from poverty?"

"What not? Is it so difficult that he can do so?" Gmasnoh added.

"Oh, you and your brother have the same purpose for school, Gmasnoh. Please stop the kidding. Are you guys becoming messiahs?" Teta said and chuckled.

"Stop that!" Gmasnoh said.

"One thing I want to say to the both of you here is that you're in the city already. I need you both a girl and a boy to keep your companionship in time to come while you may be studying still at college. Life isn't all about book matters. The both of you must put some social life into it too."

"I think you having a lay problem. Look, Teta, leave us alone now because we ain't going to be like you either. Every man or woman has his or her own style towards the life we all live on earth, isn't it?" Gmasnoh strongly worded. Teta foolishly chuckled.

"You are joking!"

To cause distraction Tesio went promptly to the tape, while playing a soft music and toned it high. He is dancing. Teta keeps laughing like she's daft perhaps. And she isn't at all.

However, Tesio still holds to keep the conversation on. He decided to ask Teta a question.

"Do you in fact have a fiancée, Teta? I don't know the reason you keep bothering us like this. Give me an answer now!" She said and got his two hands on his waist. He's a bit mute to hear her speak out.

"What do you mean . . . at my age. . .then I can't' have one either? In fact, I promise to show him to you. Just give me a lay time yet."

"Okay. But let me still put it another way, if you would like. How old are you, Teta?" He asked confidently. Teta smiled before she could make a response.

"Are you saying my fiancée or what?"

"I mean you!"

"Oh, is that a problem to know?"

"Really! Yes, I need to know because you're behaving like a teacher in some way to titter about perhaps."

"Why?"

"Yes. I want to know your age, please. It's like you have become a doctor-lover maturely perhaps for which I need to ask."

"I think you're sounding too strong, Tesio. I will advise that we leave this conversation."

"I'm so sorry."

"Anyway, I'm fifteen years old."

"Wow! But, you're still a small girl yet."

"Tesio, you're joking. My parents know about Richard my fiancée already."

"You mean Uncle Forkey knows about him? He and all is adding insult to injury by letting you behave like a woman so soon."

"Yes. And, it's really better not to hide such thing than letting it be a secret either. That's one thing we don't see most of us the parents should do in Africa, as long the person reaches at least an age of teen. Our society is full of acts of parents hiding from their children. And it's dangerous. And my father is very civilized not be of such character deficiency either. So, he doesn't really fine problem with such."

"But you're under age. I think I need to authenticate the truth from your father about this."

"Why will I lie to you? Let me tell you another thing that, since my fiancée and I came together he's been buying me very importance essentials while I'm still with my parents and in school. Do you understand me?"

"That sounds crazy. Your dad has so much money. So, what's the problem with you?"

"Can my daddy do the entire thing that I need in life? Money isn't all to life either. Can you remember when Adam and Eve had everything on earth but they failed to have obeyed God?"

"Don't make me to laugh either. Please, don't be so angry with me because, I see your early life as being a problem. You would have lots of kids soon. My cousin and I have to be careful with you. I can see that if we are not careful you may likely destroy us with your evil plans for what I see it to be."

"You are damn childish, Tesio! You talk like a country fool." She had herself come close to Tesio when she talked in his face. She has also spluttered on him.

"I think I have to avoid the argument because you are taking that too far. You want to introduce something quite differently against our plans to us. I won't expect that you approach on us on that matter again. You should be a focus with school than this."

"Tesio, maturity comes by experience also in life. Both of you can continue in the state of mental-crippled ideology which you call that, rather a good life. Bullshit!" She said and hissed.

"That's okay. Leave us alone." Tesio thought to smile after he said. He went to her and teased her with his tongue put outside, while shaking same into his mouth.

15

Interview has been scheduled for Tesio and Gmasnoh. They are going on the campus interestingly of the University of Liberia at the President's office. The president, surprisingly, he asked the administration for him to be the one to interview the two guys. And he has his funny way of doing that.

The Uncle has a Prado Jeep. With eagerness, especially seeing the new stranger-family members staying with her parents, Teta thought to carry them on campus this day. That means so much excitement for Teta because after the interview the father said they should go and refresh a little later.

Upon ridding through the traffic lights from centre city to the campus that morning, they are finally walking to the president's office at last. After like a three-minute walk they would be nested inside his office perhaps. And that the president has since wished should it be for them. He has been waiting for them since an hour ago.

Neither physically, nor any means they have seen the president or the president himself has seen them either. But the need be, purposed by the two, his office has been the point of destination. Nothing is on mind other than that.

The three minutes passed. Luckily the president was standing at his office doorpost waiting on the two.

"This is the president of the University of Liberia's office, where you're now and that, I want the both of you to come inside and have your respective seats. You're most welcome!" Doctor Dennis said.

"Wow, I've long been hearing about you. Thanks to meet you, sir." Tesio said. He decided to extend right handshake.

After that he said, "I'm Tesio, and the girl here on my left is Gmasnoh. We are both two brothers' children from Niffu to obtain higher education. Thank you ever so much having given us the audience."

"Thanks. You're most welcome once again. But boy," President Dennis excitingly smiling that moment, "you just hold on yet." He said and Tesio giggled.

"Why are you so neatly dressed? Do you want to entice me?" President Dennis had his palm into Gmasnoh's hand as he's smiling with her when he said same for fun.

Joyously, he got them seated. On his wall he decided pointing to a writing which is about the two as the nation's special students. He explained a little about that, and later told them that it's the interviews probably that have already started too, which they needed to also take a note of, where to remain well-behaved as they are conversing. Gmasnoh got betrothed right away to seriousness than anything when the President said.

"I've a letter here from the head of the regional exams," Doctor Dennis opens up, "recommending the both of you to do engineering. Are you aware of that?"

Bluntly, in response Tesio although is partially in rejection yet and he said a 'yes' in behalf of the two then. He's friendly natured, as he said with smile on his face. Gmasnoh wasn't even given a chance as usual to speak on the matter either. Anything perhaps that concerned the both of them he always wanted to show his supremacy over her that he is the man, rather speaking in their behalf. She would just smile.

"Well, Mr. President, my sister truly wants to be a doctor. And for me, you're partly right that I'd really want to be an engineer, but till I complete my first study to obtaining a BSc in Biology before I can go on for a second degree in engineering perhaps."

"Anyway," the president in a feeble he nodded, saying at last, "you can decide on whatever you want to do later but you have to follow the plan of the government for which the scholarships have been given you both. You have to studies Biology as the first degree course and later you can do the medical studies." he averred.

Dr. Dennis knows his own university rules that no student is to drink on the campuses of the university during study or interview of the kind. And for the interview which he has started he's trying to be a bit practical about the rules of the university with a little etiquette underscoring the process. He doesn't mean to shame them either. His intent is to see his country, but be as still an organized society really with a dream and respected university family. So he wants to give them an offer of a bottle of wine. And the teens so smartly however had studied the rules before going on the campus.

The last part of his interview, instead he presented a bottle of wine. Gmasnoh and Tesio smiled. It seems funny to them yet.

But tactfully, the two incoming students refused his offer then. He became responsively shame.

So, his long illusion all this while he had about lack of decency somewhat in young people by then in Liberia after the civil war came and later had ended in 2003, is shovelled by an academic spade rather into a conscience hole yet, which the two splendidly passed his very funny interview exercise.

Really, it would have been a slide mistake by the two, as he thought, even though he may not have denied them entry to the university, taking the wine from him, while drinking it as they are still seated in his office. And the two had really exercised a high level of maturity yet, as decent student to have embraced by him, proving fine by then.

Glaring, the activity of interview was so wonderful. They are home finally. Uncle Forkey has come to them while at the lunch table making inquiry as whether how did the interview go. Probably before he got the news already that they have superbly passed the interview and received full admission upon a telephone call was made to him by one of his friends on the campus. They have been long time childhood friend before in Grand Kru County when the friend left home and settled in Gbarpolu County where he came from. It's about one hundred twenty miles away from Monrovia city.

Uncle Forkey's friend, Slewion, is back again at the house. He's been urged inside where upon agreeing first to pass the night at the house. Probably, Uncle Forkey wanted to see him being around for a lay while, if he likes until a week after he could think of going back in the interior then.

Now seated, Uncle Slewion decided to disclose of his problem by way of showing his body to his friend, Uncle Forkey. He had a tragedy of tiger that almost quell him. He took-off his shirt. Uncle Forkey is viewing his body. "Wow, your body is scarred. What may be the cause, Slewion? Oh, my God! It's too ugly to see this!" Uncle Forkey had his hand on his body as he's so pithily palpating it.

"It's a long story, Forkey. I want you just sit down a little by me. I'd explain the story." Slewion said. Forkey got quietly seated. He's wobbling with his head in repudiation to his nightmare.

"I'd have been dead by now, Forkey."

"What's really the matter wrong, Slewion? This thing of your body being scarred is scaring me."

"The story here is that, I have a friend who he and I went to hunt inside the Gola National Park. First of all, we patrolled the bushes hunting almost the whole day at different locals. We couldn't just get hold of any animal either. Because we couldn't get an animal, as we were hunting around, we had decided to go to the national park furtively to hunt—and that we did. Some good friends of ours often do that too secretly as we did."

"So, what has been the problem really? That is a crime. That you know of, isn't it?"

"Look, it's so terrible to say it in detail as I'm about doing really. We were so braved and got to the area hunting. I know it's a crime but who is to blame when nature had us to? That's the damn poverty demean the problem really."

"Oh, no! It's disgusting."

"Forkey, you know the story of our country that economically things ain't just fine with almost everyone's life. The worst of the economic cliff of life is that barely was the time of Christmas near. And we needed some money to buy essentials for the season."

"Okay. Why should you perhaps violate the forest law when you know that it's a big crime? Supposed you were to be caught or killed what were you to do then?"

"I know what I did was wrong. I promise not go about that again. But like I said it's because of the hard times I did that." he said and Uncle Forkey bobbed.

"So then, what happened at last for which you're like this?'

"When we were about to hunt, sounding usually the hunting sound, we hid ourselves under the trunk of a very big tree. The roots made cave with us. We got under it so relaxed. Only from a distance we were the ones seeing afar. The first call that I made some tigers came to the call."

"Wow! So, did you bullet yourself when you saw the tiger or what?"

"No. Please listen a little. It's jeering really. I was like someone daft when I saw the tiger."

Forkey interrupted again and said, "Did you jump on the tiger back in that at the time to have pierce it with a knife or what did you really do to yourself that you are looking like this?"

"Like I started, I saw a tiger and bullet it. And I didn't know that another one came over our head to see who had fired at the other probably to harm us."

"Oh, you knew that and went out the cave?"

"No. We didn't know earlier when the one over our heads came on the ground before one of us could get out the cave to have gone to chop the other into pieces. We saw it running away. Presumably, I never thought that it has either escaped away a little in order to come back again to cause harm to any of us either."

"What? Please don't let my body creep on me in pumping up blood either. This is so scaring, dear."

"Surely that was so the terrible incident that made me like this, looking stupidly scarred."

"Did you run behind the tiger when that one came to harm you either, or what did you do?"

"No. But I was so silly to have come out of the cave in few minutes upon seeing the breath come out of the other killed."

"What? Do you mean that you did that silly thing in less than a minute getting out the cave?"

"That I did. I'd have been dead by now." He whimpered. Uncle Forkey came close to pet him. He'd the guts still to explain his own stupid ordeal again.

"Did your friend stand by while you were struggling with the tiger at the time or what?"

"I didn't listen to my friend by then. He earlier said we should wait at least twenty minutes upon firing the other tiger before could we get out the cavern of the tree. But anxiousness had made me gotten into a state of being daft, like I said, with no time to waste and I came out after five minutes. First of all, I chopped up the legs of the dead tiger, my dear. And as soon as I was looking ahead of me I saw the other tiger coming towards me, and before I could make up my mind to escape into the cave, it rushed on me."

"Oh, that's so incredible to have happened to you!"

"Surely, I was just fast to have gotten my sharp knife out my pocket when pointedly I struggled and pierced it deeply into the stomach. By then it was already on my neck chewing me up."

"Oh, no!"

"Yes, that's how it happened."

"Really? Wow! It's scaring, dear."

"That's the fact."

"Slewion, God did more than a miracle for you. He spared you a justice really. So, you mean. . . you were to be gone to the dead's world by then?"

"That's it."

"Wow!"

Uncle Forkey remained malodorous in body about the scaring thing the friend had said. For almost two minutes he couldn't say a word either. With that, being so also pathetic about his condition, Uncle Forkey promised to let him go to a hospital for better treatment immediately. You could see from Slewion's body that the sore is still the inner part unhealed apart from the surface showing sign of being healed.

Invariably, as Uncle Forkey has always done for him, a gesture when he became so now ecstatic, and woke dancing, that he is going to attend hospital by better treating himself then.

16

A very tough school day of exams taking finally came to an end. Teta, Tesio and Gmasnoh decided to pass to a refresher area for recreation. The day is so terribly bizarre. It is a day they have taken several tough tests.

There are three subjects that were for the exams taken. They are Biology, Chemistry and English.

In removal of numbed cells of the hard thinking from the brain since the exams are over, they have decided by then to go to the Robert Johnson's Resorts to swim firstly. After that they could do other things which could bring back the lost memories at the time. By that Tesio in particular thinks that the body of him could gain its normal temperature than the way he has been feeling so miserable since then. His head remained pounding on him until they were at the place and he got into the pool and cooled up.

Interestingly, after Tesio, Gmasnoh and Teta thought to do theirs turn of swimming too. Tesio quickly did his fifteen minutes after, and left the pool with them. He asked one of the hostesses to bring him a bottle of wine as he was lying in a rubber stretcher at the pool.

While chilling luckily Doctor Stewart is sitting at a not too far away a distance, and spotted them. He saw Tesio first and he couldn't just get over it that the two of them have probably come to Monrovia at last. And they should have been in contact with him since then. Truly they lost his contact since then.

"Gmasnoh," Tesio is trying to call the attention of her and Teta about Doctor Stewart pointing at them, "can you see out there, I guess that should be Doctor Stewart, who I'm looking at there."

Gmasnoh took a look at him seriously and said, "Oh, that's him!"

Gmasnoh has stupidly left the pool with just her swimming stuff on her and yelled. "Doctor Stewart, it can't be you I'm looking at right now! Oh, my God! Where have you been?"

In response Doctor Stewart said, "You mean . . . Tesio and you are finally here at the city without making a contact with me either?" He smiled.

Upon meeting the two Tesio said, "We've been wishing since then to hear from you. How are you doing, Doctor Stewart?"

"I'm fine, and you?"

"We are so grateful that things are better with us than before. There are so much good things here in the city we have been enjoying this while upon arrival." Tesio sagely and boastfully said.

Few minutes later Gmasnoh and Teta decided to keep a conversation with Stewart.

Their heavens presumably, looking at how happy they are now, seemly are good and laughter became also very huge the moment.

"M. G.K.A." That's a tattoo on the body of Gmasnoh crisscrossed vertically like a belt of AK-47 on her body. It's an inscription meaning, "Magical girl kicks ass." And that is placed on her body by Tesio because, as Tesio thought, her juvenile status is quite illuminating yet, like a gallery as the sight for sore eyes which any man with a purpose of marrying her early could then cancel such plan immediately by seeing that. It's quite a cuss but Tesio said he doesn't want any man to think of love affair yet with her. And the girl is highly plumb.

What Tesio got to know quickly is that, the life of the rural area can't be as the city's life. Certain clothes are worn by women that are fashionable in the city. They are mostly opened at the back and chest area, especially a Gucci brand. But the swimming trunk is a Tommy designed. And he had so much fear in him because he wants his cousin to be educated.

A guy by the name of Candy Browne spotted Teta and Gmasnoh from a distance while swimming at the time into the pool. He left his seat and came to befriend them.

"May I get to know you both, please?"

"Are you referring to me in particular?" Gmasnoh asked.

"Yes, you're the one, please. May I know your name first, please?"

With no hesitation Gmasnoh said, "I'm Gmasnoh Tesioti, and you?"

"I'm Candy Browne."

"Well, it's nice to meet you."

Candy likewise said same. "I saw you both from a distance and I was so attracted by your guises that is a reason I have come to befriend you particularly, then." Browne delightedly said. In response Gmasnoh said, "It's no problem really meeting with you. How can I further help you, Candy?"

They chatted a little and smiled. You could see that friendliness from the two girls, especially Teta who then wanted for Gmasnoh to have a fiancée perhaps, showing strongly her cheeks outside. She finds the conversation between Candy and Gmasnoh so interesting. All that she wants is for Gmasnoh to agree with Candy, if he happens to approach her about love matter either.

Gmasnoh, though an innocent girl for now yet, Candy held her hand very tightly then, telling her something quite desirable by him. As Candy is talking with her, however, he keeps rubbing his palm into her hands, which sometimes a street-smart guy does in seeking a girl for love affair. She forcefully jerked her hand from his palm and he smiled. It's her very first time for a man to walk up to her intrepidly wishing a friendship from her in that way.

"Well, I'd really wished that we meet than this another day to better talk," Browne concluded. He got his hands into his pocket right away when he said that.

Knowing such look by Candy at the girl's face--and she isn't either showing remorse about wanting him perhaps, but that got him railroaded to have quickly changed the subject.

Worst for him, Doctor Stewart came between and interrupted the conversation. "Here isn't the appropriate place to talk with Gmasnoh. Please, let it be another time and at a different local." Doctor Stewart unruly said to Candy.

So blushed, Gmasnoh is being obligated to have left Candy standing and came back to her seat again.

Perhaps Candy, a lover boy he is, he's thinking to one day tell her about love affairs, as he thought. No girl had cultivated him most than Gmasnoh. And the girl is so beautiful. She is such a way with her body being so young, as her nipples are trying friendly finding the way out of the swimming trunk disgustingly to titter.

However, here's the true story about Browne. The guy's father is a retired general from the US Army. Later, upon the old man's retirement benefits were paid him by the US Government, he negotiated a contract with the government of Liberia---a country that just came from a civil war and since then trying to retrain its army, rather to provide some assistances in that training partly the Arm Forces, since he's a veteran general. That's how he thought it wise by then bringing his son to his home-country. And Candy is practically a replica of him. He fears nothing and very skilful as well. As long something concerns him, he prefers confronting it right away without fear either. He has the first most bravery factor of a true general. All his days he never left any of his comrades in a battle as a general.

But Candy got as powerful, rather as a teenager. He is like living in his own world. His father wanted him to always live life as he used to live while in the United States. He's his lovely son. Everywhere he has gone he had always wanted him to be there with him. And so, he never wanted for him to be penniless in the process too.

Candy so loves his father inexplicably, too. Howbeit, he left his brothers and sisters in America to be with the father because his father always used him to always go and buy just anything he wants in the marketplace. And when he comes with a little change left over from buying items for him, Mr. Browne himself tells him to keep it, or deposit same into his personal account.

He is like his father trusted bodyguard. For this, since arrival, his account for years now has been building up by such activity. Sometimes the two times monthly shopping for the father could give him four thousand dollars unimaginably. So, he had money. As a teen yet, he got him so wide to be making love to any girl that either comes his way, interestingly. And this moment, with the Gmasnoh saga, but he got a slap from her unconsciously. Gmasnoh just wanted to be a friend but he was taking it differently by her act of friendliness that had shown by her hand into his palm while smiling with him too.

Tesio, doing that conversation he has been frowning at Candy. But luckily Candy left their presence, being so then downhearted, because Gmasnoh didn't show any concern for him about his ironic mind towards her then.

17

Their lives in the city seemed more promising daily. They are skilfully mastering everything in the city and at college level too. And four years had gone by. Graduation is just few weeks to go.

This faithful day that came, Gmasnoh and Tesio got seated in the park on the campus of the University. By then, the two decided at least to inform the elders about the planned graduation. In his start, his first contact is with the elders. And next should be the parents.

After a greeting Elder Bartee decided to admonish him about the oaths they took. "I want you not to forget that the both of you took oaths in that to protect yourself against sex yet. You all know what the oaths are intended. To hear that you're still doing well, we are so happy about that really. Keep doing your best always. We are so much impressed about your splendid performance still."

Tesio decided to put the phone on speaker. He wants his sister to listen to what the elder is saying to him. She came by his side quickly. In response yet a rebuttal is about to be made to the elder. He said, "Elder, there is no society in the absence of its traditional values will grow. The traditional values in any given society are there to bring out the real good, especially where we find ourselves now we are so much cognizant about that." Tesio said and paused.

"You are sounding very good. I must appreciate the efforts of the two of you yet. I know you both as very smart individuals that are tactful, each time making sound decisions. That's good!"

"Thanks. You said something at last for which I want you to listen to me a bit. I want to tell you that it's not time for marriage discussion for which you've to call us about that now." Tesio said.

"No. I'm just cautioning you. We are so concerned about the both of you. Where you people are, rather is a very stupid place that doesn't regard traditional values at times. That's what a life in the city is. Sometimes you can't know how you would fall into trouble either." The Elder said same.

He gave a story of how Rosa's parents decided to take a step by meeting the two of them parents yet, concerning a plan of paying a dowry in Tesio's behalf for the girl.

Tesio is a bit galled. Because of that he wants to ask him a question forcibly. "What did you say about Rosa?" Elder Bartee maintained by saying, "We need to do the early arrangement so that you won't probably or the girl can't even think of marrying another person in time to come."

"I think that premarital arrangement is too early for that yet. Or, is it part of the oath I took? I expect that you know we are just seventeen years old yet. Is it time for premarital arrangement now?

"I don't mean to say anything wrong but the arrangement has to be made in advance. The both of you are not just any individuals to take your matters of marriages for jokes either. You're part of the elder for which everything needs to be done in advance."

"Thank you for the plan but that is too early. Let it be tabled yet." Tesio said and frowned a little.

The reminder made by the Elder got his mind quickly televised about trouble that any mistake he and the sister may make would be bad for them.

To wonder, Gmasnoh decided asking a question to know exactly what he was really saying on the phone with the elder, because he got through talking while still his face is so faded. In response he said, "Nothing is much really! I was just on the line with head of the elder council who said something funny to me. He said Rosa's parents, as it's supported by the elders upon briefing our parents too, are going to meet with my parents yet to see if there could be an early arrangement for my parents to pay Rosa's dowry in the meantime before the deal day, when we shall have reached the prime ages of twenty-five, which everything could be really fine."

"That's shit! What's such an ugly plan, Tesio? It sounds so funny and early for such talk to come about now. I thought he should be praying for us to do our best still then, instead of him talking about premarital arrangement."

"Just wait a minute, Gmasnoh. I know what to do about that. We shouldn't speak with them like that yet. You know we took oaths and I expect that the gods are all over here watching us."

"Tesio, you're the one who really believe that thing still. It's not me. My life is no more the same, oh! I took my mind off that long time ago. I'm planning to get married to a person in the city than going home to marry a farmer either. Do you think I would want to go back onto the ugly path of extreme poverty when I have left home already?" Gmasnoh sounded so funny to him. Tesio smiled.

"Don't say that yet. It's so soon for you to behave like that. Any attempt by you repudiating or obliterating the premarital vow yet in your life that is, rather a crime against the tradition because you are to go home firstly to do the necessary sacrifice to the gods to abort or obliterate the oath."

Tesio laughed loud when Gmasnoh spoke. It got him reflecting a bit on the issue.

"What is it that you are you still laughing, Tesio? I beg of you to please be a lay careful and think about those oaths we took. The mess may hunt us one day."

"Hush, Gmasnoh! Don't you know about African tradition for which you calling it mess? No, I want you avoid that, please. We should deal with these people intelligently than by clamouring over any issue with them either. They are uncivilized people that take everything very seriously, if you go wrong with the tradition."

"Tesio, you need to know this. I'm already regretting the moment while I've to take that oath by then. Now, as we are in college definitely, there are lots of opportunities before us that may cause you either to forget partly the tradition. In fact, it's an understatement to say that things are now good than it used to be at home which you need to know now."

"So, what does that really supposed to me? Should we dump or cancel the tradition right now because of modernity? Come on. . . Gmasnoh! Stop the joke." It got her frowning at him.

"Oh, you call that a joke!"

"Please, you're to get that talk away from me now. I see you getting too seriously talking bad things against the tradition. It's too early. I don't want to be blamed by the gods if you fall into trouble as you're talking unruly that much. If you continue so I may communicate with our people home about what your behaviour is, for me not to be part of it. I hate that really."

"Don't you say that to me either! I'm just telling you to be that careful by opening your eyes better to see around you. Do you think the life at home is a life to say a person is living rightly?"

"I'm not going to continue talking that much with you again. You just go ahead and talk." Tesio said.

With that at least, Gmasnoh thought it wise to say sorry to Tesio for whatever she had said that got him that so galled and moving about like he's confused and downhearted for her to speak a bit against the premarital oath. She knows how strongly the passion of Tesio over his tradition is for now.

18

It's Wednesday, a very special day to remember then. They have been on campus since the morning hour till the afternoon came. To wonder, they are there awaiting their clearances. Luckily the administration thought to award them. They became exceptional in their studies really.

Before the receipt of the clearances, there is a nuance that, they would receive scholarship after the graduation immediately to travel to the United States for further studies. They are to travel to get medical degrees.

That same day upon receipt of the clearances contact has been made with the elders. They were too happy to have wished to disclose of the news to the elder council. None could wait again for the graduation to be delayed either, because of the fine news of going to the USA, which is so interesting than even the graduation they are about to have.

The wonderful day came. They are at the graduation finally. It came two weeks after the receipt of the clearances. Before the graduation the elder council sent a cow for the party. The head of the elder even travelled as far as from Niffu to be a part of the revel.

Finally the graduation came and passed. A week after the graduation Tesio and Gmasnoh decided to finally depart Liberia for the USA. It's inexplicably hard to describe how excited they are the moment.

The night before departure Tesio and Gmasnoh first wanted to chat over the trip while seated at the back of the yard of Uncle Forkey as usual. Teta wasn't even there.

"America is a land of real opportunity. I believe when two of us happen to get there and study hard we may be that so lucky to quickly find work for us to meet our dreams."

"Tesio, it's needless to say. I advise that we shouldn't speak on the opportunity that much because I'm so happy not being able to either describe same really. I'm so impressed."

"Okay. I'm so impressed than you do, Gmasnoh." Tesio said and chuckled. It's like sweetly an argument put up.

"Why? Can you describe how happy I'm right now, Tesio?"

"Okay. But for me, I know that I'm already at the door of heaven. That's how I think about America."

"That's so true. I believe you and the Almighty would soon dine together because you are saying you're in heaven for now. Is it what America is?" She asked. Tesio burst up in a huge laughter.

"It's true, Gmasnoh. Just what you said about America that's a place we will be able to get our construction work at home quickly complete."

It's following the third week. On a Friday that day the weather is humid. Every belonging has been put at the back of usually the Prado once that took them for interview, rather for the final take-off at the Roberts International Airport in Harbel, Margibi County, intended going to the United States. The area is about forty-five minutes' drive from Monrovia to get there.

The day before departure they had an arrangement with Doctor Stewart for them to land at his sister's place in New Jersey before take-off after like two days, going on the Oral Roberts Medical Campus. There is the main point of destination, rather to note.

They are at the airport finally. Other good-bye formalities are to be performed. Tesio embraced Uncle Forkey. After him, he also embraced other relatives around. His comrade, Dorsla, a man who had wished to always be part of every revel of him, he's also at the place. He lustily embraced him and they smiled together. They are done with all of that.

Now, Tesio decided to stroll in the terminal area. He's so happy going to America. He starts to dance in joy about that. His funny movement is making Gmasnoh getting a bit sheepish yet. She wants the brother to stop the dancing.

"Tesio, I don't expect you to be doing this in the midst of lots of passengers here."

"What are you talking about, Gmasnoh?"

"I'm seeing the way you are dancing isn't proper for now. That is likely to make everyone here to be looking at you that you're a country-boy."

"Gmasnoh, please forget about that. How can you look at an educated man like me to be termed a country boy? Am I a boy when you know my qualification doesn't speak of that?" Why I can't celebrate during this moment? I got to, please."

"Okay. But I want you do it quietly maturely than being as lousy as you're doing it now, please."

"Ah, what's that?"

"I want you listen to me."

"Please leave me alone. I'm happy for the opportunity we have for now. Why stop me from expressing my happiness in this way either?"

"Look, Tesio, I understand why you're doing that. But you're making all eyes to be on us. It shames me."

"Okay. I'm so sorry for that. But you got to praise the creator of the universe for now, please."

"I'm not stopping you of having carousal in body about that. But Tesio let that celebration be as peacefully done at your heart than by expressing it through dancing openly. It's good that you are happy, but if you continue dancing and smiling openly all over here, which is in the midst of every passenger here at the airport, that perhaps could cause us to be sent for medical again before departure. Someone could say you're berserk and you need a check-up yet. And it could delay the trip, if that happens."

"Don't worry about that either, Gmasnoh. This is an early presumption by you. I know you to be a very wise woman to forget about that. It's impossible to see that happen really. Please leave me alone. I got all reasons to be so that happy really."

"Okay. I would get my mouth off you. Just do whatever you like."

She's going a bit away from him yet. He's standing on another line to do his check-in. She is also frowning still at him. Tesio is still dancing with a Walkman into his ears. As far he's concern his wish has come true that he's about to be in the United States for studies.

He did his check-in formalities. He decided to pass water into a bathroom nearby. While going to the bathroom a man by the name of Elechi Olumbazi, a businessman came out of Nigeria's Airway which arrived at the airport. He went straight at him to ask for the bathroom. He befriended him.

Olumbazi is about checking out to ride into Monrovia City. He'd some newspapers (Standard and Vanguard) from Nigeria with headlines: "Boko Haram is abandoning its militant struggle finally." The other newspaper read: "As Boko Haram ceases hostilities, President Goodluck Jonathan to have a nice sleep soon." Tesio read through them loudly. His act of reading got Olumbazi to look at him in the face and giggled.

"Why are you giggling about?"

"Nothing really do I have to say that much to you either. You're just making me feel like chuckling as you're reading."

"But I'm happy because the newspapers are giving nice news about a country I love, that is Nigeria."

"No. That's okay, Tesio." Olumbazi said. Few minutes after when Tesio read through, he peacefully had requested for his newspapers and went away from him.

19

For the past one day and night now they have been in transit from Africa firstly to Europe. They are about landing into America. It's Two O'clock almost the third day in the afternoon of it.

Something so ugly is about to unfold. They landed at the John F. Kennedy International Airport and got on board a chartered plane luckily brought by the administration of the Oral Roberts Medical College upon getting into America when the news had been revealed that there is a changed of the plan for them to have gone on campus straight instead. No more are they to go Doctor Stewart sister's place again, as earlier planned.

Doctor Scott, the head administrator himself decided at the time to have come, collecting them at the Kennedy Airport. He was earlier told about them sometimes ago. And the Government of Liberia told him about the guys smartness which impressed him for which he wanted to be the first contact with them upon entering America—and which it's now.

The most memorable debacle here is that, which any human mind won't easily had described, is about to unfold. This is something which the Great United States might have really remembered in life time.

Disheartening as it may, but some disbanded US veterans from Iraq war, for years since the return to the United States had pleaded with the United States Government to settle their remaining benefits. All efforts were exhausted by the guys to amicably handle the issue with the government before and no avail.

They have decided to take up arms. And the Kennedy Airport became a target to be barricaded by them.

When Tesio and Sister landed and upon packing their things on board the Medical Aircraft and sitting inside few minutes later, now to make the take-off, a forceful change of plan, as the disbanded veterans decided to cause havoc, started. Everything became momentarily stilled. Only the guys who came on the carnage you could see posted everywhere. Some people at the airport are unruly put under gun point in a pocket style by them to be stilled.

The situation alarmed. The Federal Bureau of Investigation in particular has quickly been set in that to get situation under control. A strong elite force composed of gallant men and women in the number of fifteen persons decided to quickly put the situation under control by then.

To wonder, the first attempt by the joint elite security team reaching to the airport, in that to secure the place quickly, that is rushing to put things under control in such a roaring manner, but the entire group has been killed. It seems so incredible. Bodily men and women in a number of fifteen persons are all slayed surprisingly.

It became farce anybody couldn't easily have explained yet. Gmasnoh went into coma. Before then, she wondered, while then she and her brother had left Liberia to be in America for education, if death would have been the case they are to encounter the moment then.

But Tesio, who had got a little education during a fight at home, and learned also how to wrestle and by firing a gun at last, he's about to be tested. He prefers to sacrifice his life that moment to free the airport than for him to sit and allow the simple situation to be out of control. He had smartly left the plane. He came from the cargo area furtively and got on the ground.

He walked quietly close to one of the guys very close by the plane. And in a ruffian manner, he quelled the guy. What he did was that, at a different direction, he threw out a canned emptied soft drink. The enemy looked at it in surprise. It was then he came on him furtively and broke his neck surprisingly. He tugged him away in less than a minute.

And Tesio took-off the guy suite on him and wore it, looking as the same way the entire terrorists are garbed. He turns to another direction to knock down the rest little by little. As he's marshalling, he obtained a silent gun from the first guy he killed. He has decided to use his silent gun now for his operation. He blasted a second group with his silent gun.

He got to the third direction while furtively taking cover. And he took another canned emptied soft drink close by again, that is from a trash around there and tossed it oppositely at the guy standing, and by the time the individual took a look at it, Tesio hit at him.

Looking at the way he's behaving in containing the situation, one could say that, Tesio has a form of swiftly justice ability shrouding over him sensibly as if, he has gone to a law school before either. He's so good and swift in his style.

The particular individual Tesio surprisingly had exterminated at last, but had a communication set on him. He collected it and decided to speak with the FBI. He is now on the FBI Radio and satellite systems. He has been watched on TV Stations around the United States.

At dismay, however, the head of the FBI got on his line. Rolland Salmus is a very bossy man, who doesn't even understand that security matter of a kind couldn't just be handled in an oval office like that either. He didn't perhaps know what he was doing at all. He has a limitation for which he couldn't easily understand himself either. Everything he does as long it concerns security matter he wanted to handle with force.

But without a better calculation, letting his guys handle the situation by ease and professionally, he instructed that there should be an arm-struggle, getting the guys out peremptorily. Sadly then, it's how the first group of security were murdered by the terrorists.

He became very uncontrollable in body by then surprisingly. But few minutes later, which nobody thought to have been then, he and Tesio became communicating freely. Glaringly, as he is so happy by then, he wants to now know who Tesio is really. The entire America is watching Tesio at every point on the satellite systems, however, needless to say either.

Salmus broke the ice by saying, "May I know your name, sir?" In response Tesio said, "I'm Tesio from Liberia. My cousin and I came to the United States as student for medical studies on the campuses of Oral Roberts Medical College. At our surprise, as you can see me now on screen, we've been attacked and corralled by some guys who want to even destroy the entire Airport. And I can't just sit by with this simple operation to see these guys destroy this wonderful airport. Besides, I've so much love for the United States and its people. And so, I won't sit to see this shit." He said, as his legs crisscrossing each other while holding the gun skilfully, lambasting the guys to a judgment day come down battle of death. Adding, he's like one of the USA elite forces of Marines performing that day.

"Okay, you got it right. But do you now need a help?"

"No. Just be on the standby yet and in few minutes the operation will be over with. Let me tell you that, right now it's a situation of no escape at the airport. It doesn't really require force either. Keep your men posted away from the airport. I can contain the guys in few seconds, please."

"That's so nebulously, rather a wonderful event, dear." Salmus added.

The only sound could one hear in the back echoing symbolically is the roaring steps of Tesio's feet, as he's taking a cover by then furtively destroying the guys.

Salmus is so confused. One thing he needs to know is that such a situation should have professionally been handled than by force.

"Dammit! Tesio seems very swift. Is he an America?" Rolland Salmus worded. At the time President Walker Rosemary is in his oval office watching the incredible situation on TV. But, by the time he saw Tesio containing the situation in a professional manner his normalcy is gaining its status quo as before. Now, he is feeling as if a true state-man, who is soon to be in control of his country once again, as he's laughing and shaking hands with whomever that is found around him in the oval office.

"I'm making my way outside the airport area to get the few left gun down" –Tesio said.

"Okay. We are watching you now. That's good my boy to keep on." You could see Tesio's cheeks wide opened, but without a sound of either a laughter to have made.

Doctor Scott has since been hanging drip still on Gmasnoh. He's the chief administrator of the Oral Roberts Medical College that came to meet with them, earlier stated. He too couldn't get over what has been happening either. But he saw Gmasnoh at the time going into coma when the incident had earlier started.

An hour later, God so blessed, at least Tesio had contained the madness. Now the news about his indisputable greatness has become somehow good yet, but a grotesque. That moment, every corner of the world the news is being spread out.

By this, to wonder, I understand how benevolence has forms at times, especially when the most powerful nation's interest is protected by a single individual like Tesio.

20

The head of the FBI operation at the airport decided to meet with Tesio before the take-off by him and the cousin could be finally. By then, like said earlier, the situation had come under control. And Salmus feels so excited, having Tesio resolved the matter in a sensitive manner no one thought of him either.

Tesio decided to explain in full what has been the reason of him and his cousin of being into the USA.

"As a matter of fact, my cousin and I are here for studies at the Oral Roberts Medical College in pursuit of medical degrees. We are from the lay West African nation of Liberia--down all the way from Niffu Town."

"What did you said, sir? I want you please speak clearly so that I can better hear you." Salmus couldn't clearly understand the language of Tesio yet. His African tongue has become the problem for which Salmus can't even understand him yet, even though he's speaking to him about himself.

But few minutes later, Tesio spoke slowly and clearly for which there was a huge chat. After that he is now about getting on board the chattered plane of the college, taking off to the place, where he and the cousin are going finally.

In repudiation to his quick departure Salmus asked that he speaks with him on something very importantly yet--which he needs to know. At last he said, "President Rosemary has approved that you and Gmasnoh be given a FBI protection, while you'd be flying to your final destination now. So, let's make the arrangement, Sir!"

"Thanks." Tesio stood up waiting on him. He got a dowry from his briefcase including a pen.

"For a second, Sir," he is referring to Tesio, "when the both of you get on your campus President Rosemary would like to talk with you on a phone. And I'm hopeful that both of you may meet physically at a special honouring program in your behalf organized by the USA." Salmus said. There I got to know that America doesn't require people of riches first, as long the person is able to make him or herself important person for everyone to embrace him or her.

Salmus is interestingly being corralled by his colleagues of FBI agents, while turning the page of a diary by then in that to present to Tesio the number of the United States' President upon receiving instruction from him by then. Tesio wonderfully said, thanks upon receiving the contact; by then, he begged the pardon of Salmus and the rest of his guys rather to get on board his plane for departure.

Three minutes after, however, visually, he walked into the plane and sat for sure. His presence got his cousin Gmasnoh quickly came to herself a bit from the state of coma by then. Tesio dabbed her on the face that is how she felt the touch of a person when she left the state of hypnosis.

Gmasnoh is so confused over the incident when she woke.

"What's it that drip is hanged on me? Am I sick or daft?

"No."

"What's then the problem? I wasn't sick before leaving Liberia. Why be this that is happening to me?" Her eyes opened wide.

"Just wait a minute, Gmasnoh! I want you come to yourself. Don't you know that we were almost sent to hell? Don't you know that yet, Gmasnoh?" Doctor Scott said that to her. He had easily removed the drip from her body. He was then relaxing close to her seat, while then listening.

When he was done with talking with Gmasnoh he turned to Tesio. "Where did you acquire this training from, Tesio?" Doctor Scott asked. Tesio gasped and shrugged as well.

"I learned to protect myself when I became a boy living in Grand Kru, a place part of south-eastern Liberia. And I got a lay juju over that too. That's a traditional medicine. As such nobody can easily harm me, if he or she makes an attempt to." He boastfully said without even remorse either.

"Wow! That's so good."

"The issue here is that we've a culture that's associated with fighting, especially a man to prove his manhood at times when there is a critical need."

"But have you been trained also as military personnel? Reason being you proved so exceptional during the crisis, Tesio!"

"Hey, Doctor Scott I'm not kidding. As a culture, there is fighting often done on the beach by the population of my town."

"You mean that really?"

"Yep."

Tesio and Doctor Scott laughed. "You must really be a very good traditional fighter, Tesio." Doctor Scott concluded.

A self-importance spirit, as you could see Tesio laughing, became eminently a factor unavoidable to him the moment then. You could see how wonderful he is by the facial expression upon Salmus giving him the contact of Rosemary, too.

Throughout the month Tesio and Gmasnoh's names have become the news for most of the early morning breakfast news at every part of the world, especially the United States. The CNN became the worst of sending out the news-- and sorts of ads followed in the process too, displaying Tesio's last moment of getting at the terrorists.

The episode was replayed and replayed for a long while for almost a whole month. In that, the ABC News had a headline:

"The Hero in disguise." The Washington Post wrote: "In the valley of death, Tesio, a teenager from West Africa saved America." And the London Times wrote: "Africa's incredible hero on the continent of America."

To wonder, in China, the KTVU Prank had a story which read: "The most powerful man in the world—Tesio, from a poor nation in West Africa."

Too many headlines were interestingly monotonously made. Such headlines got most of the news networks to have accrued lots of profits in the process upon the reading world took seriously the news of Tesio. They lavished praises. It was really a fun to read about what Tesio did. His act made his country, Liberia to be adorned than ever by the United States, as a partner in progress to always maintaining its ties.

It's just few minutes left to reach the destination. Before the arrival on the campuses of Oral Roberts Medical College---the whole airport on the mission is at a gridlock with some news sight reporters again who wanted to see physically the Tesio man. Some thought Tesio is a Whiteman. Majority didn't even see the live story at the time with the CNN when it had earlier been reported.

His royalty by virtue, is a basis to say that, at least got him earned some quiet millions yet. And the United States Government is about giving them some money in the meantime yet.

By high level instruction to Doctor Barley Scott, he took them straight to their private suite on the campus upon the arrangement was made in advance.

"We are so very grateful Doctor Barley Scott for all the assistances rendered us so far since our arrival into the USA." Tesio quietly said, while extending hands as he was standing at the front portal of his villa. He had confidently held Doctor Scott's hand for almost two minutes, appreciating him so far.

"It's my pleasure hoping to see the both you later at the chapel for an honouring service, which the Oral Roberts College Administration has decided to have for you, especially Tesio. President Rosemary of the United States will also be there to grace the occasion. He would like to meet with you in person." Doctor Scott sagaciously said. He giggled over it as well.

"Thanks. We would be there as requested by you."

"Okay, Tesio." Doctor Scott left for his residence finally.

Tesio and Gmasnoh have each decided to do one or two things into their various rooms. Gmasnoh took her bath and did other things as well. Likewise Tesio too, and later they all converged in the foyer of the opened house to chat before the evening hour comes for the program.

The villa has been so much decorated by furniture and fixture. As a very interestingly festooned house, as anybody probably is about entering the house, you could really think that they are now like king and queen yet—something earlier the news world made mentioned of before in detail. It spoke of Tesio's greatness that he saved America by then. Now it has become a proof for an economic relief for them at least. Or, if I may put it another way, especially the word used before by Instructor Wea-bla, called 'restoration' has come to be at birth at least.

"Tesio," Gmasnoh came to meet with him after she took her shower, "you really put us on top of the world." Tesio took a deep smile. He rose from his seat and embraced the cousin. And he cuddled hands with her by then and led her to her seat right at the table where he had been sitting.

"Look, Gmasnoh, the creator of the world knows exactly how to work up things for the layman. And when man thinks that He's at sleep, that's when He speaks in a very special way unthinkably."

"That's so true my dear!"

"Gmasnoh, can you see now how we are? My mind inexplicability is telling me of a different world than where we have been living. I mean . . . for all those years while we have been participants in the boiling pot of poverty distress, but now we are gradually going atop of the world precipitately. Look, a real money-making life is about to speak into our lives a wonder."

"That's so true." Gmasnoh chuckled.

"The life with the both of us is altering the true meaning which we can't really explain yet." Tesio said. Gmasnoh laughed after he spoke. She laughed as if she is falling off. But he was fast to have gone to her and balanced her to her seat once again.

She woke from her seat with her hands to her mouth speechlessly again. After like three minutes she decided to speak out. "I thought when we were at the airport that was the end of us, Tesio. That's how America really looks at times?" Tesio twisted his head with a smile. "I think it was good that the terrorists came at the airport because it was the start of huge blessings for us."

"You're right but that shouldn't be a thing to praise in the manner in which it happened either. Lots of people got killed for which isn't that good at all."

"It's true. But I'm just so happy that is a reason I said that. I don't really mean to embrace the issue either. We are just sharing joke for which I said such."

"Okay."

"Even, you don't know that you were in coma at the airport when that debacle started? You need to even say thanks to Doctor Scott in particular for what he did for you. God is first--- and have him second to have at least saved your life."

"You mean that?"

"Sure!"

They chatted and dinned. The time for the honouring program is at hand. And Doctor Scott earlier talked about that before. Doctor Scott is so happy having Tesio brought a huge recognition to his school because of what had happened then.

21

The evening came. It's time to go at the chapel. Before then, a parcel from the immigration office of the United States has been brought to them while at the house. Tesio brought it at the table upon receiving it from someone outside the house where they are. He opened it and comprehended well the information and said to his cousin this: "The both of us are now citizens of the United States! This is America. . . the land of greatness!" Tesio said lousily. The two lustily embraced each other right away. They are laughing like crazy the moment indescribably then.

"Thank you! Thank you ever so much Tesio." Gmasnoh said. "No, Gmasnoh, you don't have to make huge noise about this either. I think it was right at the airport all of our paper works by the immigration office were processed and now sent to us."

"Okay. But this is really a great nation. Now it's time that we may live the American Dream as soon as possible, Tesio."

"Gmasnoh—" he called twice her name, "the real information you need to really embrace is that, we are not just citizens, but honorary citizens of the United States, we are now. That's the big news I want you to accept, dear!"

"Wow!"

"Gmasnoh, you just look at this document first and after, take a look outside the yard too. You'd see a FBI agent standing there to keep our security."

"Are you serious?" She held the documents in hand browsing through them.

"Why not, would I ever lie to you?"

Tesio is bouncing around with her as they held tightly each other. They are so happy. For five minutes, that was done.

The evening hour has come finally. Before then the motorcade of President Rosemary arrived to let them ride into it. He wants to make them feel as special. After like a five-minute ride, they are at the chapel finally.

Tommy Wilson, a very clever boy who has been state's personnel assigned to the President of the United States. He came alongside him to the program in order to read the President's message to Tesio. He began by saying, "A patriotic is a person that sacrifices his life at times for others for the sake of his or her country. By his or her act of service to be a help to humanity, he or she never grew weary of what the cause may be. Tesio, you really did lend a hand to the people of America, which nobody can even pay you back for the astounding service you rendered our people. The United States says, in particular, a big thank you ever so much in this special way." Tesio shed tears the moment. He is so elated, having been given the high recognition, full of deference perhaps.

For almost five minutes he has been dabbed. He didn't believe it that, life has a special time for every human being. And now was such for them to get the meaning of life-worthiness, being it for them the moment. It signalled the end of poverty, rather to think of that, there is no more will it be around again by then.

"We believe you've also received the document of how the two of you've now become honorary citizens of the United States, isn't it?"

"Yes, we did!" Tesio disclosed of how President Rosemary spoke with him earlier.

What interests me most is that, the President's message has been read by a lay boy like that on behalf of the United States. And what had got it to be is that, his smartness has really cultivated the United States' President by then to let him read same. But the foremost message of letting him read the message is that intended to give an opening-eye to young people, especially those of his peers that may see him on TV, where can they put up a purposeful state of being in life, working hard towards being as good people of the world, especially the society of the United States. He reminded him about little Craig in the USA, who as small as he is, tremendously helping lots of young people in the world by his voluntary programs in place.

Invariably, there was a lot of flamboyancy about the program. However, three hours later it came to an end.

The next day came. Early that morning by six o'clock, Tesio's phone rang. President Rosemary called him. At the time Tesio took the phone and Gmasnoh too woke up to listen while in her room. The two are connected on the same line yet. So, the call is instantaneously being received by the two.

With a lay contemplative rise from her bed to have then answered the phone, because Gmasnoh wasn't that sure who may have called the hour yet, Tesio quickly took the call and said, "Hello!"

"Good morning, Tah-Tesio." The president fumbled with his name in response.

"Who may be on the line, please?"

"It's the President of the United States of America calling to say good morning."

"Wow, Mr. President . . . it's Tesio truly on the line. Do you really mean to speak with me, sir? Wow! How are you doing?" In respond the president said, "I'm good and you?"

"I'm very fine for now."

"Well, Tesio, I had a good sleep last night because of you. I do really appreciate you for the endeavour to have saved the United States from such menace. If, it hasn't been you quickly to have brought the situation under control, my damn ass would have remained very hot throughout the day and night. My eyes would have got glue stuck to them purposely struggling with sleep not to come to me, while they were to remain wide opened until otherwise. Tesio, since the hour of that incident, I've been on the alert just to report to the federal states. But, thank you ever so much that you made me to have a good sleep at last."

"Wow, I should thank you ever so much, Mr. President. Imagine by your approval we became also honorary citizens of the United States. It's so much worthwhile."

"I should be the one really to say thank you, Tesio." President Rosemary said amusingly.

They chatted hugely. After a lay while he went off the line.

Tesio is so flabbergasted, having heard the President of the United States directly spoke with him on phone. He felt as though somebody in paradise. His heart by the way then is pounding in joy over the good conversation he had with the president.

One thing he ought to know is that-- the people of the United States, including the president is not of the pride to talk or probably dignify a person as long he or she deserves same. Nobleness is never a special gift for special people that may have been stored by only noble people of laudable background, or with riches either. Poor person could even get such deference based on character content. This has been the case with him and the cousin perhaps. And so, that moment he was lustily in a state as if, somebody who has won probably a popular case in court that would earn him unimaginable million dollars soon. He feels as being a worth or great so soon, as a very good citizen of the United States now. Imagine too many persons have sought such opportunity since then in the USA or outside to be, but it seems hard to obtain same. But theirs by the power of God has come through in a second. It's quite incredible!

22

The medical journey has now started. Finally, they are to the class orientation for the very first time a month after.

This first day became as if a special interview period by the time everyone happens to lay eyes on them. Every direction Tesio and Cousin have turned so far, lots of students kept forming queues just to see the Tesio in particular. It's seemed as a sight for sore eyes about the way Tesio and Gmasnoh have been corralled by the student populace at every corner of the college.

The entire day upon leaving class, walking around on campus to know their various classes, too, was an embarrassing one really. Some news reported came heavily on the campus just to speak with them.

What had helped to control the madness of embarrassing them few days after is that, warning notices were written by the college. They are placed at every corner, requesting everyone, especially the student populace to desist from crowding around Tesio and Gmasnoh.

All that everyone has so wished is that to know exactly how Tesio managed at the time when he contained such an unimaginable or catastrophic situation.

Really, there is something very interestingly to praise, for the people of the United States, especially they are smart and law abiding people. Because of that, by the time the administration wrote the notices and placated them everywhere, the content sought the indulgence of everyone, which has so then saved face perhaps of that huge embarrassment it would have been.

The third day came. Doctor Barley Scott went to class and thought to introduce himself to the students. This man is a very lovable but sexually a con. He has since admired Gmasnoh. He designed something of a stupid course he thinks he could use to test the minds of Tesio and Gmasnoh because they told him before about their cultural value they hold unto yet. He wants to annul those oaths they told him about through his medical students. Because of that he decided to openly tell about what the medical culture is in America.

"I'm Doctor Barley Scott. I'll be teaching a course call the 'Anatomy or Human Physiology Analysis.' It's something a bit passed gynaecology with focused, especially with body surgical analysis in dealing with machines too. You'll be dealing with all sorts of living bodies or things in order to prove a medical problem that may arise using a surgical machine in the process too. And so, that would so much require for a person, when the time comes, for him or her to be unclothed individually to take my final test."

Majority of people, or students, knew what he meant to say about that perhaps. The subject is about seeing unclothed person when the time comes either at a hospital or the like. And the issue of nakedness of a person or anatomically, is a course in Biology that can't really, there be big news either about that. That he knows. Why would somebody who is involved with or doing a medical has to be feeling uncomfortable to go about it either? It's a popular saying or thing about Biology or the so-called anatomic course he is talking about in the USA.

And for the medical studies it's an understatement for anyone to think of avoiding such either. But that statement is like sounding yet funny, or making muddy waters into the brains of Tesio and his cousin Gmasnoh.

Most of the Biology they even did at school while in Liberia is mostly theoretical. It's not as too informative about anatomical analysis issue that is spoken about. On the other hand, such thing of nudity in medical as a person would be dealing with either non-living or living structures or probably a human being unclothed to show parts of his or her body either affected with illness that, really is seemed, abstract for the two Africans yet.

The statement got Tesio a bit funny in body to wonder about the oaths taking which could be as destroying partly their traditional values. If the both of them are not careful perhaps, whereas they took oaths to protect same, that will surely be a trouble.

Gmasnoh decided to ponder over the assertion of the instructor with Tesio. "Did you get the issue raised by the instructor?"

"No. I really need clarity yet. Or, Gmasnoh is he saying that in the long run as he will be teaching the course is when we are either to be naked into his class or what?" It's obscured yet about the instructor's assertion which needs to be clarified.

"Yes. I believe that's what he meant to say. Do any of us really have a problem with that?"

"What not, Gmasnoh. It's funny because of the oaths we took at home."

Tesio lifted his head to look at Doctor Scott and Williams, who are in partnership with the course, while still lecturing the class.

"Look, Tesio, those are some of the best doctors in the United States." Gmasnoh said, while comparing quiet note with him.

"There is no big deal about nudity either. Failure by anyone perhaps that is either going to accept partly the act of nudity during surgical lab, he or she will not be part of the class again. So, if what I say is not good for anyone who may have come from Asia or Africa, you'll have to leave the class to go back home immediately. You are to tell your people that the medical study in America is strange or full of rudeness, intending breaking your traditional vows or not."

Tesio had his hand up to ask.

"Please excuse me, Doctor Scott."

"Yes, what's it?"

"You have said something very interesting to note." Most of the students' eyes are turned to Tesio. "Yes, I want you speak your mind." Gmasnoh had her head bowed. "You spoke of the issue of nudity, if I'm right."

"Yes. You're right, sir—"

"Look, I and my cousin are Africans. Back home where we came from we've a tradition that says nobody is to even dream of looking at our bodies, and even as we too, as you said, which is part of our studies, as long we ain't married yet. That's, we ain't to be involved with sex yet, till we get married upon the return home then. We are not to look at the body of a naked person either. This is what I want to say." Tesio said and paused.

"Can that be an issue to talk here, my dear? I'm so sorry that this place is the land of America that believed strongly in the liberty of people. But with medical studies it is a different issue the laws of America are limited about." Scott said.

"Let me just make my point, sir. Will such exercise of yours not be a problem for us?" Tesio padded.

When he asked Gmasnoh jumped up at her seat and said, "No. He's the one going to have problem with it but not me." He felt highly abashed when Gmasnoh spoke. It got him in a little nervousness in body.

"Tesio, I guess you're from Africa. But let me tell you that this place is America. The culture of Africa has nothing to do with the culture of America. Most importantly, you're a medical student. There isn't anything like avoiding being naked you've to speak about here either. As a doctor, it's a bit force that you're always going to perform various surgeries on people who may have medical problems. It could be either a pro-culturist from India or Africa where you come from, and you will have to get him or her nude to do your job if the person is at a critical stage to be at our hospital here."

The students laughed loud. Doctor Scott tries to stop them. After at least five minutes, there is perfect decorum again in the hall.

"Nobody is allowed to bypass this stage of your studies. If you fail to do so, like I earlier said, you as a medical student, you'll be denied of graduation."

It seems yet oxymoron in nature to Tesio and Gmasnoh. However, they remained silent yet and the professor went on with the lesson for the day.

After three hours of lecture and moving about from one class to another, they have decided to return home.

"Do you remember sometimes ago I told you since then about childhood anxiety and so forth? It's like God had spoken to me at the time when I had to say that to you before, Tesio."

"You're right, Gmasnoh. I can see lots of changes in our lives since we left home, especially as we have come to America."

"As long you are at the level of going to school, there can't be without the thinking that, probably modernity isn't going to bring about changes gradually, into your life. And from Africa where we come from, is already in a backward state. Can you remember the last part of our Biology lab at the University of Liberia, where we graduated, when we used a charcoal during our lab display? And it's not as compare to the studies in the United States either."

"Yes. Gmasnoh, you told me that before."

"Okay, I'm just appealing to your conscience right now so that we can go through the studies and come up success. Let's do whatever it takes to being the best students or probably the dux for our graduating class in time to come. It would be bad if we thinking of returning home without achieving our goal for the professional education."

"Yes. I do twig that very well, Gmasnoh. You made a sound point to me."

They reached home finally. Each person went into his or her room and took off the clothes on the body. After that they have each decided to do other things while at home. The light and TV are complementing each other, as entertainment became the content of most of what is on TV. There is sport and music in line too.

Three hours later Tesio took a book written by Shirley Hazard: "The Venus of Transit," and sat at a part of the house, especially on the porch of his room to read it. He had a bottle of stout emptied into a glass side him. As he was reading intermittently he keeps sipping as well.

Very interestingly the same, Gmasnoh is also on the other side of the house, sitting on her porch reading. For her, rather she's reading a book written by Irvin Wallace: "The Celestial Bed". The two books they are reading are all full of romanticism. They never knew that only matured people that are supposed at least to, when married probably, could those think of reading such books. But ignorantly, they spent money and bought them to read same. They want to feel as romantic people since in the United States. Since the day of school lots of boys and girls have been talking about their partnerships, while conversing on love's matter. And they are like babies at a stupid state as fetus yet, without a trace of the true sense of what earth is really, especially as sex became a dream yet.

Tesio read few pages of the book at the level of reaching chapter five. He started just laughing by himself. It drew Gmasnoh's concern by then.

Absorbing, Gmasnoh is also facing similar problem, as she is reading her book, too. She was just acting maturely to herself yet, not being it audacious perhaps. She is highly romanticized, unconscientiously.

"Hey, Tesio, what's going on? I hope you ain't doing anything stupid out there."

"You mean what?"

"Don't worry. And just that I want to know if, you are enjoying your book as I'm."

"Yes. The book is really interesting." Tesio said. And Gmasnoh tries to then wake up at least to go and see what he's really talking about.

Unthinkably, Tesio's inside his trousers there is a trouble, as his penis trying to force its way out of there because of the sexually stupid book that he is reading. The book tries giving him a conscience mind, though. By the time he heard Gmasnoh feet making sound, as she rose to get to him, he too quickly left for his room and closed the door powerfully. He never wanted her to enter either until his private-expanding stranger into his trousers thinks of the moment on him, settling down yet before he could open the door by then. Stupid self be him the moment, despite he had locked the door, but he laid on it still. It seems grotesque really.

23

Since the arrival in the USA three years had gone by. The confusion of a part of the course once, for which Tesio has been perplexed yet, is now due shortly. They are to go for a practical surgical test, this time round. And it's a special course that must be administered at the senior year before graduation comes. To praise, as expected, they have since been doing well at school. They have been performing lots of surgeries. Most of the surgeries are on grownups.

It's nearly the turn for internship before the graduation is due in the fourth year. Now they got to understand that the issue of body protection or nudity once spoke about by Professor Scott is no more a matter of a concern, thus since three years now they passed through the stage already. But there is an important aspect of it still remaining. As Scott and Williams who have been admiring them personally said before is that, their bodies need surgical work too. The last part of the discussion with them is that, their cells have grown, where likely of each losing the usefulness, if sex got be of no importance yet to them.

Doctor Scott decided to understand one or two things yet from the two of them. Gmasnoh went to the wine box and took up a wine branded "Imperial Gold' and brought it at the table for the two visitors. They are refreshing on it at the same time conversing, especially that concerned the medical studies.

"Tesio, the both of you have since been doing well in every course. It's likely that you may be the dux for the medical college during this graduation."

"What are you saying, Doctor Scott?"

"The both of you are smart students that the medical college wished to award in some way soon."

"It's so wonderful, Scott! I mean I can't just believe this of the kind of information you are revealing to us."

"Anyway, as the graduation year comes close to us, don't forget the last part of the surgical work."

"Are we to go for another test?"

"Yes. That's a reason the both of us are here to explain that better to the both of you."

"What is the issue, Sir?"

"Did you see how you've been working in the surgical room and saw lots of people medically with a problem? Most of those you saw are deeply cultural gurus from different parts of the world because there have been critical need to have so then performed the various surgeries on them. And there is nothing like cultural issue did any talk about either, to say, he or she wasn't accepting a surgery perhaps by you. That's something a reason why the medical school here doesn't promote the idea of cultural protection or a person who may come from Africa or Indian to talk about his or her cultural issue either."

"Yes. I know that! This is what I've been noticing all this while since our studies, especially during surgical work on people while the person is naked." Gmasnoh said.

"Can you a bit explain to me what did you really learn since then?"

"Well, there are lots of things we have since acquired during our learning process so far. And I do really appreciate the administration so far, especially the people of the United States. Here is a much opened society." Tesio added instead. Doctor Scott chuckled. Gmasnoh's cheeks are wide opened. Doctor Scott keeps looking at her in admiration. Her body is showing a worth that once the stress and pains that got her looking so wriggled before are out of existence.

"But the last part of the both of you studies will be the surgical test which is in conjunction with the overall medical state board test. When you both shall have succeeded in it probably, you'll have to work with us at the medical schools or work as both the administrative assistants at the two major departments of the hospital itself."

"Wow! You mean that?" Tesio isn't smiling even despite what he had said. Doctor Scott is so much concerned about that. "Tesio, what's the problem perhaps?"

"Like the last part of the statement you have just made I can see this thing of destroying our traditional values we long held onto." Gmasnoh interrupted by saying, "Tesio, please let's give Doctors Scott and Williams a chance yet. Let them make us better twig this other part of our lesson. Anger from you, Tesio, trying to reject the plan of the instructor may not help us at this stage of our journey either, knowing that we are almost completing the studies." Gmasnoh became very sagely position when she said.

"I thought Tesio you have since got the clarity about the medical culture in the United States? Why would you again want to repudiate, or having a reservation about the matter of nudity either again?"

Tesio didn't respond yet to the Professor when he and Gmasnoh asked for a lay excuse yet, and left the table while going inside a room to ponder. The two walked into Gmasnoh's room first to ponder over the issue, where for him to be able to better response to the instructor instead of the way he's still rejecting the plan, as Gmasnoh thought. Ignorant and innocent were yet cadence despite the level of education obtained by the two about them.

"Tesio, I told you before about childhood anxieties. It's like we made a mistake with the issue of our tradition by taking oaths. Really, I don't understand such an ignorant tendency of ours for which tradition has to make a fool of us since then. Why should our parents at the time home, sat there and allowed us to have really taken the oaths when they should have known better from the beginning that education comes with too many things anew in the life of a person?"

"You are right. But let's look at the issue yet."

They came back in the sitting room again. Discussion over the issue has been settled. Doctor Scott and Williams by then promised to take the two for an evening party which is due in three hours' time.

Williams and Scott left. These two instructors are very rich. And since the arrival of the two Africans into America they have since developed so much interest for the two. And marrying the two as Williams and Scott thought became strongly inside them. Both Williams and Scott are without a man and a woman either. And most people they have met seemed as rich as they are too, which they don't really like about love. That is, they need some poor guys as the two.

Gmasnoh decided to express her view yet on a special issue that came to her mind with Tesio.

"Can you tell me Tesio, like the way we are now in America, a lady probably wants to marry you and she happens to tell you her heart about that, especially if the person who is so rich, for example Doctor Williams may want to change your life overnight by marrying you because of your smartness, what will you do?" She asked and Tesio laughed. In a quick response Tesio said, "One thing you should know is that opportunity comes at once. And now we can see a prospect of greatness towards our lives since then. But the issue you are raising right now is a difficult one. Really, I don't know what to do about this yet." He said just to get her view too.

"Listen to me a bit, Tesio! Can you tell me," Gmasnoh woke from her seat while walking around him, "what would you have done? I want you tell me your view about this." Tesio laughed first.

"Please leave me alone and let us look at that subject matter very keenly. I think our instructors intend putting us into trouble with that so-called lesson they talked about. I'm worrying because that may be a serious problem against our tradition." Tesio said. Gmasnoh lousily laughed over it.

"Let me tell you a lay thing. I'm ready to do just anything now for my lesson. If the professors want me in particular vigorously working by taking the special test, especially if that would be Scott to administer my test, I'm prepared to go about it. I even admired Doctor Scott since then, who saved my life the other day, and if he can even propose to me."

"Please, don't bring a different picture to the table now. I beg of you, please." Tesio said and paused. He had his hands into his pocket being so confused of what she said.

Gmasnoh still wants to settle few issues with him yet. "Tesio, we've to be serious. Didn't you even figure out from the last statement made by the professor that we'll each have to be unclothed either by any of them? Doctor Williams may give you test while Scott may be the one to either give mine too perhaps."

"Yes. I do know that. We have even been looking at some cultural gurus who had medical problems since then at the hospital. It's not strange that be really, if it's such a practical situation that have been spoken about to be had."

"Okay. Then, don't take this for a joke either. That's the reality." She said and Tesio nodded.

The party time came. They are nicely garbed as planned by Doctor Scott and Williams for the party. Two motorcades bought by Doctor Williams and Scott are brought, packing outside the yard. Gmasnoh is to sit with Doctor Scott, as arranged by the two doctors, while Tesio would also sit with Doctor Williams. And the two doctors is each into his or her vehicle, while waiting still on them dressing at the time. They are now marshalling before them.

"Tesio, there is something very good about you which I can't just hold back this while without telling you what that is either." Doctor Williams broke out in words. Tesio was sitting by her at the front seat of her car while they are conversing and ridding.

"What's it?"

"Look, you're a very smart man. I probably want to marry you just in a day's time upon you saying yes to me. I would offer you just what you want in life to be that happy."

"No. Don't go that distance with me. Is it all about the party?"

"No. We are just having a date, my dear."

Doctor Williams, a very smart and good-looking young lady, a billionaire's daughter and sexually blazed by excitement from her guise, and she is so cultivated by Tesio's appearance, too, including his academic repute too, she couldn't just afford to making him her love-pulse either. That's making him her special person for life. Because of that she's beginning to tell him what her plan is since then towards him. And Tesio has since been under the professor and having the desire to see her approach him one day. It has been deep down into his heart. Now she has come the distance with him for which a date is about disclosing the intention to him.

"Doctor Williams, please take a little time with me." She had her hands on his trousers while squeezing his penis.

"Stop it! I love you but there is something serious I want to tell you about." He said.

"What's it, sweet heart?" she said that because Tesio couldn't the moment resist every mood she keeps making on his body further when he said stop but she remained stubborn in her doing. Only the issue of the oath he wants to tell her about yet. And if she sees a reason about that, they could forever be as husband and wife upon getting married soon.

"Look, this is America. No one here delays in action about anything either. We respect time. If a woman sees a man that she really loves, she doesn't have to waste time of tell him either."

"Oh, that's how the society here looks?"

"Yes. If you think you've to waste time not to accept me now as your lover, when you know that I can change your life, then no problem I can get away from you. And right now I can, but in a second, change your life for the better. I want you for real."

"You are too bold. Please stop the kidding, Doctor Williams. In Africa there is no way can a woman being rather the one to approach a man either. We, the men are the ones who do that. But this thing of yours is strange to me."

"Look, this is a different culture you have to understand. The years Jack stays within an army doesn't determine how efficient and effective he is either. A man could join an army today--- and he becomes the best than compare to the one who makes a long stay either. Let me put it another way that, love has nothing to do with how long or how well does a person stays or gets into it either. If, that love between a man and woman is meant to grow, definitely it will have to. It depends on the two the efforts to get it work rightly."

"Do you mean this for real? But look at me. Can I be your man for now, why?"

"I mean that Tesio. I want to marry you. There is nothing you have that I really want other than love affairs. Look, I got money that you may need. In fact, after this party I will ensure to buy you one of the best cars in America." She boastfully said. And Tesio almost put up an incessant laughter by then. But she kissed him and he shut up. Only smile was then unstoppable a yet. Tesio really felt numbed to himself. His spirit almost left him because his plexus shock on him.

In the process of deeply conversing, Doctor Scott and Gmasnoh vehicle is passing by theirs, and Doctor Scott had his lips on Gmasnoh's cheeks. For her, but saying a word of resistance to him that moment, is a like a dream. Her desire has since then been to marry a rich man. And it's like her dream may come true right after the party.

Most besides, since then Gmasnoh has read a part of the Transit of Venus, the strange world of a romance by her one day then to try making a transit to, had developed strongly into her mind, though. Now the time has come to make a true transit from a nonsexual status, rather to the said idiomatic world shortly, if Doctor Scott wishes to take her one there very quickly.

The party started and lots of things went on there. The fun was so great for them. It's the very first time for such a thing to have happened for their lives.

Finally, however, the party ended. As a secret between each person, especially Tesio and Gmasnoh consented on being lovers to the doctors each. They kept it secret from each other. In other words, Gmasnoh never wanted to tell his cousin, while his cousin, too, never wanted to tell her what the agreement between him and Doctor Williams had been either. You could see a chorister state as if a sweet noisy time, where their bodies are making confusion with them, rather to embrace sex soon. It's like being into an opened hall. And they need sex really. Visually, they are so much embroiled gradually by huge sexual feelings, then.

It's the first time that they were now feeling as real citizens of America. And the party had really made the introduction needed most about the American culture perhaps. Flamboyancy consciously, by then, was a captain in its hooliganism state of being, rather the moment. There was too much rich style of comfort involved with the party—something they never experienced before. It seems awarding.

24

"This thing is so early for us. Why will we continue to see a security present when we should be as students to study our lesson, Gmasnoh? Although it has been a long time since the presence of security has been at our house, but we have to change that now. Why are we living so soon as rich people when we have a lot to do for our people at home? I feel so terrible these few days when I go to bed it bothers me a lot. We are likely to miss our focus, if not careful to correct the situation now."

"What are you really talking about, Tesio?"

"I'm talking about the removal from around us now the state security yet. We came to study here, but the United States Government has allowed security presence at our residence, making us to feel as great. I hate this. We are students and so we should remain as students to complete our studies yet."

"Is that wrong to have the security presence still, Tesio?"

"Yes, that's it Gmasnoh. I'm so sorry but please listen to me. I'm just begging you."

Gmasnoh is a lay galled for the decision he's about to take. Tesio feels as if they are living flamboyantly yet. He said it means a lot of distraction.

While explaining to his cousin, Doctor Scott and Williams came to visit again. Not knowing Tesio had earlier discussed the matter with Doctor Scott. After that he told the US Government by then to remove the security presence at the house. And that would shortly happen. Later he got to know that he needed to first have told Gmasnoh before going about the cancelation plan yet. But he overlooked it because he feels still as having control over her as usual at home it has been between them.

Doctor Scott and Williams are at the front door upon ringing the doorbells. By the time Tesio and Gmasnoh noticed that they are the ones standing there, they were quickly allowed to come inside the house to them.

They are lavishly poised and refreshing on wine.

"Doctor Scott, I call you for a very important issue that I would like for you to witness about what I'm about to say to Gmasnoh, even though I briefed you about it before."

"What's the matter?"

"We want to live a simple life to continue to have good concentration while we are still here studying. We don't need the state's security presence here again. That's a reason I've called you just to tell you the plan despite I did that before, Doctor Scott." Gmasnoh jumped from her seat and said, "Tesio, you should have consulted with me before taking that decision. It' can't be by force either, my brother! I think you went too far with the decision you took." Gmasnoh walked out their presence and went outside the house ranting over the decision. She feels so hurt by the brother not telling her before he could have come up with the decision. And now he has gone so far by telling the instructor. Gmasnoh is that incongruous to herself.

Doctor Scott quietly came to her and said, "Please, Gmasnoh come inside and let us listen to your brother on the decision he wants to take. I think your brother is making a good point. Look, Gmasnoh, this is America. Why be fast to have everything when you haven't really worked for it yet on your own? And you need to always learn to respect the view of your friend around you sometimes."

Gmasnoh saw a reason by then coming inside with him. She is so happy to see him dab her by then. His hand rub quietened her. Now, she decided to ask a question as they were seated. "Doctor Scott is it right without Tesio consulting me and he took such decision? I need to really know this."

"Wait a minute, Gmasnoh!"

"But that's an affront to my right as a person. A security protection here is for the both of us. The USA Government didn't bring that only because he killed terrorists? That isn't for he alone for which he has to come up with a decision by not consulting me. Why has he jumped to conclusion about this? Here isn't Africa where men are too commanding about issue as long it becomes a problem between any man and a woman. Really the men," she is so angry speaking, "in Africa often have the final say about any issue involving a woman and a man. That is what I'm saying." Gmasnoh strongly worded.

"Cool down a little, please. I know he has removed a button of your conscience but we have to understand the concept. You're really quite correct to blow your top about this. But, please let's at least see a reason listening to Tesio." Doctor Scott urged. She gasped.

"I'm really wrong for all that I did. But it has been concluded with the President on the matter already. I should have letting you know about it before going about the cancelation plan, but I thought you were always going to listen to me on any issue about the two of us requiring a decisive position should be made."

"How can you presume about such issue like this, when the matter is a concern for the both of us?"

"Mama," Tesio came down on his knees while holding her legs, "please forgive me, okay." He said and pretentiously took a mist from her face. Gmasnoh bobbed.

Tesio's apology got her to have lamely at least accepted the decision in an interim.

"Please don't do that again. If there is any issue that is for the two of us be able to discuss the matter with me first instead of unitarily doing your own thing."

"Okay. But listen a little. The decision to say that the US Government should withdraw its security presence now is based on the simple fact that I want us to be really focused with the last part of our lesson. Graduation is near. There is so much distraction about the security's presence. And we should obtain our education, especially as we are going to India on internship soon, now doing away with this kind of lifestyle yet, where we are living like rich people. It's good to suffer now and later enjoy the life perhaps."

"Alright. I do accept with pity, Tesio. There is nothing I would do otherwise about it in rejecting your plan either. It's done already. And you are the man now with the sway in everything that is a concerned for the both of us really. But you should learn to seek my view on an issue like this before you act."

"Gmasnoh, we should learn to confront a snake when it's coming before us than letting it pass you before you can act by killing it."

Tesio is a very sugar-coated guy who believes in parables. He meant to say that the trouble of distraction that he's picturing now in time to come that may be more than huge for which they need to deal with it now before it becomes as a future problem, as he thought.

Tesio had his hand on Gmasnoh shoulders while still petting her to listen. "It's good to live a simple live than living a flamboyant life yet, when you know we have some projects home to complete yet. We are from Africa. Besides the background we have, relative to even our parents' statuses, is a backward one. And so, we have to try in time to come rather to go back there, which it should be very soon. We are here learning and at last to make some money." Tesio said. "I couldn't really have had a problem with the plan either. You just needed to inform me earlier before we could both work around it. But you didn't do so either."

"I'm so sorry, Gmasnoh. Please, we shouldn't stretch this again."

"I can't. You can go ahead now and do as you purposed to." Gmasnoh said lamely. Tesio wasn't really satisfied with her response either. He wants to still pet her.

"Alright just listen to me a little. We should plant our seed of success like we are doing now and let it to grow to harvest. When we plant and when time comes to harvest by ourselves then, we can feel as great as planters. Do you want to enjoy another man's harvest when you have the seed planted to letting it grow and harvest nicely soon?"

"I have already given you the chance to go ahead. Oh, what is the matter again?"

"Alright. Still, I want you listen to me. Gandhi said, "Live simple so that others may simply live." This is my entire plan while we are here in the United States to live simple yet. Look, this place is for serious-minded people."

"Thanks. You have said a whole lot to sooth. Just feel as fine and do what you have had to do either."

"I'm not too comfortable with you response that is such reason that I've decided to still talk to you. Gmasnoh, one thing I know about this America is that it can take a person to a higher level, and simply in time to come, letting you fall, if you fuck things up here. That I won't want should be the case with us either. Let's remain as peaceful people, managing our lives properly to avoid trouble." Tesio openly said while Doctor Scott and Williams are seated. Doctor Scott is nodding. Everything Tesio had said really moved him at heart.

Luckily they settled down with it. "You're really right, Tesio. The decision sounds so good to me." Doctor Scott amplified. Gmasnoh smiled.

Gmasnoh accepted everything he had said, having embraced him. He is just laughing.

25

There came a special Saturday Evening when Counsellor Uguche, a wonderful lawyer who is a Nigerian born, to pay a visit at their villa. He is a renowned legal practitioner, a man who had obtained a scholarship since fifteen years ago from the Republic of Nigeria. His mission at the time in America was to do law exclusively and make a return home upon that. The Nigerian Government wanted an environmental lawyer to represent its interest in a special case that has since been in court at the Hague, Netherlands, against the state of Nigeria concerning the people of the Niger Delta Region of his country who sued the government.

He came to the USA sometimes ago and graduated from the Harvard Law School. Since his graduation by then he failed to go back home for a reason other than he's penniless since he met with a Liberian girl that he had married. It's nebulous yet.

There is a complicated story he had to explain about the Liberian Girl. Dorothy Parker Williams, she's no living low kind of woman he was to marry by then either. They became husband and wife in three years and when his savings got depleted she went away from him. They are now facing separation yet.

To note, she has so much passion as a woman for pomp and pageantry. She wears clothes even that are designer made and the most recent. This is one of such unforgettable troubles he came across since then upon marrying her. Only the USA citizenship he obtained through her that he felt so happy about relating to the relationship, as he thought.

In one years' time by then, he became a penniless African-American by the time he married the woman and emptied all of his savings, while supporting her extravagant lifestyle.

Just before the guy could come to sit, the President of the USA said something very vital to Tesio on the phone once more.

"The day you decide to go and stay in Africa perhaps most of the incentives you and sister have been enjoying since then in the USA you may find a problem for the government to continue same. I hope you'd be fine with the plan in time to come not to dream about going back either. Every penny Gmasnoh and you will make in time to come in the USA, probably you shall pay just three percent each as income tax. Besides, the USA has about ten millions, a reserved amount for the both of you and decided to give you in piecemeal. First, as we speaking, two million dollars have been sent into your accounts already. The rest of it you'll receive it little by little upon request from the government. Please, let that take care of the both of you expenses yet, while still in the United States on studies. I hope you would even stay here after the studies."

"Wow! You mean all that . . . being for us?" Tesio called Gmasnoh into the room where he is to give her the message while Counsellor Uguche is still sitting.

"Mr. President, I heard all that you've just said. But with the issue of us going back to Africa I want you please give me a lay time for us to decide on the issue yet. And I would get back to you later." Tesio said, and a thanks at last.

He went off the phone. It's like the President has yet understood the plan of the two that they came purposely to America for studies upon that later to make a return home.

26

A chat with Counsellor Uguche commenced. The counsellor has decided to explain in detail yet his ordeal. "My African family how are you doing?" Counsellor Uguche said and extended handshakes with the Tesio and Gmasnoh. "If I may be allowed to speak to you really, I do the other day admire the both of you, especially when Tesio got hold of the terrorists. More besides, the news about your splendid performance yet in medical had really forced me to be here now in that to talk with you at least, if I can at least be as your personal legal adviser yet."

"Oh, you most welcome sir! That is a very good idea for you requesting to be our legal advisor. That can't be a problem either. You most welcome to be."

"Thanks. Let me first give you a brief account of my autobiography."

"You are most welcome, Sir." Gmasnoh said. "I got a Bachelor of Science Degree in Mathematics when I then acquired a scholarship from the Nigerian Government. I was the dux for the entire school that year. It has been almost fifteen years now when that really had happened. Really, I don't want to boast of this that, I was one of the smartest of my school during that whole year. That's how at last I got the scholarship awarded me by the Nigerian Government only to come and do law in the United States."

"Wow! That was so good for you." Tesio said. "Thanks. And I've since been here practicing law upon graduation from Harvard University." He said and Tesio giggled.

"My plan earlier has been upon graduation to have gone back to Nigeria but I couldn't just go back because of the opportunity here so huge that I met up with. Besides, I have destroyed my savings. But there is a reason."

"So, because of the opportunity what did you really have been doing at least to remedy the situation?"

"I'm a married man to a Liberian girl. I did that because I wanted to have a very good status upon graduation by then to have a good job which I got one. She is a US Citizen."

"Okay. That's fine. What's next was the problem?"

"Since the marriage my love for her at the time got over plus ridiculously. I don't know why I had that too much love for her really. The girl is now so extravagant. In the first one year she made us to live so flamboyantly. There the ailment of my indebtedness had begun for which we are now on separation. She destroyed all of my savings since the married. I think this thing is getting out of control with me now. Imagine I will soon, in twenty years from now, I shall dodder as result of age. I find myself too much in debts and I'm unable to make a return yet to a normal status in order to be able to go home soon. Stress is killing me also to that. It's really troubling me. Because of that I'm even dreaming not going back home probably. I don't even have a project at home yet in Nigeria. And now I'm really getting old. I got to really fine a way out that I can go home. And no money still."

"Wait a minute, sir. What do we got to do about this your misfortune now, sir?"

"No. It's none of your business but I want to admonish you to be that careful not, falling into the same mess as I'm now. I want you have a good time to be able to go home soon than the way I'm now. I have a lot of debts covering my fucking life up."

"Wow! That's so terrible. I do really pity your condition and pray that you find a way out of this perhaps. You know life becomes short when you have too much of stress on your head as a person. And you are a much educated man once to have really known better. So, you sold all of the property you had when you got broke or what is it? Please, don't be angry with me asking the question either."

"No. There wasn't any property that much I have on my own other than the pitiful house we had at the time. It was taken away by the Barclay Bank that, we since then have a two-million dollar outstanding debts for right now."

"We need to know because you are the very first friend of ours I think we need to put our trust into while we are stay here studying. Most especially, you are a counsellor."

"Thanks Tesio, having given me the recognition and permission to speak to your minds really about this serious issue of my life. Some people who don't feel like listening to me could say that from the beginning that I'm sounding stupid to listen not. I do really appreciate you both for the sense of thoughtfulness really, letting me explain my ordeal."

"I think the story is so interesting to have our ears still to it." Counsellor Uguche felt more relieved. He'd a law book with him that moment that is almost destroying his bag he had when it has been held by him. It's too heavy for the bag perhaps. He feels the law book could right away consciously say out his profession to the guys by displaying it at their house while he is there.

Gmasnoh got so attentive to him.

"I'm facing a huge problem home right now. My people home are now calling me sorts of names, especially as foolish man, a man without purpose and a dreamer for which my mother in particular is regretting why I've to be born unto her on earth perhaps. And I'm really living dead in America. I can't just afford to send a penny home either to my people since fifteen year now. Imagine I'm just praying daily to have a very good case one day soon so that I can remedy this situation."

"Oh, that's really a terrible problem or onus on your head which you have to find a solution to very quickly to feel as belonging to a family from Africa. You know in Africa we love external family affairs. Please try and clean yourself of debts now."

"That's so true."

"But let me just ask something very important yet. How can that be resolved so that you can go home soon perhaps?" Gmasnoh asked.

"It's difficult to tell exactly how to remedy the situation."

"But you've to try your best to resolve the financial problem by labouring hard. Why can't you find a second job instead of one? That would probably help for you to pay-off your debts and begin doing something concrete back home as a project where you to go back someday." Tesio purposefully said. Uguche wept his eyes off a mist almost blocking his visibility perhaps. It's like a flying bird unruly shitted on him. But that wasn't the case either. He was just pretending, having got a hit of truthful words, banking at his door-mind consciously to wake up from his slumber bed of financial woe.

"My brother, please listen a little. You're correct about whatever you have just said but it's hard to see it happen. Imagine my brother died home the other day because of my condition I couldn't send a cent home either. The worst of it is that, my home government will soon pursue a case against me for not going back home since the studies had ended. As you can see things with me now, I'm really like a stupid man living without a purpose in America. I don't know what to do really. It's disgusting to continue like this throughout my life."

"That's mindboggling about such perhaps, Counsellor Uguche!"

"Tesio, imagine I now know the entire law I wanted to know about but my life isn't a complement of the education I got.

Imagine I can work throughout the week and at last when pay comes nothing is left with me. My expenses and debts are too much. Look, this is physical hell I found myself into right now."

"But you said you wanted to live the American Dream for which you got married quickly to the Liberian girl. Why have you been crying with life still? Lots of people want to be as you, but the opportunity isn't given them either."

"It's lack of purpose for which I'm like this."

"Why should you say so, Uguche?"

"Anyway, let me say, it's lack of wisdom, if you want me turn it the other way either."

"No, you are becoming too vocal about your life. It's just that you need to make a budget always to manage your life better than this way of yours now. Live within your means. If, you don't do so in case you are confronted by either a serious health crisis, probably you will be forced to understand the need of your lack of management to yourself."

"I think you're right about this. I'd begin doing that now."

Counsellor woke from his seat while walking around inside the house like he's in a courtroom. He took up a handkerchief from his pocket since then he has been using at the courtroom to wipe his face pretentiously by then. He is shamed.

"Counsellor Uguche, we are so sorry for all the problems you are faced with now." Gmasnoh lamely pitifully said.

"Look guys, this is the America I came to. I got the education and working but I'm now like a non-living thing or an imbecile or a big fool in America right now." He said and Tesio lousily laughed. Gmasnoh also did similarly.

"Counsellor Uguche, don't get me crazily laughing please. You sounding like a convincing investigator who before his or her investigation begins, got to bring about a lay fun into a discussion of such." Tesio said. "Let me say the last thing. The day I happen to fall dead or paralyze I want the both of you help in taking me back to Nigeria. Let me feel as finally returning home to my motherland. At least my spirit may have had a lay peace by then. Especially when I'm dead, please try burying me on my father's land in Nigeria." he worded confusingly. He doesn't even know what to say either. Tesio giggled. He is a funny man that teases a lot.

Tesio in response said, "Be a little brief now because we are running out of time to go and study. If we stay here with you for long you may make us to laugh until pains come into our stomachs each." Tesio sounded with a purposeful and sage tone of friendliness.

"You got my explanation from the beginning. Tesio, I'm serious. Just take a look at me right now I'm emaciated because of difficulties. I'm just pretending like living well but it isn't it either. Look, as I'm liquidating my debts, I pray that my entire life balance sheet needs to be reshaped, anyway. I'm just asking the Almighty daily to get me out of the worst situation really."

"That's okay. We are in sympathy with you. We shall meet again." Tesio said and took one thousand dollars check from his pocket and gave it to Counsellor Uguche. He's so much elated.

Tesio and Gmasnoh at least decided to force a good-bye on him. Before his departure he called for a glass of wine. A wine called Obikwa was given to him at the table. He gobbled it up just in five minutes and left. He got Gmasnoh to smile.

"I guess he should be a very funny man, Tesio." She said. "But that I got to know about him since his entry into our villa." He said and smiled. They nested back into the house again.

27

"I'm here to tell the both of you how the final tests has been scheduled for eight O'clock each tomorrow morning." Doctor Barley Scott said. He's sitting right in the villa with them while conversing. Gmasnoh is by him poised in bewilderment. Her heart is pounding a little in fear.

At the same table Doctor Williams is seated. She sank heavily into the sofa and took a glass of wine as usual. She loves 'imperial gold'. It's a kind of red wine with an eagle on it.

"Please, you've to tell me if you're okay with this or not." Scott said. Earlier, Tesio has been figuring out before about what really would be the final test which is to come. And that is about coming to a reality now perhaps.

"But Doctor Scott, you know that we have since been doing our best in school? And probably there is nothing about the test we would be afraid of either. We shall do our best to pass same."

The whole story about this stupid exercise is that, Doctor Scott and Williams have proposed relationship to the two since then. But they keep fooling around because of an issue of traditional oath sometimes ago each of them took. Despite all the parties they have attended since then, Tesio and Gmasnoh when told to still consider accepting marrying to the two doctors, but they refused to. Each partner, that is Tesio and Williams had their own story, while Gmasnoh and Scott the same, too.

For Doctor Williams, her father has been involved with a kind of syndicate planning since then for his daughter Williams marrying to Tesio. She told him about the love she has for the guy. And each time Tesio is that accosted about the issue from

Doctor Williams herself, he had the story of his tradition to tell her still. It seemed now stupid to Americans. It is the same way with Gmasnoh too. For her, she is just pretending because she wants Doctor Scott to be her man really. And each time Doctor Scott has been similarly telling her about relationship matter. She has been between a 'no' and a 'yes' with him. It's a reason they have been trying now in taking them to various parties but no avail yet. This brought a change of plan towards them but to plan a syndicate against. And Tesio and Gmasnoh held fist to their traditional oath, telling that the gods at home may harm each of them if anything stupid is to happen where the oaths are broken. But sexual feelings got its own lesson also against their lives perhaps uncontrollably.

The Williams's father, however, is so much concerned about making his daughter marry Tesio. Since they are two doctors, Williams told her father of how she is really in love with him. But as usual, jeering to her, he keeps refusing her. But her father is just planning to satisfy her. He loves his daughter so much that he doesn't want to see her actually hurt. Since the daughter disclosed of her love about him to him too, he plans to capture Tesio in a very net of hooliganism by then. It's his whole worry. He has been so then willing to offer anything to the administration, which he knew the best person to be in contact with is Doctor Scott. He feels Doctor Scott could fool the two into a deal by a kind of surgical test taking method of deceit.

The father of Doctor Williams has concluded the deal with Doctor Scott since he's the head administrator.

"I'm now issuing you a check worth three hundred million as a token," Pratt Williams said.

Before the deal day could come Tesio and Gmasnoh are to attend another wonderful party which is a day after would furtively as Williams and Scott planned it that, they would go through the test by then.

The day of the party came. Before then here is a lady by the name of Sarah Coker, who once saw Tesio on the CNN at the party. She has since got the news about his brilliant performance at the airport and lastly in the college. She made several phones call to him about her mind for him in love. Even she had bought lots of gifts too intended giving him but he stood his ground still not love her either. He just needed a friendship but not love affairs, as he thought.

She's been for two years now planning a way out that she could come close to Tesio. Here is it luckily she sees Tesio at a distance and decided to befriend him once on a pertinent issue she had with him before and he didn't really give her a face about that.

And that issue is about marrying him. She has been trying all out to induce him at the time when she even bought a car for him, but he returned it to her. But the only lucky individuals who bought them cars and other things for which they accepted are Doctor Williams and Scott. Dejectedly since then, Tesio had shunned Coker. But she has resilience too. She has become contumacious yet to meet him on the same love matter rather at the party again.

She took Tesio at side. The guy maintained the same old saying that he doesn't need her. Because of that she decided to openly shame him this moment.

"Tesio, I think this mess is over."

"What is the mess are you talking about? Do I owe you? Tell me this?" He forcefully said.

"I'm so ugly for which you don't need me? Why you don't want to accept my proposal?"

"Please, let's leave this talk. I came with somebody at this party and it wasn't you either that had invited me."

Coker remained mute in few minutes. Surprisingly, five minutes after, she called her two friends from a distance away to come around her. Jess Samson and Brandy White are the ones. She quickly changed the discussion point as an introduction saying, "This guy is Tesio and he is blind sexually. He is handsome but a fool that doesn't want a better change of his life. He thinks America needs a fool like him to remain here forever when I know he is from Africa and without a penny?" She said and Tesio's head got bowed. He didn't believe it that the woman could be so vocal to have approached him like that either. And lots of people standing by looked at the two of them while fusing. She held his hand forcibly as he was about to jerk it from hers too. But he cowardly followed aside.

In concluding she said, "You're just passing your ass freely around here without you thinking of making love to a woman like me? Am I a crazy woman?" Coker quite openly said. Doctor Williams saw Tesio at the time while discussing with Coker. She hasn't even looked at Tesio's face again either. Instead, it is Coker's face she is looking at and at the same time she is frowning. Imagine while coming to Tesio from a distance, she asked who is Coker to him.

"Who is that woman, Tesio? And what is going on?"

"Nothing has really happened. I'm okay." He said without him giving Williams a chance either, but she held his hand and took him away.

Sarah Coker backed-off. She went back to her earlier place into the hall while then dancing as usual with a man that took her there. She's just a fussy lady blindly in love.

The party came to an end finally. Just in that time, Tesio received a call from the United States President, who then wanted a finally saying on the option he did give him earlier.

"We want to continue giving the both of you cash which you need to tell us, if you're still going back to Africa after the graduation?"

"I will go back but not to stay there anymore. The reason is that, there are some projects back home we are undertaking and need to complete by our presence there very quickly then. That's a reason my sister and I have to go back home soon."

"That isn't bad either. Okay, I think I will have to renegotiate with the Department of Treasury to increase the amount in time to come."

"Please, Mr. President, I'd really appreciate were you to increase the fund as you promised to. My town is down to nothing. I need to help my people. Mr. President, I'm so happy now knowing that the United States is a place really of so much opportunities to make every human here his or her life a better one. This is the experience we've been getting since the arrival into the USA. It's something really to thank you about." He got the president to chuckle.

"Tesio, this is America. In fact, that's how I expect for an ordinary African who leaves Africa coming to study in America should behave nicely yet by living low perhaps. There is a Chinese proverb that says, "It's good to learn how to fish then to learn to eat fish." First be able to improve your life educationally and then can you feel as pleased later, making money on one's own then. I want you also help the people back home to feel as humans too." They laughed on the phone together.

The day of test came finally.

"Brother," Gmasnoh is calling out Tesio on a serious note, "I'm going to the test finally. Please, I want you pray with me, okay."

"Don't worry yourself about anything either. I know you shall do your best still to be a success in that test." Tesio said purportedly.

Glaring, Gmasnoh desire is so to see herself succeeding in everything of lesson for which they since travelled from Africa, for.

"We've been doing well at home before for which we got the scholarships awarded us from our nation's government. There is no test that I think in any way, believing strongly now, that would be a problem either to you and me. Walk up to it." Tesio urged her proudly. Gmasnoh smiled with him innocently.

What Tesio meant is to put a lay confidence into her. And stupid self be her really, as sexually an ignorant she is yet, she nodded to everything Tesio had said in that to do her best, whereas Doctor Scott is going to test her on a different unruly thing he had planned. He has something of stupid tester into his trousers he wants to use on her body. They are only to enter a room and she would feel as pleased to expose of her own body, as he thought. And Tesio and Gmasnoh have both passed the stages of teen already. And their sexual desires are uncontainable perhaps, this time round. They are just feeling as blissful each time now that, doing something about such uncontrollable feelings.

For Tesio, not to mention, he already knew what the game is all about really. He thought it's only to see her nakedness perhaps. Surprising, however, he has built his courage at last just to go and take the test, too. It's like a no turning back stage they have reached so far about the school lesson.

28

"I'm doing a recording right now. I want you be aware of that. It's intended to let you remember this as a medical lesson and when you shall have gone back to Africa, if you would like, you can play it at home. Do you hear me, Gmasnoh?" Doctor Scott surprisingly said. She said yes.

"Gmasnoh," Doctor Scott breaks the ice on something seems as stupid, "the exercise is about teaching you something of physical surgery on your body. I want you know about sex as a means of removing those odd cells of yours since then that have been building up inside you." He took his stupid hands and touched her down part, which is her sexually exciting corner, while the clothes on her body. In concluding he said, "It does require somebody matured like me to do it for you. I used to face similar problem like that before."

"What's it?"

"Please be able to accept the exercise now. Why all this while you have been without a man either?

"Look, is it a matter for which you said I should come to a test?" She said and despite that also she smiled. She has even wished for that since then but she is pretending to him. That is the kind of man with the cash she needs most.

"Please, let's avoid the too much of talk now and get on course with it."

Very quickly before her, Doctor Scott wore something of medical robe for the so-called surgery to be conducted on her body. Innocently, she too, but wore similar stuff and got on the little bed that is inside the room. He got a special machine close by in that to fool her with it yet.

The two started the so-called test by touching each other. The first attempt by Doctor Scott on her body had surprisingly, but got her shivered instantly. And Scott knew exactly where he could have touched on her body for her to feel as awakening the moment, though. And no trace of resistance that could any thinks of each other either. Rather, she pulled herself very close to him, holding him lightly like a kid into the hands of a father, while fearing something very odd that is coming her way then. Her action seems paradoxical. Reason being, instead of fear but, it's an act of sweetness for which she is trying to position herself to him well.

Now to wonder, inexplicably, at the other side of the building there is similar thing that has been done by Doctor Williams and Tesio. For them, noticing a trace of resistance of not taking such test that seems as a dream—if so. Reason being, Tesio's head is like pumping as if a basketball. At certain time he felt numbed to himself. His soul left him. That's how he is feeling right now, as sweetly he's deeply willing to do anything as that--the moment to remedy the situation of sexual captivity he found himself since then then. He held Doctor Williams firmly like a baby girl held in hand by the time she touches his privacy-string of intermittent expansion on him. His plexus shock. He couldn't wait to seeing her perform his test of surgery on his body too.

Turbulently sweetly, too, Doctor Scott and Gmasnoh are seriously kissing and hugging each other on the other side. And the true thing about Doctor Scott is that he had kissed girls before, a lot of girls. But none has had the power to charm him most as compare to what Gmasnoh is. She is so beautiful. The worst thing about her is that, she is so anxiously stuck to him as if a cad trying to get something furtively from him, or like a first time rider into a plane. However, conscientiously sexually, she is a new rider for now to get on the train of Doctor Scott.

This is yet a moment of shame really. Reason being, the beds from both sides, that's from where Doctor Scott and Williams are with Tesio and Gmasnoh, in thirty minutes they were rumpled up. Their minds are so blissfully lost consciences the moment very sweetly.

As senses reeled, the straight instructions from Doctor Scott consciously became acceptable by Gmasnoh. Each of them feels as stupendously good about such test that, it should be of continuity then. There I got to know that ignorant is a disease in some way, in spite of a person who is at a level may have had education.

However, two hours later the game of surgical test once became a different story. "Doctor Scott, I'm just appealing to you now that should this course of yours continue." Gmasnoh wonderfully and unabashedly said. "I can see you making lots of progress in life, Gmasnoh. You don't have to really think otherwise again as we both lovers now to keep building up our relationship. And I won't even waste the time but in a year's time from now to marry you." He was sitting on top of her, rubbing her body on the surgical so-called bed, that he is performing sweetly.

None has put up any refusal either. They are innocent guys who have just gotten somewhat a lesson of something new to take seriously in life since they came from Africa and sexually once in captivity.

"I'm promising you now to marry you without delay, Gmasnoh. It would be after a year perhaps due to the internship that is due in few days which shall delay it a little." Scott said.

"I promise to marry you immediately, Tesio, when we come from India after the internship." Williams said.

Tesio didn't even ask for his cousin instead. He decided to take a ride with Doctor Williams home as usual. A new conversation has ensued between him and Williams. "Doctor Williams, you have really taken me to another part of the world that I haven't been before. I won't forget about this. You removed the stress of non-sexuality from my head. I'm really a different man now partly in the American culture, feeling more anew than before."

"Hey, Tesio, don't make me laugh either."

"No. I mean it. Really, that's how atop of the mountain looks? By this act it's like I have seen a different part of life to embrace in my life. I believe this is something of good test which the school needs at least to have it at every interval to be five times every year. Why did I from the beginning have to talk about my culture?"

"What are you talking about, Tesio?"

"Doctor Williams, I was too stupid to myself all this while I kept myself from sex. Anyway, that has ended. I'm restored. That is my primary instructor back the days in Niffu Town who talked about restoration. It's something of another face which I'm experiencing right now."

"Tesio, I'm the master for your life right now. Just anything you want I would give you it. I'd do everything for you because it has been my wish to have a man like you as husband, who is so very power and clever over it. You are not just an ordinary person perhaps."

"That is okay. Thanks for what you have done for me so far." Tesio friendly said.

On the other side while riding home too, Doctor Scott is heavily laughing. Gmasnoh keeps telling him lots of funny things.

29

The internship for Indian just came to an end after a year for true. "I've just received a call that you and Gmasnoh successfully passed the state medical exams. Because of that the administration of Oral Robert Memorial Hospital decided giving the two of you immediate employment. As a renowned gynaecologist, a title Gmasnoh you have claimed for yourself, you are given a position of assistant administrator for Paediatrics, while Tesio has been given a position of Assistant Director for the Surgical Department. May I say congratulation for the preferment that you have both been granted the opportunity to work with Oral Roberts Hospital."

Doctor Scott, as they are returning to America that day it's right in the plane that he had read that information. He was so happy over the appointment because of that he decided disclosing of it then.

By the time Scott revealed the news to the two, very quickly had Tesio then leaped from his seat. "I'm so happy for this. It's a very fine opportunity that I won't forget in my life." Tesio said. "I can't speak of it either. I really lack the words to express for this. Thanks Doctor Scott." Gmasnoh padded and kissed him. They are sitting side by side.

"As we are on our way now back to America the next day each of you'll be married. It's even in line with the graduation too. Let me make that clear to Gmasnoh. I'm now going to marry her without a delay." Scott took an engagement ring of diamond made he has since bought for her and asked Doctor Williams to join him in prayer by presenting the gift to her in the plane. They are sitting in one of the Delta Airlines. He had pearls too he has since three years ago, bought for his girlfriend.

Lusanda Mason, his girlfriend interestingly, acts too rich as he is, too. Of course, he hates that because he too is rich. Almost to have given her the pearls and the ring before, rather on her birthday, but he right away changed his mind. A poorly and smart Gmasnoh, with high respect and love for him now, she got to captain his mind the moment then. He decided to give her the gifts as his love for her.

"No. . .I can't get over this! Doctor Scott, thank you ever so much. You've made fully my dream has come true." Gmasnoh said joyously. She didn't even hide from her brother again about her kissing mood with Doctor Scott either.

Tesio is so excited. He's even speechless a bit. He was so happy as a result he got his two hands around Doctor Williams and shocked her in joy.

However, as being expected now, they are back into America.

"You mean we passed all our tests? Thank you . . . my brother." Gmasnoh happily said while they are about to get down the plane. Tesio is almost incessantly smiling. His cheeks are just outside for a while, then.

"Doctor Scott, when are we to pick up the letters from your office?"

"Tesio, we just need to get off the plane and rest a little and by tomorrow the both of you can get to the office and collect same from there." Scott added.

And an hour later, they got off the plane finally. The medical bus from the Oral Roberts Medical College came to collect them. They drove off and went to their abodes. Gmasnoh embraced firstly Doctor Scott, kissing him on the cheeks. His plexus shock as usual. But shortly, after the marriage they would be living together. And that is due in a week or two from now.

A week after, two colourful weddings by the two partners are held all together. Doctor Scott and Williams, as they had earlier promised about marriage, the said plan wonderfully came to pass. Without any delay after the marriage that day, everyone moved into a single building. Tesio and Doctor Williams decided to stay on the first floor, while Doctor Scott and Gmasnoh, both as husband and wife too, moved up on second floor.

Doctor Williams woke up one morning feeling so downhearted. Tesio decided asking her a question to know what the reason is. And that has been since one year now.

"Sweet heart, what's really wrong with you these days?"

"Tesio, it's interesting to me, but I guess you may be angry over this yet."

"What's that?"

"I'm damned pregnant."

"What did you just say?"

"I'm pregnant!"

"Oh, that can't really be a problem to me. You are my wife and so why worry about that either? I thought it was something differently you wanted to tell me either."

"Thanks. I do really appreciate it. We should now think of how to handle the pregnancy because I don't want you to destroy same. Would you want me keep it?"

"Yes."

"Thanks. I will do that." Williams said and Tesio smiled.

"But why should we in fact be thinking about the pregnancy removal when we are husband and wife?

Do you think I'm still in poverty when you know I have money now? Besides, I'm now a professional man that is economically being also restored. I don't think of what I would eat as the day comes either. I have the money to buy whatever I want, isn't it?"

"I'm sorry, please."

"Okay."

"Let me say something a bit to you. Tesio, like you've done well already in your studies, and obtained a medical degree I believe your people at home may be so much happy even to hear that you and your cousin have done well. Even the marriage issue will be a great importance to them if they hear that the two of us are done with it."

"Wait a minute, Doctor Williams. You just brought something to my mind that is very important to consider for the future."

"What's that . . .the problem, Tesio?"

"This issue of marriage the two of us have undergone here in America is a problem with our tradition at home."

"Oh, you still have a problem about the tradition when you have already broken the vow you talked about before after being married already?"

"No. Things don't just work like that. Gmasnoh and I'll have to go home to tell the people what's going on now."

"Why is that so important to the both of you? You intend going home for what?"

"It's traditional in nature. We know what the matter is for our African traditional issue. We broke the vows given us, before by the elders from the gods. And if, we don't go back to tell the traditional people, who should be able to perform a sacrifice in our behalf in that to unfetter our souls from the trouble with the gods at home, which the latter punishment may be so dangerous. My spirit keeps telling me this."

"You keep talking about gods, but what's this issue of god has to do with the both of you when you're here in America? You just need to keep going to church like you doing now and let the people fast and pray for you to spiritually obliterate that thing. As long you're here that whole thing by itself would be annulled. It's something spiritual to destroy through prayers."

"Stop it! You just need to support me so that when the time comes I and my sister can make a trip to Africa. No joke about that either. A sacrifice has to be conducted to the gods in order to cancel the shit."

"Alright. Please, I'd be there to support you now to leave and meet with the people."

"Thanks. I really appreciate it."

He giggled over it. They exchanged kisses too profoundly.

Williams in that process of kissing Tesio a call came in, rather on her phone. Doctor Scott called her. She asked an excuse from Tesio yet to receive her call.

Tesio said okay to letting her go her way, receiving the call elsewhere. She went quickly to a part of the house, relaxing so nicely, receiving her call on the phone for almost ten minutes since then.

"I've just done the test of Gmasnoh and she's two months pregnant." Doctor Scott said.

"What are talking about, Scott?"

"Gmasnoh, my wife is now pregnant for me."

"Are you serious about that?"

"What not?"

"No, just that I'm so happy to hear that, Scott. Let me give you also a true picture of what is now wrong with me, too."

"What's it?"

"I'm faced with similar situation of yours, too."

They smiled on the phone together. At last, she made a return to Tesio again.

30

Since the return from Indian, however, several things have been happening in their lives new. Marriages took place. And most importantly graduation is held. Next they got fabulous jobs.

And three months had passed since the return from India.

A wonderful day has come when a guy came with a funny tape. Tesio has been relaxing in the sitting room reading a very interesting novel as usual. At least his maturity has spawned its state of worthiness than before. I guess, teasingly thought, the test has added to that.

The guy rang the gate bell. And he's allowed inside the house. At the time Gmasnoh is upstairs in her apartment. Tesio and family are downstairs.

"I'm Thomas Thug."

"It's nice to meet you, sir."

"Thanks."

"How may I help you, sir?" Tesio said in an enthusiastic way as he was a bit hunched to receive the tape from the guy's hands. He modulated in a soft tone. He feels a bit yet appalled about the tape issue. And the two tapes are clamped. Only the various names could differential who be who owns this or not.

Thomas is a guy that is street-smart. There is no day any of friends ever play smart on him either. And his doing is just simple means in which he gets lots of cash unto himself each time.

"A guy gave me this parcel, as you can see it sealed up, but is a tape. He said I should hand deliver same to the both of you. So, where is Gmasnoh by the way? I guess you should be having a cousin living upstairs of this building with her own family, too, probably called Gmasnoh. And the both of you long time ago came from Africa."

"Oh, yes! How did you get to know this?" Tesio, in a congenial way by then he has asked.

"Just relax. Then, the tape here is intended for the both of you families. They are two separate tapes. Please be able to give her what is hers, as you can see every tape has a name to it."

"Okay. Thank you ever so much. But what is about the issue of the tape did you bring here?" In response Thomas Thug said, "I beg that you view it to exactly know what it is, please. I'm just there to deliver same." Tesio received it from his hands and said good-bye finally.

The tape that's given him needs to be tried. The guy with no further comment he left his presence. After ten minutes, he played the two tapes and saw what he did with Doctor Williams. On the other hand, what Doctor Scott and Gmasnoh did is displayed on Gmasnoh's stuff too. He got so restless for a moment.

"Dimmitt! What are we going to do about this mess now? We are from Africa and we don't know about these people legal system yet. Why have we trapped ourselves sexually into a scandal like this?" He said and tears fell from his eyes right away.

"This thing is a syndicate the two of us really need to take a note of. That's how I'm feeling about this thing. Oh, God! How did this thing happen?" he complained to himself and hissed intermittently yet. And he has quietly also whimpered.

Even so, the evening rolled in finally. He received a call from Doctor Barley Scott and told him of how he met with Thomas Thug--the same individual presumably. And the guy sent similarly tape to Scott and threatened him to a rape for which a case is pending against the entire group if, especially

Scott doesn't meet with Tesio for the two of them the men, to handle the issue quickly. He said they need to find a lawyer and that he and the lawyer will do business without their involvement. That is all they needed to do, as Thomas mused.

"Tesio," Doctor Scott is speaking, "I received a foolish tape. I believed strongly that you know something about this."

"What's it are you talking about Doctor Scott?'

"A tape is here into my hands containing a mess."

"Oh! I just got similar tape delivered to me here by a guy of the name of Thomas Thug. He came sounding stupid to me at the time. At last, he said, I need to meet with you on this matter or else we may be sent to court. Isn't this inanity? Imagine my sister and I haven't understood that yet, about the legal system here. Why then should someone talked about a case?"

"Yes. He's the same guy who brought mine too." Scott began sweating unimaginably in the kind of cold evening air. It's fogy at the time. His situation is proving worst on him, as if a different temperature other than a cold atmosphere he's experiencing. And Tesio told Williams about the tape and she didn't believe it. She is paralyzed shamelessly.

"We need to clean this mess now. Failure to do so, as I see it to be, it may be a big crime probably as a rape case to disgrace us in group. If, you happen to mess up for us letting us not act probably now, everything we have since worked for in America will be lost. We'd be jailed."

"So, Doctor Scott, what can we do about this?"

"You need to think about it and in three days let's converge to discuss it better with our various suggestions being put into place to deal with it."

Tesio nodded. "In fact, if nothing is done now our professional certificates would likely all be revoked by the state government. And where will every one of us work again as professional doctors? This is really a piece of shit!" Scott said.

"That's okay. Let's work things out now to resolve the matter." Tesio wonderfully padded.

"Look, Tesio, this is a shit. I can't get over this either. Who did this to us?"

"I don't know. You should tell me because you and Williams have teaching that shit of yours."

Scott became restless too. He didn't even say a word further.

In two days' time he couldn't eat and he's getting emaciated.

"Gmasnoh, I think Doctor Williams is rich. She'll be one of the best persons to help us quickly in our plans of development back home. We'll try to haul some money now from her to build our town." Tesio happily ignorantly said to his sister. He's now feeling a bit relief after he disclosed to her the tape issue. He is relatively not understood yet, how dangerous the tape issue is, if that happens to really blow out of proportion what is the consequent that should be either.

"I think it's about time that we go home. For what we did here, where we are married without the approval of our people back home is a serious issue that we need to go and handle same with the gods by conducting the necessary sacrifice required of this. It's better to go home now and settle that traditional issue with our people."

"What's the traditional issue are you talking about still, Tesio?" Gmasnoh asked with a frowning face. She seems faded.

"Oh, you meant to ask me again? You don't know that we took oaths at home since then?"

"Tesio, there's nothing much about this either. We are married already."

"But it's a problem still against our tradition. We took oaths for which the two of us swore not to get married anywhere, and not even to a stranger-person at all, except back home. And what we did here has changed the story around for our traditional marriages. Let's go and tell the people what had gone wrong for which we did this shit." He said and opened his mouth wide to bray out.

Quickly Gmasnoh came to him to dab him. "Look, Tesio, forget about that thing! Nothing wrong for which you have to cry either. I want you stop this shit now! Do you want my husband Scott to shoot the shit out of me now? Let sleeping dog lie yet. Let us just help our people at home. We should just be that focused with our profession here. I don't really have a mind of going home now. I beg of you to lay low on it yet."

"Please, don't just say that either. A sacrifice has to be performed in order to clear ourselves or souls of the traditional onus of the kind, please. It's not by mouth either and by sitting in America can resolve the matter. It needs our presence and participation into a ritual."

"I heard what you've just said but I'm satisfied to be as this about the situation. Let it be as sleeping dog must lie. I keep saying this to you. Did anybody ever approach you yet, on this matter from Africa?"

"No. But there's seriously a matter of concern for you to note."

"Tesio, isn't life better here than being it back home?" Gmasnoh furiously said. She is behaving sheepish, as if she is conjuring him to desist from talking about the oath issue. Tesio remained very speechless and contumaciously, as a fool in state yet. He wants to convince her.

He stood up before her. But after Tesio came to himself a little of thinking on what to do perhaps, he decided to say something differently to her.

"We just need to keep the secret when we get home for the elders and gods won't get angry with us either. And I want you really think of following me. Don't desist of going either."

"No. Tesio, that's a lie! I will, but earlier I told you that modernity comes with too much problems we needed to be aware of in life. And this proved me rightly, isn't it? Why all of the tragedies have to come our way either? We should have remained home than coming here, as you know."

"No!" He said and changed his statement again saying, "Now I know that you're right, Gmasnoh. But the desire for western education is necessary for a better change of our poverty condition once a problem before. Imagine I don't even have the spirit to go back home either. Anyway, what do you think we need to do now? Can we go back and report the situation without hiding anything about it? Probably the people and gods will see reason to pardon us if we do so now."

"Yes. You're right, my dear. We got to go home now."

In a week's time the two sought excuses at their working place to go home then.

Several nights had gone by since then no sleep could easily be into their eyes either. Gmasnoh keeps having funny dreams. She couldn't get over it. Each time the gods keep telling her in a dream that they have violated the traditional premarital vows for which they need to get home quickly. Sometimes they would scare her with a sword and she would just jump from bed stupid. It happened several times and she kept it secret with a mind to have telling her cousin Tesio know about it.

Now she has agreed strongly to go home then. Before the departure could come, Counsellor Uguche came to visit them again.

31

Counsellor Uguche came as a surprise at the house. Tesio and Gmasnoh often don't go that far from each other either despite they are married perhaps and needed to always give each other a space.

Counsellor Uguche was about to enter the house on the first floor to Tesio. While coming close to the house he decides to call out the names of Tesio and Gmasnoh intermittently before reaching inside in a squeaky way. He hasn't yet got a seat even to relax himself. The gateman took him all the way inside upon the instruction from Tesio, even though he's inside his room and making his way out quickly to him at the living room.

Finally Tesio met with him and took him to a special seat finally. "I'm seeing the both you of living the real American Dream as expected right now. Why I can't also be a participant?" He had teased in breaking the ice.

"Counsellor Uguche, it's hard to say, but we appreciate what you've just said."

Uguche looked quickly on the wall and noticed that they are married already. He rose from his seat and went to the wall, pointing at the pictures of Tesio and Gmasnoh being separately that married.

"I guess you didn't mean telling me at all . . . since then you got wedded? Why?"

"I'm so sorry that we didn't inform you about this. But it was a quick joined-wedding we had upon returning from India at the time."

"But I heard about it in the news. And you know nothing about you and sister, as special individuals in America that would be a secret either."

"You're truly right."

"Okay."

"We are so sorry for all that."

"But where is Gmasnoh right now?" Uguche posed the question in a sage manner to tease again perhaps. But before he could relax to his seat again upon looking at all the photographs on the wall, Gmasnoh came down from upstairs. She heard him with his husky voice of a courtroom's man.

"Oh, I'm so sorry, Uguche. My dear Counsellor, how are you doing?"

"Fine! I have just asked for you not too long to know your location perhaps."

"I have been upstairs."

"Oh, you were upstairs? There you live?"

"Yes. I want to say sorry that the both of us had our weddings since then without a notice to you either. I'm once more so sorry for this." He hugged her profoundly. "I should have been part of the signing of the wedding certificate of each of you. But you didn't instead invite me then. But don't worry yourself about that either. I've been praying that you both should have a good husband and a wife. And that you have done or have had. It's marvellous. Thanks a million!" Uguche said.

He has then decided to ask for once the red Obikwa wine he often drinks seriously in velocity because of its quietly sweet power of fooling him, but sure to reach his distance slowly. It's brought at the table before him as usual. He took two glasses of it. He felt like his senses more sharp again, as fully then he is about conversing with them.

"We've longed to seeing you since your departure that day."

"Well, that's okay."

"Counsel, we've a serious problem on our heads right now. Probably you can assist us in this mess."

"What's it?"

"It's something of a tape we received from a guy identified as Thomas Thug."

"'What?"

"That's the situation now."

"But the guy last name is scaring me, oh! Anyway, is it a tape about the both of you . . . embroiled into something funny or what?"

"Probably you are right. But you'll have to view it first, rather in our behalf and advice. It's troubling!"

"You mean . . . did you call that a mess? Then it must be so that very seriously a problem to talk about. Don't scare me either."

"That's true!" Tesio said.

"Wow!"

"Yes. It's really a serious story, Counsellor Uguche. But I know with the both of us concerned, I believe we can have it resolved undercover." Gmasnoh added. Tesio went inside the room and collected the tapes from there.

"You're the only person that I really trust in America to disclose of this to either. It's a tape that contains a mess about the both of us. Upon you viewing it, we are of the conviction that you would properly advise us on what to do next in addressing the problem. The guy who gave this thing threatened to go to court if, he can't be given some money. He wants us to give him money or else he would tarnish our reputation while the news media may blow the issue out of proportion. So, will we sit here and allow that?"

"Wow! I won't want you to talk that much yet. Let me go now and view it first. I would do that as soon as possible and inform you about what it is." Counsellor Uguche padded.

Tesio starts to picture what would be the result of Uguche upon viewing the tape.

"Thomas Thug is believed may have been facilitated by the cleaner at the surgical room of relaxation, where we went for final exams upon that result was obtained which later we graduated from the school."

"Could you just give me a lay time yet to view same and later I would make a return to you guys."

"Counsellor Uguche, I would advise that you check the tape to please get to know what I'm talking about."

"Yes. I'm surely going to do that now. But I want you to just give me a lay explanation about the matter yet, before I can leave to view it. I guess the story is interesting as you are sounding about it."

"Well, during a particular test—something of surgery in nature on our bodies, while exposing same to two of the doctors of our college, took place. There is a surgical test that was between Doctor Scott and Gmasnoh, while Doctor Williams and I were paired, too."

"What's that explanation of being pair is all about? Can a doctor and student at medical school do something of test together or what is it? Are you guys sexually ill for which you have had the surgical tests on your bodies? I hope," he is pointing at Tesio's privacy, "you didn't use that thing."

"I'm saying we took our test two by two. It's something sexual."

"You mean you and Doctor Williams sat together for the same test? Please, don't scare me up. This story of yours about a lesson is scaring me really." He said and smiled.

"Yes, that's what really happened."

"Wow! How can that be?"

"But it's since that test that you see each of us married today. We wanted to start fully living our dreams upon those billionaire doctors got us to do something like this."

"You're joking! You're trying to give me a different scenario about life really. You have gone beyond the level of a student-and-teacher relationship rather to an affair by each of you."

"Look, Counsellor Uguche, let me confess that it was stupid. And now we got to know that it's stupid."

"You mean . . . it was a love affair of test each of you took?"

"Yes, oh!"

"What? Oh, this is really America, Tesio. Both of you have socially flunk. You don't know anything about the culture for which you got hastily messed up."

"It's true. But what's so much about America?"

"At least, you got to know a bit about the fast life of living well in America by what the both of you did for which you're now married to rich individuals."

"But lots of the students were involved. It's not only us that took the test."

"How you got to know this? It was a syndicate to have said that to you. The instructor fooled you."

"It's a general test that took place."

"Then what's this issue of tape into it?"

"It's hard to talk about really. But, I don't know if this thing of tape is spread, has been done to us, out on every student that had done the test that day either. This is a reason I have decided to call you here at our home to assist us by twigging this thing before it becomes a real mess of disgrace to us now." Tesio concluded. Counsellor Uguche shrugged.

"You mean, you took-off your clothes and taught each other woman and man business to have been considered as a school lesson? Oh, this is stupid! Why, you the Africans in America are often too quick at being into trouble? Anyway, I'd try finding a solution, okay. Please, I'll get home and view it." Tesio nodded. Counsellor Uguche took-off.

Tesio felt a bit relief. Before then his Madam had given birth to a boy. His wife said the boy should use her father's name instead of his African name. That day he got so galled about that but nothing he could do to stop it.

And Gmasnoh, too, but had given birth to a girl. Now the sore, as the condition detects, is that the traditional vows have been broken.

Tesio had developed so much love for his Madam and the child. He's in the kitchen with his family. This day, Counsellor has for real, a week after since then upon viewing the tape, established a very, very serious crime about it.

A very interesting call is about coming on Tesio's phone. He ran on the stairs right at the doorpost to receive it. "Who is it may be on the line speaking?" He asked in a surprising way. Now there is no response yet despite the person answered the call to speak. The number seems strange to him. But by the time he said hello again, the voice he later heard was Counsellor Uguche.

The counsellor without saying hello, but burst up in words saying, "I've owed about two million dollars now on bills--the Barclay's Bank. I expect you to pay-off my debts soon. You and Gmasnoh may be able now to let me cover the hole I've been into since then, where I can be able to go back soon to Nigeria," he's saying that the debts he owed since then, "because of the tape you gave me." He said and Tesio's eyes beeped wide. He can't yet comprehend what he meant to say either.

Really, Counsellor Uguche has been looking for the slightest moment where to clear himself of debts. Now is the time. Cases are not coming as it used to be either. Only one other case given by the Government of the United States the nature of it he's still studying by himself. Partly his group of investigators at his work place are yet brainstorming with him too on the matter of how to handle same. And they are still praying that they sign the contract soon with the US Government.

Now the time has come upon viewing the take to make a huge disclosure of the legal implication of it. Tesio thought the counsellor is referring to someone differently. Because he couldn't be cleared to tell him what he meant to say, surprisingly, which he has quickly then, not to his senses of whom has made such a funny call, he aborted the call to figure out the person who had made the call perhaps. He feels so stupid really about that.

He said to himself it's an error perhaps the person who called him had made by calling him. And that person is impersonating as Counsellor Uguche. In a second's time, however, the phone rang again. He took it and asked for sure.

"Hallo!"

"Yes. It's Counsellor Uguche on the phone."

"Okay. You are most welcome, Sir."

32

Counsellor Uguche decided this time round to talk loudly and clearly for him to understand what he meant.

"Tesio, you're fucking things up! I said before that I'm in red. And now the tape you gave me to view shall greatly assist me at last, as a crime has been established into it, rather to settle my debts soon."

"Please, don't create problems for us. There is an issue in part, which we have violated our tradition we are now thinking about than what you're saying, please. We need to settle that matter with our people. Don't bring another trouble on our heads here in America."

"Tesio, we've a very big case. How are you talking as if I'm the one who had really then produced the tape? It's someone differently that you know who brought to you the tape and you asked me to view it. Now I have viewed it to tell you something very importantly you would like. You should be concerned about what the guy said than for you to be looking at me as if, I'm a problem man. I'm a counsellor for which I have to tell you what it is about the tape, and which I'm doing." Uguche laughed and Tesio is petrified about same. He did it rudely.

"Are you playing joke or what? What are you talking about, Sir?"

"Am I a joker, Tesio? Now I have a rape case against the four of you who went to the medical test sometimes ago. It was after that mess I guess you people got married, isn't it? It's a cover up, if you don't know for which the two doctors married you and your cousin. I wish I could have had such an opportunity from the beginning to have married a rich woman like Doctor Williams. And she had raped you."

Tesio interrupted him and said, "Why should you say so? Please, change your language because the woman is mine."

"I'm sorry. I was just trying to tell you something firstly by an example and the crime she has committed against you. Look, my brother, this place is America for which legal issue can't be handled undercover either. It's in Africa you can find most of that by doing things undercover but it isn't here either. No amount of money can bend the legal system here. I want you to know that now."

"Okay, please calm down a little."

"I will but we need to earn some money right now from this mess. You and Gmasnoh might have to get rich soon. We don't have to delay that. Doctor Scott in particular will have to pay you both some cash because he is the chief administrator of the medical college the both of graduated from and did all sorts of shit."

"Please, don't give us another worry."

"Okay. For what I can see about this tape is that, there is a big dollar involved for which the rest of you need to cooperate with me. Go and tell your so-called partner-instructors about this."

"What's the meaning of that saying, sir?"

"We must go for the case against the two elites Americans. They will be scary when they hear that you turn the tape over to me. I'm sure of the evidence on the tape; you and Gmasnoh have already won the case against them if it goes to court, for what I can see here about this thing. I want us to sue. I want you just give me a chance to handle it."

"But let's do that now Counsellor Uguche. But we shouldn't go to court either. I'm begging you because we are scaring for our reputation, please."

"Oh, don't you know that all of you foolishly took off your clothes upon blindly telling each of you to? But, I'm really angry about what this Scott did to Gmasnoh in particular. First of all, let me say congratulation yet. Reason being this particular tape would make me to settle my debts and be able soon to return to Nigeria. Don't be a dumb still this while when you know this is America."

"Please, Counsel, let me talk to you later. Call me in an hour's time," Tesio reluctantly said and put down the phone. He is feeling so sheepish. He knows the matter is a sensitive one which he didn't expect it to have been either. But it's now a terrible one. What to do about the situation has become a complex one. He tries complaining to himself.

Gmasnoh, however, upon being told she instructed him to quickly call Counsellor Uguche now and tell him immediately that they should find a time to meet now very quickly. Because of that, he decided by then calling him back again.

"At least could you please tell me where we to meet now?" The counsel heard the voice and hung off the phone without saying anything further to Tesio. It got Tesio more serious than anything. Because of that, but in a confused manner he looked on the right side of him, close by, and saw his cousin relaxed. He quietly hissed regrettably. He thought his cousin didn't care about that. He's so much downhearted about the incident.

Gmasnoh is looking at his eyes. She noticed a message of downheartedness from him. A moment later, she woke from her seat quickly, and went to pat him on the back. He bowed penitently by the time she lays her hand on his shoulders.

"Are you okay?"

"Yes, Gmasnoh. I'm okay, please."

"Is it the issue of going home a matter? Did you get an ugly word from back home or what?" Gmasnoh tries to get his mind away from the tape issue. Tesio couldn't respond to her yet.

After like six minutes he broke out saying, "Gmasnoh, it's serious. If we don't do something about this thing now, which is the tape, it's like we may lose everything here, including our professional licenses and at last be jailed for almost our life time. It's a mess we find ourselves into right now."

"Are you serious, Tesio? Is it about the tape?"

"Yes, that's it Gmasnoh!" Tesio looked at her face for long, while bowing and said,

"We've truly defecated on ourselves---the four of us. This thing we did is a very serious crime." The funny saying got Gmasnoh serious to the face more.

"Do you know we should have gone home to marry without doing any wedding, but Doctor Scott and Williams got us into mess here and we are even that married?" In that agitated tone, Tesio bluntly put it. Gmasnoh is yet speechless. She tries to give him a balance in mind yet.

"It's not mess, Tesio. I earned so much money since then, and my marriage has also been done. Doctor Scott, my man, he had shown me life during the test exercise and that is really good for me. Can you even see that he and I now have a child? That's okay for me!"

"You don't understand the subject of conundrum that's now on our heads yet. But you'll soon get to know it, Gmasnoh."

"But this man," she's referring to Doctor Scott, "you know is a very rich man. So, it's really good for me the way it had happened. In Africa, especially where I come from we don't call this a crime either. He loves me for which he did my personal body surgery, putting me alive that, I'm into the state of having a feeling about sex in time. That is so fine for me. And I really needed that. Which of course, I got it and feeling so better in body than the way I used to be before. Please, don't take my mind back, rather on anything ugly either. Let sleeping dog lie. What should be a concern is for us to continue to work and wire some money back home as usual. The guy is rich,

Tesio. And we shouldn't make any issue with this. Plead with the Counsellor now to lay low on the matter."

It's like Gmasnoh couldn't understand what Tesio is still talking about relative to the oaths. That's the matter that is really worrying him perhaps.

33

The plan to go home has finally come. Both the wife of Tesio and the husband of Gmasnoh consented to let them go home and return to America later. Explanation about the tradition from both Tesio and Gmasnoh got them by then agreeing to the plan.

They have sought excuses already at the workplace. Before the said departure they took a flight quickly to Minnesota to speak with some extended family members they got to know of.

In the act of going to Minnesota, they are brainstorming on the secret tradition which upon return home that would be to perform a sacrifice then.

"Do you think that sacrifice that would be should call for at least three cows each?" Tesio asked. In response Gmasnoh said, "Whatever number of cows it will take for the sacrifice to be a success it won't be a matter for me to provide the money either."

"Okay. But if the both of us don't hide this thing our partners both in America may know and at last the issue would blow out of proportion. None of us should tell them that we are going purposely for weddings. Gmasnoh, we've a legal issue in America now and at home is a traditional problem for which we need to be that very careful with the both sides of the coin."

"No. Wait a minute yet. Have you gotten a word from Counsellor Uguche first concerning the matter on what we should do next? Probably we need to wait on him yet." Gmasnoh begrudgingly said.

"You're truly right. We got to wait."

They came from Minnesota four hours later.

While sitting at home, Tesio decided making a call. "I'm the one calling you," Tesio is on the phone talking with Scott, "that my sister and I must go to Africa now as you both have agreed to let us go so we can have an assize on the issue of breaking our traditional vows to plead with the people. Since we are married here in America we just need to go and do the necessary sacrifice that is required to unfetter our souls from trouble. If we don't go quickly to let this matter be handled with the traditional people, it may be too bad for us at last. We are from Africa for which we know a lot about our traditions. Please try and see to it by allowing your wife—Gmasnoh to go with me concerning the said issue." In sorrow, Tesio pleaded.

Doctor Barley Scott, who knew already how sensitive the issue is about his wife Gmasnoh, he happily said 'yes' to Tesio right away.

"I've since been wishing to see the both of you on this matter because your sister long ago told me about it. And this is for a reason since then she has had any good sleep either these days. It scares me. She's just behaving like someone so downhearted."

"Thanks! But let me say again that, we know how African's matters can be about the tradition and the gods."

"You're right, Tesio."

"So, we got to go now! I have to picture a deviltry about that thing since then we did by breaking our vows really."

"I'm even getting scare over her behaviour. Anyway, happiness by virtue matters in anyone's life, which you both need."

"Don't worry. She's just a woman, who worries over little thing a lot. She would be okay."

"Tesio, I'm so sorry for what every one of us did sweetly yet grotesque now. We have to solve the matter quickly, especially the legal issue concerning the tape. It should be handled so that it won't be as a double-headed sword situation with you and her."

Tesio further said, "Don't you worry! Just what I want you to do is that always be willing to support her while she may even be in Africa."

"Tesio, what's about the issue of the tape? You've not spoken to me on the matter yet."

"No. Be it a bit relaxed about that, Doctor Scott. We have earlier told you that Uguche would handle the matter with you while we may be away yet. Please don't find a problem with that. He's a very kind-hearted man of wisdom and power to do the right thing, as expected of him. He is damn smart and influential. Don't get a scratch of your mind about that either. Please be a lay patient. He'll do just what we say in a professional way." Tesio soothed him. But his face spoke oppositely of the acceptance yet.

His statement got Doctor Scott into a state of enigma yet, wondering about what to do next in case thing gets out of hand since they are about going home on another issue very important to their lives. Of what he will do, rather that became an incomprehensible or hollowed question in mind though.

"You mean . . . your Counsellor Uguche is aware of this?"

"Yes. He is."

"You must be serious! I thought we were going to handle it among the four of us. Why you went that far telling him? That isn't fair! I told you before about learning to keep a secret as a doctor. But you failed to, just in this simple situation. Why, Tesio?" Doctor Scott worded. He stormed his legs on the floor acting confused of what to do next. Tesio remained mute despite that.

The thing for which he fears Uguche is that, he's a fearless lawyer. Before he won a case in which a woman went on three months maternity leave. And it was just barely one day left without her knowing she shouldn't have been at work. Her own records at home fooled her on the rightful date she was supposed to be at home. Surprising, a special day that came, she left for work when it was just one day left into her maternity leave. When she got to the work place she was told that the particular day wasn't the time for her to have really come to work either. But she requested that she has a work to do that day in a railroaded sweetly state of being. And she is a worker the management so much adorned because she knows how to work. But the company was just thinking about the critical nature of letting her work when just one day is left into her leave time.

She persistently pleaded with the management of her company and her request was granted based on certain condition. She worked in financial department for which there was a critical need for her to have been at work. Due to her persistent plead, however, at least, she was allowed to work that day. And she worked so tirelessly and interestingly, pleasing the management of the company. She was given a special purse apart from her pay.

To wonder, the company had a special accounting figure that was making the financial statements to be in error by then. Other accountants of the company tried discovering the error by tracing each accounts from the beginning, but they couldn't still find the problem. What is so jeering here is that, the company is to report to the Security Exchange Commission (SEC) that day for its stock to have been listed on the stock exchange option.

To wonder, her presence has blessed the company at last not to have missed the opportunity because many investors were to lose confidence in the ability of the company's management team by then to withdraw their investment from the company or layoff most of all key management staff. But

God had spared the company a bit of grace that moment indescribably then.

After the day work, she was about returning home. And while making her way home but at the company's ground she'd an accident. She broke her left leg. Just in that time, because the employer never wanted to take the full responsibility, even though the company was still struggling to recover from the economic downturn of 2001 that hit the US since then, the woman was told that the entity isn't fully responsible to do anything concrete about her case because that day wasn't the day she should have been at work. It seemed stupid with the company's decision. But her salary alone was threat in payment with the bi-weekly salary section's budget because her salary could pay-off the salaries of about ten middle staffers in a six-month period.

However, she was taken to a hospital upon the order of the company. She was paid off quickly for the day she worked and extra little fund was given her for the number of years she has been with the company, as her pay-off, too. She stayed at the hospital for about two years. Because of that after half-year the company decided to lay her off because it's against management's policy by then, working against one's maternity leave in such a manner which had led to a huge trouble.

It's one of such cases, Counsellor Uguche took on for her since a year and half now and she won. She was blessed to have really had won the case because luckily for her she signed in that day and worked. She won two million dollars after the case was ended, and the company paid her off straight down the amount.

And there are several of cases, too, which Uguche won for others. They promoted him a lot. But the thing that often suffers him most is his lifestyle. And when he had got married before his wife lavished spending spree became worse than ever. Besides that, he too loves the big show-making of life too. This is the social immoral plague, as he thought, that has shrouded his life.

Scott, visually, had heard about him before. His brilliant legal power is truly one of such promoters of his greatness. And he has really cultivated Scott who has been reading a lot about him since then when he heard his name. He wanted each time probably to learn his style of pleading or probably be as Uguche someday. So when he heard about him this time round, a fever, of nebulousness in body by then had showcased. He wanted maybe to be a barrister, wherein the two could meet elsewhere as legal-minded people by then, they could seek a gentleman path on the matter than what it seems to be now, instead.

34

They have returned home wonderfully in Niffu Town. Their belongings are taken to town by young people. Civilization by virtue had showed its proudness of power over other friends who they all came up together before. For them, not to mention, they have improved greatly. But lots of their friends were still collaborators to the danger of poverty in some way. Life seemed difficult for them to have then taken a better step for education. So they have accepted somewhat to work for poverty then. But Gmasnoh and Tesio had truly made it.

They have been taken to town seated in the palaver hut. The wonderful historical tree is still standing close by the meeting area. Tesio took his eyes at it and nodded for its past history.

Lots of welcome statements were made by some elders. After that they were urged home to take a rest yet. Later they are to come back at the palaver hut to meet.

And they took a lay rest in few hours waiting at four at least to go and brief the elder council. Every gift items they have brought for friends were given out. One thing good about them is that they have changed the entire town structure. Even the house they are staying is where they parents' muddied houses used to be. But all those have changed to a compound hosting the entire family.

By Four O'clock Post Meridians the elders (Gbarku) convened a meeting upon calling Gmasnoh and Tesio into their midst. Needless to say, they are about firstly speaking on the misfortune encountered in America. And lastly is the issue of traditional marriage that should be by the same time, too.

In a very interesting faction, some powerful individuals, part of the elder council, having since had been involved with incantation at the shrine and when the news got in that they were on their way to West Africa, heading for Niffu Town, they got ready since then. But upon Tesio and Gmasnoh's arrival, few of the guys at the shrine came to town firstly that, welcoming them in the meantime yet. Astonishing crowd has once more kept pouring at the house playing traditional songs. It's like a day of feast to remember again.

"You've just returned home. We're so very grateful that you've come home safely and purposely to honour your marital vows. We appreciate firstly all the assistance so far the both of you rendered the people of Niffu, which is your own town. We are highly grateful to you." Elder Bartee said. He usually speaks for the elder council during any time when there is a public gathering. This, he is doing as usual. Tesio and Gmasnoh smiled. They felt the start of the conversation is a hint of that positively the result that would come out later shall be despite they haven't even reported the trouble of breaking the premarital vows yet.

"We've to take you around first to see your own work in town. When you shall see all the development projects, we are of the conviction that when you get back to America again you shall do more than what both of you having been doing since then. We have made used of all the money you have been sending." Elder Bartee lustily said. Most members of the elder council have encaged them, while taking around on foot. Every corner they have so far gone the women and children kept greeting them in happiness.

They were done with going around. Federation, as youth and women, elders and other eminent people all formed thought to be at the place, has once more come to being at the hall. Tesio has stupendously rose from his seat and stood at the podium.

"My Elders, we are very grateful for all that you've said you have done concerning our common town and its people. One thing I want you to know is this, there is constantly the complaint by lots of Liberians in America that Liberians at home majority can't be trusted to manage funds well, especially when that purposely intended for projects. And now it is becoming a problem about trust these days with those in the diaspora towards the people of our motherland. Imagine all the illusion held about that---I don't want to say that much, but you have proven me wrongly, as I held such negative feeling too before. But I would desist from such to keep trusting you---the people here. We tried you all and you proved beyond all reason doubt that you're developmental to refute the negativism about those in the diaspora towards those at home here. Never did I ever see on earth the kind of earnest people as you're." Tesio said and Gmasnoh deeply smiled. He tries to beg the pardon of his countrymen. After that he would put forth the real issue they have experienced, which has become a worry of their souls since then yet.

"Thank you, Tesio. A writer says that the human character is like a condiment. For good without the condiment there can't really be a taste of the food either. And for the human being his condiment is his character which gives a true sense of his being as human too. " Bartee said. The whole crowd went wide laughing, ah, ah!

Interesting he is quite a wonderful man of trust of no nonsense feature in him either. He regards the voices of the gods as long a decision is reached about anything for the public good. So when he speaks his voice is regarded as a lay god that is physical to be watchful about.

"The desire for unity is a journey still too long. I want you continue to walk towards unity. It's such a reason you have since built upon yourself on the establishment of customs by the gods in the land to legally control the activities of our human world, at times, the acts of evil which can be beyond measure perhaps."

He's interrupted a little by Elder Koffa.

"Bar-tee-oh. . . bar-tee, bar-tee—" Such battle cry slogan was sounded thrice by Elder Koffa. It's a way which perfectly helps in establishing decorum in an instant, which is popularly part of the culture. And that was then being achieved. Imagine on the bare ground as a person drops a pain, the sound could be that loud for the others to hear it perhaps. Visually, there is perfect calmness by the people to listen to their wonderful son and daughter that have come from a civilized or developed society, as the United States of America. It was as if the congress of the United States the presiding speaker taking over his duty. And the quietude that exists in letting him speak on the first act of making welcome statement, that is so great to praise.

Pleasurable to describe, as women and children are clinking together, is how the condition is the moment. Everyone at the meeting place has been wishing to see the return of Tesio and Gmasnoh. Their guises, as they are before their people, are by far telling a conscience story of how greatly they are. Money and power were symbolically pictured from them. The studies in America proved really good with their lives. In a null shell, they have become rich people and quite marketable to any economic society of the world by virtue.

The watch on Tesio is a brand of Polo Assassin. His clothes, from head to toes, are a design of Georgia Armani. And for Gmasnoh, she had on a Forbes watch and a T-Shirt and sneakers are the design of Polo Ralph Lauren. She had on a head tie by Tommy, folded on her head like a character from the movie: "The Soldier Boy".

Tesio is about receiving an urgent call. He and Gmasnoh thought to go outside yet. The call is from the USA.

"Hey, how are you doing?" The unknown individual said. And Tesio is yet to really twig who the voice is on the phone.

"Could you please tell me . . . who is probably on the line?" He wobbled his head, as the phone was placed at his head.

"It's Counsellor Uguche."

"Oh, what's a great man! How are you doing, sir?"

"I'm so good and you?"

"That's fine. Well, we are now in the midst of our people discussing the issue of the tradition."

"Good! Be able to convince the people to understand the circumstance the two of you faced for which you broke your vows."

"Thank you, sir. We will ensure that the proposed thought by you is followed."

"Anyway, let's talk seriously a matter right now."

"What's such an important matter, sir?" Tesio's heart broke on him instead.

"I want to tell you that, I and Doctor Scott are now on our way to a meeting point to reach a final saying on the matter of the tape. I feel for you and Gmasnoh so much that I want us to handle this thing once and for all, perfectly and quietly. Besides that the Thomas individual and I had a discussion already that I have to give him some money for him to forget about disclosing of the issue to any individual other than us, rather he has met already with this thing."

"Right! That's what I since had wished for about this."

"Tesio, is it true now that Scott resigned his post?"

"Yes. He did."

"Oh, my God! He must be an imbecile."

"Please don't say that either. He isn't as you thought."

"Why is it that you are backing him always? Is he because a husband of your cousin? Whatever you feel about him, but one thing I want to talk about here is that, he needs to now behave in stopping himself to this kind of hooligan behaviour, which is highly sacrilegiously against most people cultural values, then. He is too knobby. That's one thing I know about. A person can't be doing medical work involving sex. It's strange to me."

"Please, Counsel, I'm aware of the destruction Doctor Scott brought upon us since then, especially which is against our tradition. But somehow he did some good too, despite the incident. We intent at least remembering a little good thing he had so far done so that, we could probably now forget about this damn bullshit."

"What did you just say? Tesio, do we need to lay this thing to a rest in just a stupid manner like that? You are joking!"

"What not? There is a wise saying by our people in Africa that, when you have your hand into the mouth of a lion, don't you the person force it out of there. Instead, you should be able peacefully to get it out."

"Yes. That's a reason I've since planned for us to handle it with ease. But he has to pay us some money because the guy, I guess got so much money from this thing he, especially did because he is the general administrator of the hospital who may have personally designed this shit."

"No. Just that I want us to speed up the process of dealing with the guy. Really, Counsellor Uguche, I have something very important to think of at this moment the other side of the world than that. I beg of you, please. That you know about that the man is now Gmasnoh's husband. We should understand that to resolve same peacefully. It is an earnest request that I'm making." Tesio pleaded.

"Now, I do know that you're truly blind to the American setting yet."

"What do you mean? Do you mean to cuss me or what?"

"No. Being a novice about issue doesn't me you're stupid either. Please get what I have just said."

Counsellor is like frowning a bit on him while still on the phone. "I wish to call you back in an hour later, Tesio."

Despite Counsel Uguche's tough-saying to Tesio, but he feels a frustration in Tesio's voice. He knows that the guy is bombed in body to a huge stress since he's home with his people.

Interestingly, in a state of heroism, Uguche is making his way to a special location he's supposed to meet with Scott. Now it's like a condition very funny to see really. You could see the muscles of Uguche on the wheel standing strongly while driving fast, purportedly, to see Scott.

Tesio and Gmasnoh returned in the hall at last. They are more mindful about the issue than anything else. He's standing at the podium in seriousness to give the detail of the omen of breaking the traditional vow by each of them.

"My very interesting people of this town, our dear Elders," he's trying all out to appeal to the consciences of his people by way of toadyism, as you could see him standing erect and looking so purposeful about the speech-making, "I know you've always been there so greatly of promoting unity at all levels. But, it's a trifling situation right now about us, if I may say that Gmasnoh and I came home to tell you about as we are all seated here. I know you people can handle it in few seconds to free our souls from the trouble with our lives."

He is interrupted by one of the elders again. "Thank you, Tesio. You now have the podium for us to accept that you're special son or a hero in our midst. May you have the consciences of our silence, as you're being permitted already to speak to us in a very fair manner right now! Just go ahead and speak your mind." Tesio smiled. Proudness has made a monument that moment with him. His cheeks are wide open as he was turning here and there with his head talking.

"Well, I do know for sure my people that you are going to give us your assistance to this, by going to the gods performing the needed sacrifice. We have truly violated the norms of our culture. But forgive us."

"Before you continue to speak with us, may I please say something to you, Tesio that I want you to listen keenly." Tesio paused to listen to the Elder. Gmasnoh had quickly used the time of pause and she came close to Tesio's ears, urging him to explain the situation in details.

The elder did what he could at the podium and gave Tesio a chance to speak again. Tesio, majestically, he went back to the podium as usual to give details of the situation that had befallen them in America. Majority of men and women present, well-seated, stupendously they are listening to him. Impatience to hear the true story has pancaked their minds strongly. They are purposeful just to know the rightful issue in America and the traditional marriage soon to be, for which they have all since then prepared for it to come shortly.

Pomp and pageantry in Niffu is so much associated with having a wedding. So, it' has been the interest of everyone that their separate weddings, even though the names of both the woman and man they are each to get married to haven't been disclosed of yet. Usually that is kept secret until the last day to the main wedding day at least at night before the names of the persons are disclosed of. As that, everyone was still in bewilderment yet, to know who be who or so, marrying to Tesio and Gmasnoh each.

The chief elders have had the note compared already. Even, the guys who went to the shrine are yet to come. And it's almost one day gone since the arrival of Tesio and Gmasnoh. And it's about four O'clock for which the chief elder asked that they should meet the next day since the shrine men haven't come back yet to town.

Each day a cow was being killed. The night plays are behind mention as it's arranged by the chief elder in collaboration with the elder council.

35

It's the following day. Tesio is permitted to speak his mind still. "Gmasnoh and I had caused damages to the tradition. We have already briefed you all about it earlier. It's an opened secret you all know about now. We are married in the USA. My wife name is Doctor Shirley Williams, and Gmasnoh's husband name is Doctor Barley Scott, and both of whom are Americans. In our marriages, we are separately blessed with each a boy and a girl. Get to know it that they are now your grandchildren. We pray that one day they shall come to meet with you all." He said and there was laughter. Some elders held their hands to their mouths in astonishment to what he had said. It's scaring to many by then because that is seriously a violation of a major tradition like that.

There is a huge laughter. Somebody in the midst of the audience surprisingly said, "That can't be! You must be punished by the gods. We shouldn't laugh over this either." The person couldn't be identified either. There is perfectly a decorum the moment. Glaring, the individual has talked about sentencing them rather than just accepting same like that for each to go unpunished. Jeering, the situation is more than the condition of Sayon perhaps. But what should the punishment be upon any of the customs is broken, that depends wholly and solely on a decision from the gods. The incantation must be performed in order for what the sentencing could have been that can come to being then. Momsio has the power to chant at the shrine.

"Please, let's keep quiet about this. What has happened to our son and daughter isn't an issue to sit here, opening a state of debate, either." Bartee said.

"We are home because of this serious problem." Tesio lost a lay balance when he said and paused. He's wiping his eyes. He feels like whimpering but he's able to control himself---which he did.

"Thank you. We have since then got the information. Be patient! Now that we are awaiting the result from the shrine concerning what the gods will say about this. Since three days now the elders are at the shrine and they are soon to be here while we are at the meeting hall. Let's all be patient to wait on them." Bartee said and Tesio bobbed. They had kola to chew. Some coconut fruits were brought at the meeting place in the meantime. Both Tesio and Gmasnoh are really feeling fine, especially being at home--for sure. There is so much respect that is being given them. An old lady from the crowd came to wipe his sneaks of a little dirt that got on it. He tries stopping her but she insists on what she was doing and wiped the dirt instead. He was forced to have looked at her and smiled.

Interestingly, an hour later those that went to the shrine came back finally. Cheering audience by then rose to welcome them.

Upon arrival, but since then about thirty minutes---the elders are comparing note. Heads are grouping and chatting. The result from the shrine seems yet good to the elders ---but on the other hand is a danger for Tesio and cousin perhaps.

Worst of all, Tesio and the cousin took from their bodies before all the various chants that were given them since then. It's not as the way the gods' protection used to be with them again, rather before the departure to the city came.

Now fear of death overthrew Tesio's sanity. The way he saw most of the elders behaving, brought that morbid fear into him. His eyes are beeping high, as his guise is also changing like someone fading out.

Tesio couldn't just wait the moment upon reporting what has been the problem faced. Why should the verdict of the gods on the matter be that delayed? That became an issue into his heart, pondering about it. He became incongruous to himself, thinking about what he expects the problem would be, which a negative result is that now presumed.

"I and Doctor Scott are now about to speak on the issue. Just give me a minute and after our talk I'd call you later." Counsellor Uguche called Tesio on the phone while he and Gmasnoh quickly went out the hall to chat with him on the phone.

Tesio got more infuriated. Why is this so much delay for a decision to be reached either? Forgive him and the cousin, as he had thought. He wants that from his people. But it's a roaming talk into his mind he couldn't just over either. But he had his own answer each the foolishness came over him. And he wants to tell his sister how he is feeling now but he couldn't. Nobody knows while he couldn't either.

So mournful to say, but Counsellor Uguche is also complicating the situation on the other side in America. But for him the issue in America is his interest most. Tesio is so vexed. But one thing about him is that, he knows how to control his emotion despite the situation the both of them found themselves into since then. That's the mental-power he has so interesting about him.

"Counsel, you just go ahead resolving the matter and later call me up upon that has been done." Tesio said in an incensed state of being but maintained his balance. He had frowned. He didn't allow Uguche to either put down the call. He didn't even get the phone from his ears too, while he keeps saying hello. Right after that he called Gmasnoh and said something very pathetically; this proved there is mental-upheaval perhaps.

"Why is this Counsellor complicating this thing? We've a big trouble now on our heads this side, and he's just calling me. He should be very mature to deal with that issue in America since then, but he's slowing to. You mean every time he'll just be calling . . . slowing in his steps? It's bullshit. Definitely it's bullshit, oh, my God!"

"What's it, Tesio? I can just see you frowning and complaining to yourself on the phone. Please be a lay careful about everything that is happening right now, okay." Gmasnoh pleaded. She took her right hand and placed it on his left shoulders while moving him inside the hall again.

It's the day coward was like about to die many times before its death. "That's Counsellor Uguche. He's another trouble to our lives. He is complicating things than before. This is what I'm noticing about the whole thing right now in America about him."

"Wait! That's that?"

"Please, let him stop stressing me up! Can't the guy see that our culture on this other side is hanging us gradually to death? This is a whole memory link of unforgettable menace if not careful here perhaps could that be more trouble than expected. It's not a joke either."

"Tesio, I know how is the issue so sensitive, but we are to now allow him handle that problem in America in a very professional way than by force. He is just in his legal formation to soliciting facts. That's all I can see him doing, if you don't know now. And it shouldn't be as the way you wished right now. I beg of you, please. Like I said to you before, when a person gets his or her hand into the mouth of a lion he or she needs to be careful to get it out. And he's a professional man who has been in the business of law to resolve the problem with ease than by force. So, let's take our time in speaking with him on the matter." Gmasnoh said wonderfully.

"Please," unconsciously rotating, "let him leave us alone," Tesio arrogantly replied.

"Tesio, you need to be a bit gentle about this and avoid the life-threatening emotion in you. This whole thing is like a chicken egg right now, which we've to handle same with the necessary care needed. If, you behave harsh as you are behaving on the phone, the whole thing may blowout of proportion. And my husband and ours profession too, like I see it may that be in jeopardy. I fear such. Look, if you ain't careful there would be a future debacle about our lives."

"Fuck!"

"What not?"

"Gmasnoh, it's true but what can I do now? He's a legal man to be able to handle issue as soon as possible. And it isn't like that either."

"No. Don't say that either. Legal practitioners and professional doctors all take turn with any issue that confront them. You're a doctor to prove that perhaps. Do you go into rush when you have a case at the hospital? I really want to know. Contrary, you do everything with ease. Why we can't exhibit the same patient?"

"That's good."

"Okay. You might take a little time-off now at least talking with counsellor, who I believed would see a genuine reason gently and carefully to handle this thing with Scott." Gmasnoh, not to mean same yet, but she's frowning at her brother. She now feels that he's down to a huge stress for him to rest his mind at least, being careful to express himself on any issue for now.

One thing about Tesio is that he's very fast to acknowledge his mistake at times when he does wrong. And so, he saw a reason upon talking harshly to Gmasnoh, while complaining and he walked away by then, leaving the phone with her but he later said sorry. They walked back into the hall. Giving them attention as usual became indiscernible by way then. Faces expressed more seriousness and to punish them. But most people really want the history of what went wrong in America and they didn't really had made a call home earlier to have told the elder council either.

"We're now calling you and Gmasnoh in again. The final decision is about to be reached. Our shrine men are here at last." Elder Bartee purported.

"Thank you, sir." Tesio added.

"The both of you're very good son and daughter of our town which we can't afford to express how good you have been to us by way of a speech either. We've even built a monument in your honours for all that you've been doing for generations now and those to come to remember you always then. We accept the life threatening problems you were confronted with for which you dumped the traditional value. It's modernity. We should have known better earlier to have repealed the customs by sacrificing to the gods, especially by telling what school life is for a person at times. But we are so sorry that none of us could tell of what the future, the distance this thing would have come either."

"Yes! You're truly right sir! But is it late to do that now?" Tesio asked.

"After a consultation with the gods we now have the decision to be reached that says, that the both of you've to be married again in our African way. It doesn't matter since you both got married in America. In spite of that you might get married still here. As far the gods and the elders here are concerned, you've yet gotten married despite what you did in America. The continent of America is a different one, which the African society is also different from. That is obvious you must do new marriages now to free the both of you souls firstly by a sacrifice from the trouble of the gods that would likely come, if not."

"Thank you." Tesio said.

"Give me a lay chance yet. For what we do know in Africa, a man can get married to, as many wives he wants, as long he's a strong wealthy man. Only a woman isn't allowed to do so."

Tesio giggled and said, "That's true!" There is a lay relief from his face. He and Gmasnoh are now feeling amused that his people are with them still to come up with the final names soon of whom they are each, at least to marry few moments after upon the announcement has been made. That's the most sensitive part of the issue they need to know most.

Counsellor Uguche decided to meet with Doctor Scott and Williams finally. He wants to speak with Tesio and Gmasnoh on the phone concerning that after.

"The tape given me is full of lots of crimes. And the both of you could be charged with sexual assault and rape. Your behaviour resulted to touching, fondling, and fingering or oral masturbation, and so forth. As a medical practitioner you really need to be aware of this. At the time you committed your medical testing or exercise, the students (Tesio and Gmasnoh) were yet of innocence when it comes to sex. And these are Africans with strong beliefs due to their tradition. But now, you've made them to break their traditional vows or destroyed their values because you thought that they are innocent Africans yet, and very strong about school and wealth creation than anything else. The both of you: Scott and Williams, the sexual act is sacrilegious to their tradition. This is even criminality. And the laws in Oklahoma City have to hold you both for forms of felonies!" Counsellor Uguche had seriously said. He's with Doctor Scott and Williams while lashing in his legal terminology or philosophy.

"Counsellor Uguche, you have all the best about this to seek our prosecution. But it's a two-sided situation that may either damage the profession of your African family . . . that is---the Tesio and Gmasnoh, if we go too strong about this."

"Look, it's stupid! Are you to suggest to me about this? When and how did you become a legal man? Let me tell you that, it is because of preserving their characters' sake, if you don't know, for which they are now begging and saying that the whole thing should be laid to a rest. That isn't you to demand that from me either. But the only way this thing now, finally, but laid to a rest, is by you paying to each of them a twenty-million dollar. You've to make a total of fifty million dollars ready now, or else you'll be sent to court to justify your action." Counsellor Uguche strongly worded.

He got Doctor Scott and Williams to sweat. Right away upon seeing how Doctor Williams is behaving nervously about the issue he asked her to leave, wherefore he and Scott alone are to handle the problem, if she likes. She is so happy to return home. And Counsellor Uguche accepted and Williams quietly drove-off as she is told to.

But as far Counsellor Uguche is concerned he'd at least banked at the consciences of Doctor Scott and Williams, using his legal-mind.

You could see him opened up like he's in a courtroom. He'd his face so sobered. When it comes to doing his legal job, he behaves too harshly and forceful, rather in speech to put fear in an accused. And his questions in examining are always interactively entertaining.

"I'm begging you. Please let us forget about this." Doctor Scott appealingly said. He took a check book right away from his pocket to write a check for the amount he needed to give out.

"Excuse me, sir," Doctor Scott is seeking the attention of Counsellor Uguche at the time, "am I going to divide the amount evenly between them?" he asked. Counsellor Uguche looked at him strongly with a pucker brow and said, "No! Just wait a minute. I would tell you what to do next." Scott peeped up at his face because he's standing over him upon leaving the car he brought.

"You're to write for me at least a separate check of ten millions particularly, and while twenty each is for Tesio and Gmasnoh. Upon completion of this, I'll be the one to handle the delivery. I'd better deal with my clients than you do."

"I won't even delay doing that now, sir." Doctor Scott said.

Doctor Scott is at least feeling that euphoric that the trouble is soon to be over with. And an agreement at least has been reached which got him feeling a bit good in body perhaps.

Mind-tumbling, as the news has been seemly, quite indescribable for Tesio and Gmasnoh, is about to be disclosed of. The shrine men are about telling what the final result is yet. He got so purposeful by the way then, wishing that they should try and do whatever they intend doing about them. Impatient solidified itself into him than ever.

Since three days ago, Rosa and her parents are since gone to a nearby town to seek the help of a traditional medicine man. They are just going about from one town to another finding out from the spirit's world through performing various chants. Their aim is to see that Tesio marry Rosa. And since Tesio left Liberia by then he has been helping her in some ways by sending lay cash home to her. There she developed the confidence that he has to marry her.

For heaven's sake, probably the way the gods have been consulted by the elders in Niffu since then, the decision as to whom each is to marry, hasn't been disclosed of yet, and that meant to the Rosa and family that, Tesio would likely be getting married to a different woman maybe other than the Rosa. Usually she should have been told since then that she and Tesio will get married for which her parents should be aware of same. But it's not the case either.

It is just endless presupposition they keep making perhaps. All these beautiful years, visually, Tesio had been away, Rosa has been waiting long endlessly since then too. And another family member of hers and the parents they have since three years now been rearing a cow and goats for her wedding. But it's like they have been betrayed. It's like her cake is about leaving her mouth, because she really loves Tesio. And Tesio, since him and Gmasnoh arrival, he has been asking about her. He had a parcel to give her that he brought. He bought lots of good things for the girl.

But will the consultation be of value as purposed by her and parents at last? As thought, the best step is by quickly embarking on the act of conjuring the spirit of Tesio. And Tesio and Gmasnoh are still awaiting the final verdict of the gods in Niffu since then. Jealousy, as condition depicts, is highly at its feverish stage. Reason being, juju men from every side of the coin are working to ensure that the spirits of Tesio and his cousin are in agreement to their chant-culture.

The fourth day came. The head of the shrine, Momsio, he came to town finally. He is seemed nostalgia. His result of what the punishment should be about the issue of marriage, are now with him. He and the elders are once more at an assembly first. After few minutes of the brainstorming by most of the elders, Momsio stood up at the podium to speak on what the final decision is finally.

He's a funny-looking man with lots of beads on him. He also has chalk lines all over his body. He had a wrapper made as a diaper-like and no shirt on him while standing before the audience. By his outlook, you could think that he and

Satan often sit on the same bed, conversing daily. And it's like Satan had nurtured him a lot in chants shamelessly and contumaciously. He's damn fearful on an overall.

He broke the ice. "The incantation has been performed for the past four days. The final decision by the gods now is that, Tesio and Gmasnoh, for the sake of preserving the culture of our land in keeping the integrity of the town, including keeping the bond of unity in their family-line too, and lastly preserving their wealth, they are to be married to each other since they are two cousins. The gods are saying that such decision is intended to protect the family in time to come, where to avoid the infiltration of strange individuals probably those that are outside the family arena for any not to either think of marrying any of the family either, especial the two in question. Tesio, as this is said, if accepted by the two of you now, that would be as a basis for the future of the family not to be into any trouble of division either." Momsio said.

In a ninny stage unruly, Tesio jumped up from his seat saying, "No! The decision is highly unacceptable. So, help me God! This girl, for what I do know," he's referring to Gmasnoh, "is my blood. What kind of society is this? You want me keep her as a wife now in life? I hate this kind of intermarriage situation. It's disgusting!" He said. Every soul at the place couldn't get over it. They thought the decision is the best ever the gods had come up with for safety in their family's behalf. But it wasn't instead.

Being so furious, Tesio asked Gmasnoh that they should leave the hall right away. And he's saying that they are going back to America. Truly, they are gone away from the presence of the elders by force. This became a very serious trouble with the elders. They are feeling so insulted, having thought of Tesio and cousin doing that to them either. Because of this few women in the midst of the elders rose to run behind Tesio and Gmasnoh, begging to reconsider the decision, and do whatever the gods said to the elders.

They are at a distance moving fast away. The elderly ladies are so downhearted and scaring about the disrespectful manner in which they are leaving. Some tried reaching them to beg for their pardon to desist and make a comeback instead. "We must leave now. This community isn't safe for us anymore." Tesio, while holding Gmasnoh hand said. They got at the house and took the most essentials, put into their various bags and went away to the airport.

"Yes. We got to go!" Gmasnoh added. They are bumbling going away. They are surely set to leave all together for the airport and never to come back to Niffu again. That is what it had shown.

36

Counsellor Uguche has finally concluded a deal with Doctor Scott. He decided to phone Tesio on phone about that.

"Look, Tesio, the deal is now perfectly done."

"What's the deal are you talking about?"

"It's done. Didn't I and the Doctor Scott plan to meet as I told you earlier?

"Alright."

"The deal is perfect, Tesio! Doctor Scott has given me three checks right now, which I'm traveling to the bank to put into each of you --the account."

"Wait a minute, Counsellor."

"Yes. Tesio, what may be your problem again?"

"Is it fair?"

"What are you talking about concerning the issue of fairness you spoke of? Do you want to determine my level of professionalism or not? In fact, have you been to heaven before where there is the tree of fairness? Bullshit!"

"Please cool down a little. I want to know how much did you take from Doctor Scott--by the way?"

"Take your time, Tesio. Let not you sympathy disease catch me either." He said and twisted at the point he's standing.

"I'm so sorry, sir!"

"Okay. But he has been able by giving the both of you a twenty-million each." Counsellor said.

Tesio is so angry for the amount he said he got. He is a guy who really adorns Doctor Scott because he's his boss and lastly a husband to his cousin. But Uguche cares not about how he's feeling the moment. As far he's concerned he got the money from the guy which would help to clear him off debts.

All this while that has been his worry then. And his heaven has lavished on him the blessing he needed most.

"How much did you just say you took from Doctor Scott?"

"Why are you so concern about that amount? Don't you want to get rich as he is, too? Please, I don't want that your sympathy fever from Africa to either grip or make a fever with my body either here in America. I got to live better now and be able soon making a return to Nigeria, my home-country, please."

"No. I was just making an inquiry. Why are you fuming about what I have said?"

"I know. And I should be the one to say so. Not you! Perhaps the way you asked me is infuriating. Please, I know the problem you are both faced with, but you've to be a lay polishing in words. I don't want you to bring my profession to a public dispute either. I'm just helping the both of you."

"Counsel, don't even pay attention to my words either. It's just a joke."

"Okay. Let me say something very interesting you have to know about right now. This place--America is a land of fortune or full of opportunities by a chance sometimes can anybody get across so easily to live a better life. I made a mistake first and I got to correct my mistake right now and live better again."

"Wait! Are you saying we should live a life full of trouble by collecting from someone in a knobby style or what are you saying?"

"No. I won't entertain your wrongful or hash assertion either. And you need to try and ask Doctor Scott, if he did get anything in the process of the silliness he put you both into. He should be the one for you to really ask in that silly talk of yours. He's a man living already flamboyantly about this thing, if you don't know."

It got Tesio gasped. He's a bit restless again the way he saw Uguche made a life on Scott—something he didn't know that it doesn't even mean anything to the life of the doctor either. And Scott's main concern is to see unanimity makes a comeback as usual about his life. And it seems returning gradually, because the matter will soon be handled.

Probably Tesio's thinking is that, there would be a backlash from Scott which the situation may likely get out of hand for Scott to either quell him and sister furtively. He's always thinking fast ahead which sometimes is behind imagination.

Gmasnoh is really set. She's done with packing her things since the return to America. Tesio too had sat in the living room with Counsellor Uguche since an hour, chatting differently on important issues. Peace had presumably returned in an interim to their lives yet.

Now a week after things started changing. And they are considering a question to know why the issue at the time wasn't handled with the traditional people and the gods and they came rushing from there. It has become a waterloo the moment then.

Dumbness inexplicably, is showcasing little by little, especially in their minds to maybe go back home again.

Gmasnoh, a special day which came, she is downhearted after being at work almost the whole day upon performing lots of surgeries. She is upstairs in her apartment crying to herself, wondering while they took such a decision of leaving Africa without settling the matter with the elders.

To wonder, she is about receiving a call from Tesio's father on the same matter, as the old man wishes to know what the next step of the way is with them, especially if they can thwart the decision of the gods.

"My daughter, please talk to your brother Tesio about the decision of the gods. Since the two of you left for America, we too left town to see a juju man to a different town who knows about juju powers. We consulted with the gods there. The result of the chant is that, you and Tesio might probably have made a quick return home again. But I'm not in agreement with that either. And a twenty-one day has also been given by the gods to tell you both to make a return within those days. At last, they gods said any failure by the two of you not returning then, that would be an untold story for our families and yours too. But it's stupid to me. Because of that when I was told by some members of the elder council, I cussed. And they fine me to pay a cow, which I did provide in time. Glaring, they are jealous of the both of us success for which the gods brought up that saying without any rebuke by even the Momsio man, either."

"Thank you. But we have a hope of meeting with a prayerfully powerful man of God. He's Reverend Howard. He's been told to do a very fast prayer for us within twenty-one days also. He is really a strong man of God."

"Surely?"

"Yes."

"Okay. Take the necessary steps quickly to meet with him so, if there can be a deicide with the gods here to unfetter your souls from the trouble that might likely befall you both."

"Okay. We will double in our steps on that."

While Gmasnoh is on the phone Tesio came from upstairs to meet with her. He met her on the phone and decided to ask her who really she is talking with perhaps. He saw on her face tensed.

She gave him the phone to talk with the father, too.

"Dad, hello!"

"Oh, Tesio, my very good son, how are you doing?"

"Dad, things seemed a bit okay. But the only problem on ground is that issue with the tradition. We need to work out things against the gods. And a good prayer would get it well for us."

"That would be very fine. Let me tell you a story which you are a bit forced to know about."

"What's it?"

"Rosa's parents went to a neighbouring town before, and brought news to me and Snoteh that the gods in the land are saying you and the sister should come home in a twenty-one day schedule given by the gods in Niffu. As they said if--the both of you don't do something about this it would be as a serious trouble with the gods."

"A trouble could be from the gods, what is the meaning of that saying really? Please help me understand such."

"I can't tell exactly what the meaning is really about all that perhaps."

"Okay. Don't you people even worry yourselves about this either. A pastor, in collaboration with his colleagues of prayerful clergy would handle it with ease, like I said earlier."

Tesio and Gmasnoh returned to work. The second week of being at work they are urged to sign a contract with the administration of the hospital, if possible, after a month to get ready for a trip whereto, coming back to Liberia soon.

Accordingly, the United States Government wants to assist Liberia by then in containing an Ebola outbreak since then. So, the hospital has been given the responsibility for such. And the two are to lead the team of doctors, especially to Lofa County which had been the origin of the virus upon leaving the Republic of Guinea and came into Liberia.

"Gmasnoh, this kind of ugliness in Africa has to now really stop. I regretted while left our jobs before just for such a thing. Why should it be for cousins or extended relatives in this modern time married to each other? We will ensure that as of today . . . no more will anyone family of ours get married to each other again. We shall work with some human's right organizations to stop the awkward part of the tradition. For that marriage issue it's so ugly to exist anymore. I see that as being uncivilized."

"But Tesio, I'm getting a different understanding about this thing."

"What's the picture are you figuring out really?"

"The concept of the tradition is about maintaining a peace within our both families in time to come. For me, that isn't bad at all. Do you remember the story of the Pierre, once the best gardener in the USA of what caused his family to extinct?"

"It's such intermarriage!"

"Okay. But what should that be to you a good thing, Gmasnoh?"

"It's about unity, especially for our lives. That's how I think perhaps."

"Intermarriage is it about unity--like how?"

"But you since got to know this. It isn't strange either that be, or me saying it now. You know about that since then."

"Okay. I can remember all of that, but we now find ourselves at a different continent which isn't as Africa to hold onto traditional values like that. I'd rather like for us to wait for the prayer result at the church with Reverend Timothy Howard yet."

"No. Listen to me a minute, Tesio. Didn't I tell you that before? I said sometimes ago that modernity is associated with better changes in life. But see this disruption instead!"

"Gmasnoh, there is a parable that says that two heads are better than the one. Now I got to know what has been your point. But since Howard has been consulted to help us in the prayer time, I'm strongly of the conviction that things would be better as expected of the prayer at least for us to shortly be at peace once again. Those very unhuman and ugly gods of our home might die. Imagine in the past lots of people die because of a simple cultural value that has been violated either like this. It must stop. Why should we be forced to marry to each other?"

The two are really confused still. Neither Tesio, nor Gmasnoh has a sound mind either the moment presumably. Once the comfort in life is like turning into a sour stage. But it's like they have been deceived to the new culture of America. And this has been something of traditional nature for which they left America to resolve the matter. But they have developed so soon something of a different story about their own tradition perhaps. It's mindboggling really.

Culturally, the materials that should make the wedding, as it was planned, are being divided amongst the people, especially at every quarter level. Those that are in part supposed to provide the soup kind, liquor, and food, firewood, and others, all did before time. The disclosure, earlier said, which should have said who each person was to marry then, came at last oppositely.

Glaring, the issue of getting marriage to each other that which the gods talked about then, but Tesio has remained so soured in body about repudiating it. It seemed so ugly for him because he doesn't even have the slide thinking that it's possible. He and the cousin have become civilized man and woman.

Presumed, they are feeling that, of such intermarriage as something daft in nature to their consciences for now. And the very good thing for Tesio and the cousin is that, since the entry into America they have been part of an ecumenical, where they have since then been participating into church activities strongly as well. Once the charm he took from home he has thrown them away through that too.

More besides, the lives of the two had really since then altered aspects and directions. Ultimately prosperity became strongly an acceptance conscientiously. They want to bring a change to the culture of their people in a funny way. However, but it is a difficult situation that requires lots of sacrifices to be conducted before such thing can be done or adjured.

Reverend Howard and his church assembly of five people have been fasting and praying since then. Almost few days are left surprisingly to come up with a result. Will this result be as pleasing to Tesio and Gmasnoh, of the long awaited plan? And his prayer time is the only hope. And if, nothing perhaps is being done quickly to come up with a plan that there is a deicide at home, where their lives could be freed, but morbid fear of eminent death is probable to increase in time.

37

Howard has since nineteen days now been fasting at his church. Everyone with him is like rolling off here and there seriously praying. Noted, a grace period of twenty-one day that is given Tesio and Gmasnoh upon the gods' instruction to return home is almost to the end. Surprisingly, they have refused to still go home while trusting the abilities of Reverend Howard and his church council. It is this same church that he and the cousin got convicted since then, when he took from his body the juju or traditional medicine he took from home before. For Gmasnoh long time ago she burned them at home.

"Howard is a very strong man of God. We've to wait on his prayer decision yet. What he'll say perhaps that's what both us will go by at least." Tesio has built confidence already into the process. Howard assured him that he's going to battle against the gods of the land for which he had so much believed that it's possible --truly that would be by the prayer.

"No one can battle against the power of God Almighty for which anybody can think that the traditional gods are able to have a battle against me or the church of mine either. We'll destroy them through the prayer time shortly." Howard pompously said. Tesio is so contumaciously dumped by nihilism even against his own culture. He is rather accepting his assertion yet in good fate.

For what the condition detects now, Tesio's body is more than increasing in fear of death than the cousin inevitably. He is between having a good spirit into him as well as a bad spirit. He's behaving brave when he knows that such a problem is so serious. He knows that a traditional issue like that between the gods and human can't be taken for a joke either.

Unhappiness by virtue is tormenting him more into a state of getting emaciated gradually. By that his eyes went into him a little as if he is suffering from a prolong fever in the body. But it's all stress.

"As we are now at the church with Reverend Howard, please be factual by explaining the situation to him in detail. Don't hide it any longer like we did by not telling the people how we broke the vows. But the other issue of going against the laws of America please avoid talking about it. I know he has been praying for us but we need to now be truthful to him too."

"You're right, Gmasnoh!'

"Thanks. I know for that it's soon to be handled." Gmasnoh said.

She and the cousin are seriously seated by Reverend Howard for the past nineteen days at his church. They usually go to work and in few hours make a return to the church. And it's barely two days left rather to pass for the gods' decision on them to prove otherwise, if possible.

Reverend Howard wants Tesio to explain at least in full the circumstance that had really led to such an incident of the tradition.

"We were very small when we were forced to traditional oaths. We can't even explain it, why did we do that at the time to ourselves? It's so crazy to me."

Gmasnoh interrupted him. Reverend Howard by then opened wide his eyes to listen. "Tesio, we can still make it that, for the both of us to go home now and plead with our people. We are Africans. Staying in America can't really solve the problem without us going home. When the people see us by then perhaps the gods would see reason, pardoning us upon the sacrifice is conducted by then." Gmasnoh added.

The moment the first river of tears in the world was discovered. A bucket of tears poured from Gmasnoh's eyes. She's just talking and talking. Nobody could understand her that much either.

"Why, Gmasnoh? Should you perhaps be the one to cause a distraction right now by saying, as you know the Reverend is at the zenith already of completing his task of praying for us? Why stayed between two minds? There is no pessimism that should be into someone praying for you. The Almighty won't hear you. This is what you have really introduced here." Tesio said while moving about wondering of what she had said.

"Dimmitt!"

"Look, Tesio, this isn't about your so-called civilization you have obtained here in America I'm talking about. We must take steps home again now!"

"Gmasnoh, the elders and gods should know it now that things have changed in our lives greatly. The gods should be able to know that every society will never remain culturally the same forever. The entire human world of planet earth has changed since then. Why are we not to note same? And we should know that in the world there is no society that lives the same as before either. Why are these so much abnormalities these days should be for, rather against us?"

"Wait a minute, Tesio!"

"Yes, what's it?"

"Why can't the Reverend be able to tell us little by little since then he started the fast and prayer at least, what may be a hint about the final result like yet? It's almost the time of the gods to act, if possible, by reprimanding us, if they can really."

"Gmasnoh, there would surely be a positive result about this matter for what I know soon. Howard is highly prepared to give us a positive result of the matter."

Counsellor Uguche came also to meet them at the church to discuss something very important to them. For him, he feels that they are ignorantly betrayed to civilization, now forgetting about their traditions in Africa. Since he came from Nigeria there is nothing called a civilized state of being which he is supposed to lust to either? And now most importantly, Uguche is about coming to discuss the issue of the tradition with him at the church first and later at home.

He's seated inside the church with them. He cornered the two of them yet. "Look, Tesio, did your sister agree to the elders at the time for the both of you guys to marry each other?"

"Yes. She said we should just fool them by marrying each other. After the wedding we could later then, make our way to America and never to go back again. But, Counsellor Uguche, I see that as nonsense, especially Reverend Howard promised me immediately he was contacted and informed about the ordeal to pray for us to destroy the home gods." He said and Counsellor Uguche laughed.

"I'm so sorry for this. But, if I can give you a lay light on what usually happens at my home, would you like it?"

"What's it?"

"Like what you are saying for me---I don't really see a problem with that either. What is it about marrying your cousin that should be a problem to you? I beg of you, please! Talk to the girl so the both of you can quickly make a return home. Leave this church matter. I don't think the Reverend will want to destroy the tradition of your people by spiritually battling against the gods. Can you remember when Christ Jesus said in the New Testament which said that, he didn't come to have destroyed the traditions of any society or Israel either! But he came in that to teach the people of the world the right way to live? So, why then your conviction by modernity has to be a problem by you rejecting or obliterating your people's culture now? Can any man change the culture of his people without the help of the creator?" Uguche said and Tesio got soured in body about his assertion.

"No. I have a different picture about this. Counsellor Uguche, even though when we were at home each of us supported the tradition somehow ignorantly, but now we got to know, as matured we are now that, we did make a mistake then. So Uguche, should it be, because she is a woman when she said we should go about the marriage, I should accept to be a marriage that rather may stand between us? She wants me to marry her. How can we fool the traditional people when there are lots of things that may be involved, including taking an oath again? We may be that also forced to take something similarly as juju powder or water---which is meant as commitment in the relationship that may be between us. This is the plan of the gods of the land. And I hate the plan really. Why should she then, wanting us agree to an undignified and callously a bogus covenant or marriage out of sympathy? I know my people are very strong about the part of the tradition for anyone of us not to take that as a joke either."

"That's okay."

Uguche, who had an appointment with Thomas Thug almost the same hour he asked for him to leave and later make a comeback perhaps. He and Thomas are joyously going to meet at a secret location for the guy (Thomas) at least, as Uguche since then promised to give him a million dollar from what he got from Scott, getting same as his lay share too. The good thing that has happened to Counsellor Uguche is that, he has paid off his debts and he's like a new man with a good credit record now in America.

Entertaining the moment to watch, is the way Counsellor Uguche took-off. And he promised upon meeting Thomas to phone Tesio as soon as possible on the matter then.

But there is a lay story about Uguche. His chief investigator at his law firm is about concluding a long-awaited deal with the government of America for their private law business office on a special case that the evidences have been building up by the United States Government. It is a case involving a very special unidentified and undignified murder yet, the United States is working around the clock since then about three years now, identifying him to be booked for multiple crimes he had committed.

This particular guy has allegedly murdered two friends since then intermittently in an instant. And the big question is about the guy and America, which prosecutors have since been piling evidences against the guy is that, his where about is yet unknown upon escaping from America for years since then, a complicated issue to note. But there is a hint after five years is that, he is somewhere in Nigeria. Therefore, Counsellor Uguche, since he's a Nigerian born he has volunteered to collect all of the evidences on the guy by going back to Nigeria with a team of investigators---something his private firm has taken the responsibility to do for the USA. And it has yet been approved between the firm and America the contract for the deal perhaps.

The guy name is King Mathis. He is a very notorious murderer----believed killed his own black brothers in succession. He was a friend to Barclay Stephenson. Mathis left his compound one special morning hour to get his money from Stephenson upon a deal had been crossed since then between him and Stephenson.

And for Mathis, he's in a financial tumult for which some of his colleagues of gangs on the other side of his life pendulum, promised to get rid of him if he too, as they are more desperate for money----couldn't pay them off the particularly day that ensues by evening hour. This is a reason he went to find Stephenson. Even to get to Stephenson became a very serious issue for months. Before he entered the guy house that morning, the garbage collector of Stephenson's compound furtively and smartly, pretended with him like he was going to collect some garbage in his yard as usual, upon placing him into a very big barrel and rode him inside Stephenson's compound. Before then he got five thousand dollars from the deal to have taken him inside the compound. That is how he secretly entered his compound and hid himself.

That morning he entered unruly and unknowingly on Stephenson and put him on gun point. "Stephenson, could I have my share of the money right now?" He said. Lightly, you could see that Stephenson is sweating. In response he said, "Should you please at least give me a day from now and I'd try to settle you." Persistently Stephenson was urged by Mathis to give his money now--- or else he's going to blow his head off. Stephenson took it for a joke. He couldn't still have given him a dime despite the colleague fearfully and persistently urged him to.

Anger has rumpled inside Mathis. And the Mathis surprisingly, inhumanly, he bulleted Stephenson on his forehead and his blood smeared onto the floor. Because Stephenson is so big in body his blood poured out of him like water pump.

Mathis became very confused the moment. He is thinking of a way out he could have then dispose of the body. While in the state of an enigma, trying rather to dispose of the body, wiping the blood even splashed on him, surprisingly another friend of him, who amazingly thought to find him too, by the name of Daniel Williams, came on him because the two were to go on an operation that morning.

D-Will, as he's commonly called, became so torched and said furiously this: "Why did you do this to Stephenson---our very good friend?" In response Mathis said, "I want you now wrap up this body as I'm pointing the gun at you to assist me get the shit out of here now!" And Mathis didn't even touch the body either. But D-Will was forced to. Why then still whimpering, D-Will is wrapping up the body of Stephenson. Later, he was done after like thirty minutes.

The evening came on them while in that terrific state of being. Mercy has found its everlasting exit from the life of Mathis when mercilessness wonderfully became a new fellow for his friendship.

Mournfully and forcibly, they drove off with the body late that evening to throw it away while D-Will held under gun point still.

Immediately they got to the point of throwing away the body, with just D-Will alone is caused to do everything upon the instruction of Mathis, who had the gun at him still, he threw away the body of Stephenson. It was so sealed. D-Will became very nebulous because he didn't think that his colleague could be that wicked to an extent killing a colleague of theirs.

By the time D-Will was almost to leave the area upon throwing the body of Stephenson away, Mathis bulleted him, too, on the forehead and went away from there. And he left America altogether. He was sitting in a lay village in Nigeria for the past five years now and nobody could really figure out his location until lately Counsellor Uguche got the hint. The guy is gone to a village where the Uguche also came from.

Upon Uguche got the clue, as he's asked since then by the United States Government for him and a group of investigators to try going to Nigeria soon to do also a blood sample, and DNA test secretly on him, comparing it with a lay blood sample they got since then from the hospital at the time when Mathis went for treatment upon an illness attacked him before. Besides, the gun he used to murder his two colleagues is found at his house and his hand print is obtained. It was a hectic task to get a hint about him really.

And so, Uguche is gone at his office first to sign finally the contract with the US Government for him and the investigators to plan going to Nigeria soon. But would he be willing to go to Nigeria, whereas he is also soon to face a problem at home, when since then, he had obtained a scholarship from his home government and he failed to make a return home? Besides, noted, his family is already against him because he hasn't started anything concrete as project home yet. As thought, he abandoned the family since he went on studies about fifteen years ago now. He didn't mean to really have done that--but it's because of the woman he got married to by then who got him into the problems of his life. And luckily, since he got the money from Doctor Scott and Williams, economically things are okay with him. And he promised after a week of the transaction to start building his personal mansion where he would soon go home.

Therefore, his going back home once became a big question that has created hallow yet and paradise for him slightly in mind, though. He's done with penning the contract with the US Government finally. And he is now on his way from the office to meet with Thomas Thug at last.

Surprising, he sat at his office for almost one hour ago from the time he's supposed to have met with Thomas Thug. It got Thomas galled that he may punish him. Counsellor Uguche is driving fast to go and meet with him. Before then, he decided to talk with Tesio on the phone.

"Hello, Tesio."

"Hey, Counsellor Uguche, how are you doing?"

"Well, I'm now doing excellent after paying off my entire debt."

"Okay. Let's be able to discussion serious matters instead of that."

"Alright. Let me tell you something very fine but yet ridiculous, if you would like. On the issue of not marrying your cousin, if you don't reconsider your decision now, you may be sacrificed by the gods. If you think you're stubborn so much about the issue then, you can go ahead. But no one plays with the gods in Africa."

"No. Counsellor, what makes you think this way?"

"Tesio, don't joke with an African traditional issue either. Look, you're my good friend, and I expect that you know better about African traditional powers. Let me give you a lay story which I believe you would listen to-- and probably make a change of mind, though."

"What's it, sir."

"My father is a juju man in Africa. And so, I don't take African's matter for a joke either, especially the both of you the kind of oaths you took about the traditional marriage. It's like pulling a trigger gradually at your throat really."

"Please, we have a Reverend almost to complete his prayer time for us soon. He's about given us the rightful step to take. Don't place us between a scissors either. Wait!"

"Tesio, I think you're the one who is putting you and your sister at the face of a scissors if you don't know. In fact, what's about the Reverend that you have so much interest in his ability?"

"He prays well, and that's all!"

"Okay. I do agree a bit with you but let me ask you a question still."

"Yes, go ahead!"

"Where was that man's father, Sylvester Howard, when he became a preacher long ago while he was still a servant of his master on a plantation in Virginia during the days of old, upon witnessing or participating into lot of uprisings that led to the death of his own master? Is he a guy from heaven for God's sake that, for us to trust his mouth when his father is an evil?"

"How did you get to know about him?"

"I read a biography about his family where that Reverend came from."

"Anyway, that can't be the subject for our discussion right now because the man isn't his father either. The sin of his father can't be a sin to hold him by."

"Alright. But you need to open your ears and listen to what I'm saying this so that the both of you can quickly make a return to Africa." Uguche said. Tesio in response said, "We are doing our best already. Things would be okay."

"If that's what you say, but I'm about making my way to meet with Thomas Thug. I hope to talk with you after the interaction later." Uguche concluded.

Tesio pretentiously wiped his eyes. They are so red, full of tears.

38

Counsellor Uguche decided finally to be at the place where Thomas is. Thomas, being so blue for the delay, hauled his gun from his pocket and pointed it at him.

"Hei, Thomas, what's that?"

"I will blow your fucking head up now!"

"Wait a minute please!"

"How can I wait when I know you should have since been here?"

"Okay. I'm sorry. I'm begging you that I didn't leave Nigeria for my parents ever not to see me again. Please put down the gun. I don't like this American Culture of yours that is full of too much guns. You are a very decent individual I since believed in."

"If you know what I do really know right now, please give me a million-dollar of the deal. I got to celebrate as well as you're doing now, that you are so freed from debts."

"Hey, my God help me! Thomas, you are a good man. Why should you bring gun here? Am I to deceit you? Stop this, Thomas! You have been good to me."

Uguche has delayed so much to have been at the meeting place on time. For almost one hour now, Thomas has been standing at the place, wishing that he come quickly. Thomas, as a smart individual, who knows so much the street-life too, after like every fifteen minutes he keeps changing persistently the shirt on him to a different one. He was doing that intermittently not be identified in any way either. He had pessimism that Counsellor Uguche would have planted somebody on him. And Uguche wasn't even thinking like that either. But for him, he thinks so fast. So, he tries to put fear into Uguche. Second, he wants chastise him in his own way before he could accept the money he's about giving him perhaps.

The guy is feeling so dull or defiant of not maintaining his sanity any longer. Before then, he took in something stupid which has been making his mind telescoping on him with evil. And he was prepared to go the extra mile. A forceful knockdown of Uguche is all that he had on mind then.

"I want to leave you now to go and collect the cash from the bank as you're giving me this check right now."

"No. Just be assured that you would get the cash as soon as you go to the bank. I'll even make a phone call right now at the bank to facility your easy obtainment of the cash. The bank shall be informed that you working at my law firm. I'm about to say that you're responsible for operation affairs at my law firm"

"That's what I expect you to do now! If you fuck up with me, attempting to crib me either, I want you expect my colleagues in business with me to deal with you." he said. He described where Counsellor Uguche works and lives to him.

"Thomas, I know you knew me well from the beginning that's a reason you have since had called me up for your share of this deal. I won't cheat you either. Do you know what you've done for me? I see you as the famous philanthropic, a big man, which the world had ever produced for the 21st Century for now. You got me out of debt and that's really good! It's something to befriend you more about than deceiving you either." Uguche paused. Well, silent pleasure was a bit inside him.

"I need not entertaining much of talk from you again. Give me my shit now and let me get out of here." Thomas unruly said, while being so very incensed with him pretentiously. His face made bundles of veins on it.

"Alright. Just give me a minute yet." Counsellor Uguche worded friendlily

He is done with him. The guy is gone away finally. After Thomas left his presence two hours later, at least Uguche gained his conscience, and now to talk with Tesio on his phone.

"Dimmitt!"

"What has happened so?"

"Oh, this would have been a different story really about me." He said and hissed. His call is gone through finally. He is about speaking with Tesio; he said, "Tesio, I just met up with Thomas and he wanted to fuck things up with me. But I'm so happy that I'm still alive to talk to you again."

"What's it, Uguche?"

"No. The ten million that I received from the deal since then, I should have given one million dollar to him like I said to you before. And I have been looking for him all this while for which we made an appointment for him to get his little share of it."

"What are you talking about, Counsellor Uguche? He tries to strip you off everything?" Tesio said.

Gmasnoh interrupted.

"Thomas is right. He should have nailed him to the fucking gun." Gmasnoh said, rather without Uguche hearing her either. She sounded very low.

"No. You shouldn't have said that either, Gmasnoh." Tesio took-off the phone from his ears and said same to her. She just pushed up her mouth.

Due to Tesio's assertion, rather she declined from commenting further. However, Tesio turns to Reverend Howard again. He was done with talking with Counsellor Uguche already.

"What are you saying right now, Reverend Howard? Really, this thing is bleeding both my cousin and I souls. For the past three weeks now we highly have had good sleep either the both of us at all again. I think it was necessary that we were to remain at home rather than coming for advancement when trouble was to be the game at last against us."

"Okay. Tesio, I'm sorry for all this. Just give me a little time yet, and by the evening hour today I will tell you what the result is about this thing after the prayer." Howard said. Tesio felt a bit happy. He feels something positive would be done during the prayer time for which Howard could surely tell him something very nice to embrace deeply. But it's an illusion perhaps.

Tesio and Gmasnoh ears, probably as condition depicts, had grown wide into a fanner shape. They are achy in body to see a better result. The evening hour came. Any mistake by even a rat to cross before them, especially for Tesio, he would have gotten his head crack probably to a wall.

They left the church. And they are home finally. It's barely a minute pass seven post meridians. Reverend Howard decided to walk to their home in order to give finally the result of the prayer after the fasting. Howard said they should leave the church instead to be at their house in order to deliver the message.

"We did pray at the church and the both of you the experience now will never be as the same experience of your children in time to come. No more will any traditional gods attack your generation. If, like the both of you came, you weren't going to come for the prayer, to be frank, there would have been continuously a trouble-bond, like a curse, over the lives of your generations by the gods of your land. But now, they would never and ever be as children of the devil, as the bond is snapped. The prayer revealed something very phenomenon also that I want you to beware of." Reverend Howard said and Tesio bobbed. He'd quickly interrupted by asking questions spontaneously without halting in speech, as he spluttered by then even while speaking.

"What are you saying to me? Is the tradition too bad to be against us? There can't still be a solution that mine and cousin's souls be unfettered by this nightmare so we can live our lives here once at peace? Reverend, where do we stand now, when the time given us by the gods has been far spent? You now give us the right mind to do something better about the situation. We should have gone home but you gave us an assurance since then that you could do something about this positively. Now you made me to be felling stupid to myself, Reverend. I can't believe this!"

"Cool down a little, please. I know it's so terrible! However, you and Gmasnoh need to go back home now. Go and plead with your people."

The two have right away burst up in tears profusely. The good thing here is that none of the husband or wife was home either. Only the two were home as they went on an evening shift too at the same hospital where they all work. Scott went to pack up his things upon that later to resign his post. Even though he did that before but had lots of unfinished stuff he needed to do for the hospital in a week's time to finally, letting go his resignation.

Their eyes got red and winking fast in bewilderment, especially as Tesio in particular is wiping his faces off tears. His posture turns as if he's swallowing some bitter pills that moment.

"Tesio, I'm calling you to please listen to me yet."

"What's the matter really, Gmasnoh?"

"I think it's never too late yet to go back home now. I'll have to marry you without a mind of us doing anything stupid but to make a comeback to America. This would better free our souls from the trouble upon fooling the gods." Gmasnoh said.

"Don't say that, Gmasnoh. That decision would me as still a bond. There will be a relationship that would forever be established between us. I can't. I won't definitely do that either."

39

The twenty-one days' time of the gods elapsed for sure. Howard decided to also offer special five days prayer after that they can make the return home finally.

Surprising news has come. The parents of the two left the town and went to another town in order to consult some juju powers at least to dwarf the decision of the home gods. Still, none has been able to obtain any favourable result, except to say that they must still go back home and plead with the elders to do the necessary sacrifice required to the gods, honouring the marriage that was proposed. Besides that their forceful departures was very insulting for which there must also be a fine to that and sacrifice oppositely to obliterate it.

"Tesio, this is really so absurd. It's a very stupid thing we have done. We should have remained home earlier to fool them and do the marriage as usual. We are from Africa for which we should know about obeying our traditions."

"That's true, Gmasnoh. But what should we do still? Now the result of the Reverend is given us at a dangerously, a late time. Are we to pack up to go back home still?"

Reverend Howard sat, looking pathetically at the two. He's lacked the words to say again.

"Reverend Howard, we never knew what the life had for us since we started going to school earlier at home. Our people in Africa love this too much of oath-taking which is usually companied by juju power."

Gmasnoh quickly interrupted and said, "If man could tell of the future, I believe the future won't be any more. Look, we're forced go back now. But I can't get over this why did we since then delay? We got to go home now!"

"No. Gmasnoh, you need not to talk like that. In fact let me ask Reverend Howard a question yet." Tesio said and turned to Reverend Howard the moment.

"Reverend, upon saying all of that to you now, there is no way could that be still for free us from this menace?"

"Probably I can say no. I took this thing earlier for a joke. But I believe there is no way will the both of you die either. There is nothing really that would cause a death about this thing."

"No!"

"Why?"

"Our people tradition doesn't work like that. I think, in particularly, you must preach my funeral now. I have had so much confidence in the ability of your church since then. It's one reason I couldn't even honour the request of my people. And forcibly and unruly, I took my cousin out of Africa while the elders were seated, presenting the mandate of the gods. That is highly forbidden what we did then."

"Wow! I feel for you all. But it's left with you now at least making a quick return home. If you decide to do that, however, you have to be a lay mindful with your relationships here."

"It's true. But let me let you know that I'd never and ever do it by marrying my cousin either. The way the tradition wants it I won't do that either. It would be better for me to marry a girl who I have since then put my trust into by the name of Rosa. My sister has been an admirer of a friend of mine too, called Dorsla. She could marry that guy by the instruction of the gods. Even though, I can remember some time ago when we were home, we participated in other wedding ceremonies in similar case of inter-family in nature, but things have now changed. I just got to know that such is an ugly thing. The happiness of the two parties who supposed to get married should be that important than traditional principles that may be too forceful and doesn't really support happiness of a person either." He said and Howard was obligated to laugh.

"Don't laugh at me either. It's serious, Reverend."

"Tesio, I'm so sorry for all that that had happened." Reverend Howard said.

"But let me give you a lay story still. We wanted just to be part of our people's tradition at the time while we were very small and took oaths not to be married yet until at the age of twenty-five. We love them and did so much for the development of the town."

"It's true for what I see it for which the two of you left just to tell them what has been the situation which both of you guys were confronted with by then in the United States. That's an act of esteem for your people's tradition."

"Reverend, the story here is that, imagine I got married to Doctor Williams, while Gmasnoh is also married to Doctor Scott too," he said, while pointing to a picture on the wall in his house. Tesio is that mountainously galled. He's just talking off head and bouncing around.

"Let the two of you listen to me. We are all black people. Just that I'm born here in America but I know that my origin is Africa. We should have the same tradition as you saying it here but it isn't the case either. But the evil of slavery you are to blame for this."

"That's true."

"Since you people knew about such oath as Africans, it's good for you. But spiritually, for what I do know . . .it's dangerous, because for you to go home and do another marriage, that is highly unacceptable in the arena of a civilized world and spiritually."

"It's true but we are human that live in the physical state of being instead of the spirituality which you are talking about.

So, being it married in two ways to me that isn't a problem as I take it really. That's good." Gmasnoh said.

"But the spiritual trouble is that, as long you and your partner are living here in America, you can't go to Africa again for another marriage. What kind of marriage culture is that? It's a double-headed thing so ugly to accept really." Reverend Howard said. Tesio pretentiously wiped his eyes.

"Reverend, like you have said, is it about us dying or what?" Tesio said. "No. You are to just return home doing whatever you can, but I won't be held responsible either for the spiritual factor in time to come when both of you shall have left the face of the earth either. There is life after death, if you don't know." Howard said and paused.

"Please, Gmasnoh come close to me. I want to ask you a question." Reverend Howard couldn't believe what he is about to do either. Gmasnoh went very close to him the same way he requested same.

"Gmasnoh, it's from my heart for which I have to ask this question. Like the gods had proposed, even though it's late now, but do you really love me for a relationship matter like that?"

Gmasnoh with tears blurring her eyes, she said 'yes.'

"Why?"

"That's such a reason of maintaining our peace between us and with the gods about the tradition at home. That isn't bad at all. I told you already that we should do that and don't even think of going back or doing anything stupid. But you refused to---why?"

"But then Gmasnoh, should that love be between us as husband and wife . . . the two of us?"

"Yes, it's just make-believe we should do it for."

"Oh, no!"

Gmasnoh is this time hesitant to make a respond yet. She folded her hands so dejectedly around him.

"Please, Tesio, let's make a reverse course on this matter by going home. We saw such thing taking place at home before which we once partook into. This isn't strange that be really, either!"

"No. Gmasnoh, I love you but not for relationship matter now. Don't support that thing. That proposal of the gods is so odd. I have so much a different feeling about it, please. I want you know that my conscience is all that I have as a human to stay at least happy. If, I marry you that means I won't be happy throughout my life and I may die. Why should my conscience be controlled by another human?"

"Tesio, you can't out rightly say that. The logic that I see about this is to protect us in time to come, especially upon returning home someday so that our African culture, which is our family line in succession won't be either destroyed. After the both of us there would definitely be another generation. And that generation must see what we leaving with her now by the foundation we are setting. Would you wish for a foreign woman or a man to be part of our family upon each of those marrying us especially that we have done by marrying the Americans?" She said and Tesio remained yet adamant.

"Please, Gmasnoh, I beg of you. I want you be happy now that you find yourself into a different and glowing relationship here. If, your husband and mine also get to know about what we are saying here they may blow the both of us heads off. That won't be the same as the journey of death you fear could we quickly face by then? Let the resistant, not honouring it remains as it is now. Let me really call all matters short that, I'm so much prepared to face death because I was once declared a party to the tradition when I took the oath."

He made Gmasnoh bitterly burst up in cry. In that time but President Rosemary called him up on the phone. He ran into his room to answer the call quickly.

"Hello, Tesio!"

"Oh, Mr. President, how are you doing?"

"I'm okay. However, I just heard that you and your cousin just return from Africa. How is the condition with you and the people there?"

"Mr. President, we got a shit hanging us up gradually to death right now."

"What's it?"

"It's so sensitive. And I won't feel as please to really disclose that to you on the phone now. There is a matter about us in Africa."

"How ugly is that issue you are talking about really?"

"It's about my tradition at home."

"Okay, Tesio, could I come over to get the detail of the issue, or we meet at a different local?"

"Yes. That would be good that we meet at the basketball game this evening."

"Are you talking about the game at the Legacy Court?"

"Oh, yes!"

"If that is the case I should be there too. There would be really good for us to meet." Mr. Rosemary said. Tesio put down the phone after talking few minutes after.

He was restless still. He's just complaining at heart of what to do next. In the process one Tina Woods called him too. She has been a very good friend of the two of them since then.

"Tesio, may I wish to invite you and Gmasnoh to my birthday party due tomorrow?"

"Oh, that would be very fine! But why that can't be now?"

"No. It's for tomorrow's pleasure, please."

"Okay. Don't you even worry we shall be there live." Tesio and Woods chatted on the phone satisfactorily. After that he gave Gmasnoh the news.

Almost a month now the CNN has been reporting about the basketball game. Most of the local radio stations in the USA, especially in Oklahoma are spreading the news. It's the Sooners Basketball Team versus the Miami Basketball Team having a playoff. And that match would determine which team would go for the NBA Tourney due in one month's time.

Anybody who perhaps living within Oklahoma or the entire United States, hearing about the game at the time couldn't even wait to see it comes about either. There are so many world class players composed of the two teams which most of the young basketball players everywhere want to see the big guys live too. So, lots of young professionals around the city of Oklahoma keep buying tickets for the game.

It's the twenty-fifth day of June. Howard has asked to pray with them that day before the take-off to the game come. And he advised that after the game at least in a week's time they should leave for home.

He did as requested. This time round Tesio and Gmasnoh are using the most sporting cars made from Japan to go at the Legacy Court.

The motor the two are both into moves, as if airplane ridding on the ground by then. It's very fast for which they landed at the court joyously thirty minutes after they picked up from home. And the distance from their residence is about one hour drive. There was so much pageantry about Tesio and Gmasnoh's movement at the court purposely to remove stress about the tradition, while walking flamboyantly. Lots of fens for the two teams were seated. Tesio held his cousin's hand and began walking with her to sit at the stadium wing.

Interestingly, the game started since thirty minutes ago. While the game is in motion, the president decided to chat with the two on the side yet at the court.

"I'm seeing the both of you looking a bit stress up." Rosemary presumed.

"It's true just what you have said, Sir." Tesio said sagely lamely.

"Then, what is such factor that got the both of you so downhearted? The people of America, who I'm serving won't feel fine either to see the both of you---be living like this."

"No. Don't bother yourself about us either. We are fine. It's just that we have been having a very stressful time at work. You know we are newly admitted to the field of studies as medical doctors. It would take sometimes to see us being alright yet until we are well-schooled practically to the working arena yet." Tesio said and Rosemary chuckled.

"I want you both please try managing yourself well to avoid being into this statuses. You have money already and why will you want to work long? Look, this is a developed world for which people don't really have to work long hours either."

"Thanks. The reason is that most of the surgical work we have been encountering are terribly pathetic for which we have to conduct same during extra hours. We couldn't just see most of the patients be into such terrible state of being either. We intend saving life."

"Okay."

"Sir, that's the reason really."

"It's no problem either."

They had real fun! Now it's time to return home. By Nine P.M. they are set. The president went his way. And Gmasnoh and Tesio are going their way, too, riding first pass the Ouachita Mountains area to take some photographs.

While on the way there, passing the Kiamichi Mountain ranges, right over the little river bridge in Honobia, a great spot for photograph, Tesio is bending a special terrible curve without reducing his speed by then because he was enjoying the music playing inside the car.

Surprising, while bending the terrible curve, because it's a long curve, not knowing a tow truck had since broken down at the place. And it has been since forty minutes ago. The police have just arrived to the sport trying to remove same.

By the time Tesio left the curve--and while concentrating again changing his music by plugging a memory stick instead, because the first music skipped, and when he lifted his head by then he surprisingly spotted the damaged tow truck. Very promptly he tried applying the brakes but that couldn't really hold. Gmasnoh yelled. "This is the end of us!" Truly it was too late. Only the echoing of her voice you could hear from a distance away during that moment.

The police came strictly at the spot. They were taken to the same Oral Robert Hospital where they had since been working. Nobody could believe it. At last, unbelievably, the two went into coma for nearly a year now. And the both parents of theirs left home to see them at the hospital.

However, on the twenty-fourth day of the following year around July, they have been surprisingly pronounced dead. Mournfully, however, Doctor Scott and Williams in collaboration with the family and the US Government peacefully buried them.

Everyone is in turmoil at home due to the incident. But the elders knew the matter that the gods might have forced them to return home in the spirit world. That is how some of the elders said. Momsio, the head of the shrine chanted and he got to know it. But it's certain individuals within the elder council that were briefed about the incident.

Family members decided to have the final burial ceremony by cutting hair at home. It's a tradition where closed relatives had converged to shave at the base of the forefaces their hair. It's such a ritual. As it is so believed, at last, the spirits of the deceased Tesio and Gmasnoh had peacefully joined also the world of the dead, called the gods.

ABOUT THE AUTHOR

The Author hailed from Niffu Town in southeastern Liberia. He grew up in a very poor family. His early school years began in Niffu and later to northern Liberia on Zorzor Rural Teacher Training Institute Demonstration School. In 1992, during the heat of civil war which erupted in 1989, he and his family migrated to Monrovia, where they lived in Logan Town, Monrovia suburb, and grew up. He's from a father of one child and a mother of eight children, but both of whom are now dead. He's a graduate of the D. Tweh High School on Bushrod Island in Monrovia. He holds a Bachelor of Business Degree in Accounting from the University of Liberia. Also, he since worked with the National Electoral Commission as Administrative Secretary, where he has assisted in many ways the offices of executive director, Commissioners, chairman and the finance section with some services. He had also on several occasions helped organize, monitor, and observe elections both locally and internationally.